D0823416

# THE
# GUNSLINGER'S
## GUIDE TO AVOIDING
## MATRIMONY

# THE GUNSLINGER'S GUIDE TO AVOIDING MATRIMONY

*USA TODAY* BESTSELLING AUTHOR
MICHELLE McLEAN

Entangled Publishing, LLC
644 Shrewsbury Commons Ave., STE 181
Shrewsbury, PA 17361
Visit our website at www.entangledpublishing.com.

Amara is an imprint of Entangled Publishing, LLC.

Edited by Liz Pelletier and Lydia Sharp
Cover art and design by Elizabeth Turner Stokes
Photographer: Chris Cocozza
Stock credits: VJ Dunraven/Period Images and
Digital Storm/Shutterstock
Interior design by Toni Kerr

Print ISBN 978-1-64937-212-3
ebook ISBN 978-1-64937-226-0

Manufactured in the United States of America

First Edition August 2022

# AMARA

## ALSO BY MICHELLE McLEAN

### THE GUNSLINGERS

*Hitched to the Gunslinger*
*The Gunslinger's Guide to Avoiding Matrimony*

### BLOOD BLADE SISTERS

*A Bandit's Stolen Heart*
*A Bandit's Broken Heart*
*A Bandit's Betrayed Heart*

### THE MACGREGOR LAIRDS

*How to Lose a Highlander*
*How to Ensnare a Highlander*
*How to Blackmail a Highlander*
*How to Forgive a Highlander*

### OTHER BOOKS BY MICHELLE McLEAN

*To Trust a Thief*
*Romancing the Rum Runner*

*To all the horrible decision-makers out there—take heart. Sometimes we get it right! I mean…it might take a while…but just statistically speaking, we'll get it right eventually!*

*And for those who never felt wanted. May you all find your happily ever after.*

# CHAPTER ONE

If there was one thing Adam Brady was good at, it was making monumentally asinine decisions that landed him in a world of hurt and regret.

And he was almost 100 percent certain he was making another one. Then again, he didn't have much of a choice. Because thanks to his last asinine decision, namely an ill-advised entanglement with a beautiful woman of dubious character, he was on the run for his life. Again.

Now he was riding through the Colorado wilderness to God knew where. He hadn't seen a town or ranch or another human soul in two days. On the one hand, that wasn't a bad thing. It meant he'd shaken that damned Marshal Spurlock off his trail and was probably safe for the time being.

But he couldn't keep wandering aimlessly forever. He'd run out of food the night before, and while he'd be able to find water, he was getting mighty tired of sleeping in the dirt beside a grumpy horse. He needed some real shelter. And a meal. And, if the aroma coming from the direction of his armpits was any indication, a bath. A man *should* be able to distinguish between his own scent and that of his horse.

When another two hours of riding had brought nothing into sight but more hills and trails that led nowhere, his hope of finding anything resembling civilization faded. He sighed and dismounted, needing to stretch his legs and work out his numb backside for a few minutes. He'd only taken three steps before his boot caught in a hole, and he tumbled ass over head, landing on his face.

"Ow," he groaned, pushing himself up to see what he'd tripped in.

He frowned, looking down at the hole. The deep, oddly square-shaped hole.

His eyes searched the brush around him until he saw what looked to be an old post that might have been used in part of a fence. Or signpost. And beneath the overgrown brush and grass, he could just make out the faint presence of an old trail. *Huh*.

"Come on, Barnaby." He straightened his hat and tried brushing the dust from his pants—a lost cause at this point—before mounting again. "Maybe we'll find some place with a roof we can sleep under tonight after all."

The horse blew out a nostril full of air and plodded forward. He wasn't much of a conversationalist.

Adam changed their course and followed the direction the old trail would have led. There might be nothing at the end of it but, even if it was an abandoned ranch or settlement, he'd take it.

He kept his eyes and ears open, watching for any sign of an elusive house or town. After another mile or so, he reached an apple orchard and pulled up, stuffing his pockets and saddlebags with the fruit. At least he'd get to eat that night. He munched as he rode, keeping to the outskirts of the orchard. He still hadn't seen a scrap of anything to show that any of the land he traveled through was owned by anyone, but better to be safe.

And then the vegetation grew sparser. He emerged from the orchard to find a well-worn trail that he followed to the top of a small hill. His heart thudded as he pulled to a stop, gazing down at the town that loomed ahead of him.

Well, "loomed" was a bit of a stretch. There wasn't much to the town. Several homesteads dotted the small valley the main town occupied. The town proper seemed to have a general store, a tavern that looked to be doing good business, a blacksmith's shop, barber's shop, and a two-story structure that was under construction and little more than the studded walls at the moment, though it did have a fully finished roof. Odd.

"Where the hell did this place come from?" he muttered.

Barnaby didn't have an answer. Neither did Adam. If it hadn't been for tripping in that old signpost hole, he'd never have found the place. There had been nothing, anywhere, to indicate a town was down there.

Yet there it was.

He nudged Barnaby into motion again, taking his time getting to the town. The closer he drew, the more heightened the tension in his body became until he had to force himself to relax his grip on the reins. He kept on high alert as he rode into town. The people he passed stopped and stared at him. They weren't hostile, more curious. And wary. Given the location of their town, they probably didn't get many strangers riding through.

That was both good and bad for him. Good, because it meant he should be safe there. Bad, because his presence was going to stand out. And standing out was the last thing he wanted to do.

There appeared to be something of a celebration going on in the town square. He'd steer clear of that, thank you very much. He did *not* like celebrations. Or organized joviality of any sort. Or people, really, not to put too fine a point on it. He used to. In fact, he used to be a downright delight. Couldn't get enough of crowds and conversation. But at this exact point in time, people were danger. A man could just never be sure who might be in a crowd. Safer to just avoid other folks altogether.

Unfortunately, he didn't see a way around what looked like most of the town's residents clogging the street. The tavern was his best bet for answers about the town, but that was where the largest group was gathered. Maybe he could blend in long enough to get his bearings and slip out before anyone noticed.

He tied Barnaby to a post in front of the general store and tugged his coat into place, slapping at it a few times. The cloud of dust that emerged went straight up his nose and set off a sneezing fit that drew more attention than was healthy for him. He swiped at his nose with a somewhat clean hankie, then made sure the chain on his pocket watch hung straight. Three days in the saddle was taking a toll on his carefully curated wardrobe. He scratched at the half-week's-worth of beard growth on his cheeks and grimaced. Hopefully tonight, he could find some decent lodging and start setting things to rights. A trip to the barber would be the first thing on his list.

Adam paused, letting another man enter first, before he pushed his way into the bustling establishment. He slid onto a barstool farthest from everyone else, hiding behind the crowd as much as he could.

"What can I get you, Mister?" the barkeep asked.

Adam pulled his hat down low over his eyes and ordered a mineral water. A stiff shot of whiskey sounded better, but keeping his wits about him seemed like a good idea.

The barkeep chuckled when he pushed Adam's glass toward him. "I think the only other person in town who orders straight mineral water is the sheriff," he said.

Adam just grunted, but his stomach dropped. There was only one other man he'd ever met who never drank anything but straight mineral water. But there was no way that man would be sheriff of some hole-in-the-wall town. Of *any* town. Even if he was somehow still alive, which, as far as Adam knew, he was not.

"You're new in town." It wasn't a question. And it confirmed that these people didn't see strangers all that often.

Adam nodded but avoided eye contact, hoping the barkeep would leave him be.

No such luck.

"You mind telling me how you came to be here? Desolation isn't the easiest place to find."

Adam's head jerked up at that. "This is Desolation?"

The barkeep frowned a little. "You didn't know?"

Adam shook his head, his thoughts spinning like a bored dog chasing its tail. "I was just riding and sort of found you. Didn't realize this place actually existed. Heard stories here and there but none credible enough that I'd have thought to come looking."

The barkeep nodded. "Good. We like to keep it that way. Gotten more than our fair share of strangers the last couple years."

Adam frowned at that, though his attention wasn't really on the barkeep anymore but on the implications of being in the notorious town of Desolation.

"If you're planning on sticking around, you might want to stop by the sheriff's office," the barkeep said. "Town Council's got some rules the newcomers gotta follow."

*Interesting.* "Thanks," Adam said, lifting his glass before quickly downing it. "I'll do that."

He pushed off his stool and headed back outside to Barnaby. Looks like he needed to go see the sheriff to hear whatever these rules were. Because if this really was Desolation, he absolutely wanted—no, *needed*—to stay. It might just save his sorry ass.

Despite the citizens of Desolation taking some obvious pains to keep their location off the map, word had slowly trickled through the dark corners of the Western states and territories that the little town was a safe place for retired…let's call them ne'er-do-wells—"criminals" was such an ugly word—who weren't…ya know…criminals anymore. Pardon—who were ne'er-do-wells who wanted to start doing well. 'Er-do-wells?

Anyhow. Thieves who were done thieving, drifters who were done drifting, gamblers who were (sorta) done gambling, gunslingers who were ready to hang up their guns. If any of those applied to a person, word was Desolation was safe. The town supposedly had a soft spot for folks with a dark past who wanted to live in peace.

And if that didn't fit Adam to perfection, he didn't know what did. If there was one spot on earth that he'd have an actual chance of evading the long reach of Marshal Spurlock, Desolation was it. Spurlock wouldn't put any faith in the tales of Desolation, if he'd ever even heard of it. The few stories Adam had heard had been whispered behind closed doors and even then, only rarely. No. If Adam was really in Desolation, he was probably safe.

And for the first time in months, he took a long, deep breath and let it out again, then looked around his new town with a smile. Despite the crowd, nothing much seemed to be going on. Folks were just milling about. He caught snippets of conversations here and there about nothing much in particular.

Someone who looked to be the town preacher stood with a small group on the raised sidewalk. Maybe it was a prayer meeting or some fire-and-brimstone Bible thumping. Not usually his type of gathering, but he could probably use a bit more religiosity in his life at the moment, considering his circumstances. Though something about the whole setup didn't sit right with him. He wiped his suddenly sweaty palms on his pants. Maybe he should—

"All right, quiet down!" a voice boomed.

Adam's gaze flashed to the man in front of the tavern, all that beautiful peace that had been coursing through his veins instantly disappearing. A feeling not unlike when he'd jumped into that ice-cold lake a few weeks ago and his balls had sucked so high into his body, he'd nearly lost them altogether.

He cursed under his breath as the unfamiliar sensation of butterflies ripped through his stomach. He wasn't exactly lily-livered in most circumstances and certainly wasn't proud of it in this case. He'd faced down more than his fair share of men literally gunnin' for him and obviously had lived to fight another day. But thanks to his ridiculously terrible intuition, he now had a whole new worry to deal with.

Of all the towns in the west he could ride into with his tail between his legs, he had to go and pick the one that was apparently inhabited by none other than Gray "Quick Shot" Woodson himself. A notorious gunfighter who, by all appearances, had become...the town sheriff? Damn it all, the barkeep *had* been talking about him. Shock and terror aside, Adam had to stifle a laugh. One, because of all the people in the world who'd end up becoming a lawman, ol' Quick Shot was the *last* Adam would have picked.

Two, if that were true...well, suffice it to say that the sheriff wouldn't be too pleased to see Adam. And purposely intruding on the territory of a man who would *really* not want him there and had the skills to remove him—permanently—fell into that whole "monumentally asinine decision" category. Of all the rotten luck.

At this point in his life, he really shouldn't be surprised that the place he chose to hide out from the person who wanted him dead was run by another one who'd love to see him six feet south. If he survived his little situation, he really needed to look into making some changes that would minimize the chances of more people rooting for his demise.

Woodson glanced around the crowd, and Adam ducked back behind his horse. Damn. He needed a disguise or something. Leaving would be a better option, but the crowd had spread out enough that it would make a bigger commotion to get his horse through them than just lying low for a few minutes. He pulled off his jacket and embroidered vest and carefully wrapped his silver pocket watch inside them, then stashed the lot in his saddlebags with a sigh. That vest was brand-new. It was sure to get completely wrinkled stored in his bag.

He looked down at himself and then partially untucked his shirt. That…wasn't much of a disguise.

"Hey, kid," Adam said, waving over a youth who'd traipsed by. "Trade me hats."

He pulled his nearly new, expertly made, and lovingly cared-for hat from his head and held it out with more than a little hesitation.

"Really?" the kid said, ripping off his own oversize, floppy hat and holding it out.

"Really," Adam answered. Though he couldn't quite make himself let go.

The kid frowned. "You sure you wanna trade, Mister?"

"Yeah. Yep. Sure. Here you go," he said, relinquishing his hat.

"Thanks, Mister!" The kid scampered off as fast as his feet could carry him. Probably afraid Adam would take the hat back. As well he should.

He looked down at the dirty hat in his hands with distaste and gingerly put it on his head. It smelled like…well, like it had sat on the head of a sweaty, dirty little boy who spent his time rolling in God knew what. On the bright side—well, "bright" was a bit bold—on the slightly optimistic side, the hat, and therefore Adam, would stand out less. And with Quick Shot Woodson roaming the streets of Desolation, that was a good thing.

His scraggly beard would help conceal his face. He could guarantee Woodson had never seen him with such growth before. No one had. His mother would be horrified if she saw him now. He should have listened to her and stayed in Boston and become a banker or lawyer or some other respectable citizen. Instead, he'd gone west, when he was barely old enough to shave, in search of adventure. He'd learned quickly enough that adventure wasn't everything it was cracked up to be. All it had left him with was a dark past he couldn't escape and a deep and abiding distrust of damn near everyone.

"Let's get this over with," Woodson said. "I don't have all day."

Adam flinched at the harsh voice of one of the men who'd instilled that deep and abiding distrust in him. And the last thing Adam wanted to do was let the bastard know he was in town. Before he could change his mind, he bent to rub his hands in the dirt at his feet…and then smeared it across his cheeks. His nose wrinkled, and he glanced down at his hands, fairly sure there had been something more than dirt on the ground. He shook his hands a bit and then sighed and rubbed them down the front of his shirt. If he was going to attempt the filthy hermit disguise, he might as well fully commit.

"All right, everyone who's goin' to, gather around. You all know the rules," Woodson said.

There were nods and murmurs of assent all around him, and Adam had to keep from raising his hand like an absentminded student who'd missed the teacher's instructions. What rules? He hadn't made it over to the sheriff's to find out what they were yet. He almost laughed again as he realized that Woodson would have been the one greeting him at that office, and Adam probably wouldn't have gotten two words out before he was tasting iron.

No matter. This whole thing had been a horrible idea. He pulled his hat down farther. Time to get the hell out of town. Not that he had any other place to go. Maybe he could come to some terms with Woodson. Or maybe he should just slip out while he still coul—

A grown man's body hit the ground near Adam's feet, causing several people to turn toward the sound—toward *him*—and he cursed the unlucky star he was born under.

# CHAPTER TWO

Nora Schumacher blew her hair out of her face and glanced up at the man currently staring at her. In fascination. Or maybe it was horror. Those brown eyes were wide enough, the whites showed all the way around them, so really it could go either way.

"Sorry," she muttered, turning her attention back to the heap of man at her feet. Otherwise known as her father.

She'd managed to haul his considerable ass out of the tavern after several minutes of trying to rouse him had killed the hope he'd get up and walk out on his own. As a last-ditch effort, she'd even taken the remains of his beer and dumped it on his head. He hadn't even twitched. So she'd looped her arms around his chest and dragged him out of there. Barely. Getting him into the back of the wagon was another matter.

She let out a long-suffering sigh. Apparently, she'd need to get someone's attention after all, and she'd really hoped to avoid that. The pity that inevitably followed was more than she could stomach even on a good day. And today was not a good day. She was strong, but lifting his dead weight was a little more than she could handle on her own. But she'd have to wait until the town's little get-together wrapped up.

She sighed again, wiping the sweat from her brow with the back of her hand.

"Looks heavy," the man in front of her said, having apparently recovered his delicate sensibilities enough to speak.

His eyes raked over her, from her trouser-clad legs to the open vest and tucked-in gingham shirt she'd swiped from her father's wardrobe, in what she could have sworn was abject—and unusual, in her experience—appreciation before he returned his gaze to her face. He tipped his hat, flashing her a brilliant, gleaming smile that was completely at odds with his dingy—and stinky—exterior.

"Excuse me?"

He pointed to her father. "You'll put your back out trying to lift that."

She wasn't sure whether to laugh or curse at him. "Noted. Unfortunately, I can't just leave him in the street."

He frowned and rubbed his chin. "I suppose not." He looked her father over like he was appraising a side of beef at the market. "Husband?"

Her eyes narrowed. "Father."

"Ah." He scratched at the scraggly beard on his chin. "It's never the skinny ones who get sozzled, is it?"

She choked out a sharp laugh. "No."

"Any chance he'll wake up and climb back there of his own accord?"

"Going by past experience," she said through a grunt, "also no."

The stranger nodded, his face set in dismayed but determined lines. "No one else around to help you?" His eyes darted to the lingering crowd forming to their right.

"They're all busy," she said.

"No help for it, then," he said with a grimace. "I'll have to give you a hand."

She folded her arms. "I wouldn't want you to trouble yourself," she said, laying on the sarcasm as thick as his comment deserved.

"Truthfully"— he leaned in a bit and lowered his voice, like he was the town gossip telling her a secret—"I wouldn't under normal circumstances."

Before she could think of an appropriate response to that eyebrow raiser, he frowned and pursed his lips. "At least not right away. I'd have helped," he said with a placating smile. Then he shrugged. "Eventually. Most likely. Maybe. To be honest, it would have been right amusing to watch a little girl like you try and haul his considerable backside into that wagon."

Nora's eyebrows hit her hairline. No one, and she meant *no one*, had ever called her *little*. She was scraping six feet, which made her a good hand or two taller than most men in town. Sturdier, too. A fact most of the men she'd met didn't find too attractive. The man before her had her beat, in height and muscle, but not by much. He, however, wasn't looking at her but kept his narrowing gaze on her father.

"But…" He shrugged again. "A man face down in the street does tend to draw attention, and since I'd like to avoid that as much as possible, your and your father's quick departure works very well in my favor. So…"

He gestured for her to take one of her father's arms. She sputtered, not sure how to respond…until he winked at her and gave her a half smile that had her heart hopping around in her chest like a rabbit through a lettuce patch. The charming gesture didn't fit with the grubby man before her. Neither did the manicured nails and soft hands that grasped her father's arm. Something was definitely off with the man.

As was her reaction to him. What the hell was wrong with her? She wasn't the sort to get muddle-headed by a pretty face. If there even was a pretty face under all that dirt. The bone structure was definitely there, but the rest was a bit…smudged.

But there was something about him that had her sitting up and paying attention…and she was too busy for that kind of nonsense.

The glare she attempted to aim at him misfired, as he'd already turned away, rendering her reaction moot. She'd have to remember to glare at him doubly hard next time he looked her way. Though… maybe she'd wait until after he helped her load her father into the wagon. She did need his help, after all.

"Well, come on," he said, grunting as he half lifted her father.

His tone tempted her to take her time, but her father was not a small man, and she wasn't sure how long her would-be-savior could hold him. Best to get him in the wagon before the poor man's spine gave out. Her lips thinned, but she grabbed her father's other arm, and together they hefted the front half of him into the wagon.

The man surprised her again by jumping into the wagon, grabbing her father under his arms, and pulling him the rest of the way in. Then he hopped down and removed his hat so he could mop his brow with a handkerchief.

"Will you need help getting him back out of there?" he asked.

Her eyes widened. "Are you volunteering?"

"Absolutely not," he said, his eyes darting around the crowd that had grown enough that they were only a few feet from the wagon now. Though no one was paying any attention to them. "No offense, but I've got my hands full trying to save my own ass," he muttered, his gaze fixed on the sheriff, who stood at the front of the crowd with the preacher, who was addressing everyone, and their mayor, Mrs. DuVere.

Nora didn't hear what Preacher was saying, though, as her ears were too busy ringing with the man's vehement rejection of her request. Not that it had really been a request.

"If you had no intention of helping me get him out of the wagon, why did you ask if I needed help?" she said, her temper rising.

He looked back at her, brows raised. "Just being friendly."

She glowered. "I'm not sure you're understanding the meaning of that word. 'Friendly' would be helping me get him back out. Not telling me you have more important things to do."

"But I do. I thought women liked honesty." He clapped his hat back on. "I already helped you once. Claiming more of my assistance is rather forward of you."

"Excuse me? I didn't 'claim' your assistance in the first place. You offered."

"And you happily accepted. And I haven't heard so much as a thank-you, by the way, not that I'd expect someone of your...your...your..." He waved his hand toward her, implying all manner of things about her person, her upbringing, and probably a number of other attributes with that stuttering indignation of his.

"My what?" she said, folding her arms and glaring at him.

He snapped his mouth shut and glared back.

"That's what I thought." Like he was one to talk, standing there covered in dirt and horse shit and looking—and smelling—like he'd spent the last month rolling around with coyotes. Not that she'd be rude enough to say so. To his face.

"At the very least, you owe me an apology for your appalling behavior," he said, his tone rivaling that of the snootiest prima donna.

"My *what*? You really think I owe you an apology?"

"Yes, *I do*," he said, his words seeming to echo around them, though he hadn't spoken that loudly. Or maybe it was a real echo, because he frowned, his eyes roving over the crowd again. But she wasn't finished with their conversation yet. Not by a long shot.

"First of all, I didn't ask for your help. I was doing just fine on my own."

He snorted, and she held up a finger to stop him from making any other sound. "I was!" she insisted. "I am perfectly capable of handling my own problems. I do it all the time."

"Do you now?"

"Yes, *I do*! But I don't have the time or patience to explain myself or— Don't shush me!" she said, swatting at the hand he held up to stop her tirade.

His frown deepened, "Is everyone repeating what we're saying?"

"What?" She narrowed her eyes. "Has the heat gone to your head?"

She'd actually heard a few echoes as well, but she wasn't about to admit that to him just then.

He opened his mouth to say something else, but she pushed ahead. "I would have figured out how to get him in the wagon on my own eventually." She ignored his derisive look and kept going. "But since you decided to butt your big head into my business, I didn't see any reason why I shouldn't take advantage."

"My head isn't big," he said, his full indignant attention back on her.

"It's huge. But that's beside the point. Where was I? Oh yes. Secondly, and more importantly, I am usually a delightful person—"

He scoffed loudly at that, and she glared again. "I am! You can ask anyone in town. But I apparently have zero patience for men such as yourself, who for some reason seem to feel the need to goad good people into losing their temper. No, I didn't thank you for your assistance, yet, because you didn't give me the chance—"

"It's really not something that is all that time-consuming. I help, you say thank you. Not *hey can you help some more* and then get angry when I say no."

"Well, fine then, Mister...whatever your name is—"

"Brady. Adam Brady, not that you bothered asking in the first place."

"I shouldn't have to ask. You should have introduced yourself when you approached me. It's the polite thing to do."

His eyes widened slightly. "I'm surprised you know that. You don't seem to have any sort of manners whatsoever."

She gasped. "I have plenty of manners, just none I feel deserve to be wasted on you," she said, poking at his chest. Well, at the air just in front of his chest. She wasn't going to touch that filthy thing he was wearing.

"Of all the ungrateful little—"

"You know what, you're right," she said, pasting on the most saccharinely sweet smile she could muster. "I offer my sincere apologies—"

"Thank yo—"

"—that you're such an insufferable jackass."

His jaw dropped, and he clapped his hand to his chest the way her grandmother used to do when something she considered truly horrendous shocked her. Nora had to bite her cheek to keep from laughing, the heat of her anger tempered by his truly comical expression.

"I take time out of my busy day—"

"Your busy day doing what? Holding up that sad excuse for a horse?"

The horse in question turned and blew a nostril full of air at her, and she mentally apologized to the poor beast.

"Don't drag Barnaby into this. He didn't do anything to you."

"You're right," she said. "My apologies, Barnaby."

"Sure, *him* you'll apologize to."

"Well, he's not being an unreasonable, insufferable—"

"Sign this please."

Nora and Adam briefly glanced at the young man who'd thrust a sheet of paper and pen at them, and then they went back to snarling at each other.

"I am the epitome of reason," Adam said, drawing himself up so he stood another fraction of an inch taller than her. "And I am very sufferable, just not when faced with a—"

"Please just sign this," the young man said again, waving his sheet of paper at them.

Nora snatched the paper from him, balled it up, and tossed it over her shoulder, ignoring the twinge of guilt that pierced her when the poor guy went scrambling for it.

"Did you say you're sufferable?" she asked, her forehead creasing as she squinted at Adam. "What's that even supposed to mean?"

"If you don't know, I'm not going to take the time—"

"I'll have to get another form," the boy said, holding up the now-soggy ball of paper before turning on his heel to make his way back up to the front of the crowd.

"What was that about?" Adam asked.

"What was what about?" Nora said, folding her arms and looking around.

"Never mind, I was just wondering..." He waved it away and got back to berating her. "Where was I? Oh yes, I'm not going to take the time to explain myself to a complete hypocrite. I need to be on my way before…"

He stopped, apparently noticing that she was no longer arguing with him.

"You know, you could at least do me the courtesy of looking at me while I'm insulting you," he said.

She ignored that, her brow creasing in a frown. "What was he trying to get us to sign?"

Adam frowned as well and looked around for the boy. And then he seemed to notice what she had… the crowd that surrounded them were mostly paired up. Couples. Who were now looking very pleased while others congratulated them.

A two-ton brick dropped in her stomach, and her mouth dried up. "Oh no," she muttered.

"Oh no, what?" he asked.

"I think…I think…" She swallowed against the sudden upheaval in her panicked gut.

He raised a brow. "Thinking isn't your strong suit, is it? Does it hurt?"

She scowled, too focused on keeping her breakfast down to give him a proper retort. "I think…we may have just gotten married."

# CHAPTER THREE

"What…what do you mean, we just got *married*?" Adam said, his mind sputtering to a halt.

She just stared at him, her face completely blank. Then she sighed. "Oh well." She turned on her heel and started pushing her way through the crowd.

"What do you mean, *oh well*? Wait a minute. Miss…" Shit. He didn't even know her name. "Miss!" he called after her before noticing that he was being noticed. He tried to draw his neck farther into the collar of his coat, but he kept following her shapely backside, conveniently displayed in a pair of men's trousers, through the crowd. What the hell did she mean, they just got married?

A braid of thick chestnut hair swung across her back as she moved, and he had to stifle the urge to reach out and tug on it. Pulling hair was rude. Unless they were in bed, of course, and… Good God, what was wrong with him? He didn't want to explore why *that* thought had just popped into his head.

He would never willingly get married. Someone with his poor decision-making skills could not be trusted to choose a life mate. Something he'd proven on a semi-regular basis most of his life.

Hell, the last woman he'd been mixed up with had turned on him the moment she found out about the price on his head. He actually didn't blame her. Much. The kind of money that damn lawman Spurlock was offering for him would have tempted his own mother.

Still, he'd be lying if he said it hadn't hurt when she'd betrayed him. He'd damn near married the woman. Sure, he'd been drunk at the time, but it had still been the closest to matrimony he'd ever gotten. And would ever get again. Lesson learned. For real this time. The whole mess only solidified his determination to avoid any further entanglements with the fairer sex. This latest mistake had just been the last in a long line of romantic disappointments he should have known better than to get involved in.

He finally caught up enough that he could reach out and pull her to a stop. "Explain yourself. What do you mean, we're married?"

She scowled at him again. "I mean, Mr. Madam, that—"

"Adam," he said through clenched teeth. "And that's my first name, not my last. Adam Brady."

She squinted at him like she couldn't figure out why he was telling her his name. "Fine. I'm Nora. In any case, Mr. Brady, we just—"

"Brady?" a voice bellowed.

Adam closed his eyes and blew out a breath, every prayer he'd ever heard whispering through his head. "Now you've done it," he muttered to her.

"What?" she asked, eyes wide as she glanced back and forth between him and the sheriff, who now stood on the platform just feet away, gawking at him.

Adam slowly looked over toward Woodson. Who stared right back at him, his face blank with shock.

*Uh-oh.*

Adam backed up a step, his hand tightening on

Nora's—his wife's?—arm when she made to step away. "Oh, no you don't," he said to her, though he didn't take his eyes off Woodson. "You don't go anywhere until we finish our little chat. I just have to deal...with that...first," he said, glancing briefly at her while nodding at Woodson.

The sheriff's eyes widened, and Adam knew his luck, such as it was, had run out.

Woodson's hands immediately went for his holsters, and Adam lurched back, but the crowd had grown too dense. And once they saw who the sheriff was sputtering at, several pairs of hands grabbed him and hauled him forward. His little missus followed of her own accord, her arms crossed and amusement shining from her eyes. So much for Desolation being a friendly, welcoming town.

Woodson slapped at his holsters, pockets, and jacket, and Adam relaxed just a hair when he realized that the sheriff didn't appear to be armed. Odd. Quick Shot Woodson—er, Sheriff Woodson— walking around town without a weapon? Not that Adam was complaining, mind. But still...odd.

Woodson whirled on the woman standing next to him. She shrugged before he even said a word. "They're in the carrot patch."

The sheriff's face turned thunderous, but it didn't seem to bother the woman a whit. Instead, she raised an eyebrow and gave him what Adam could swear was an amused, even fond, smile.

"Dammit, Mercy, what good does it do to keep hiding my guns when you always know where they are?"

She laughed. "I don't know. I've been trying to

tell you that for nigh on three years now."

Woodson threw his hands up and then looked around. "Someone give me a gun."

Adam tried to jerk away from his captors as several people pulled their guns to give to the sheriff, but Mercy—Woodson's wife?—stepped in front of him, blocking Adam somewhat from Woodson's line of sight.

"That's not necessary," she said. "Everyone calm down. Gray," she said, turning to the sheriff, "what on earth is going on?"

The sheriff took several deep breaths and then jerked his head toward Adam. "Remember when I told you that I only became a gunfighter because after my first gunfight there was a loudmouth who blabbed about it, so everybody knew what happened and after that my life was a miserable hell of everybody and their giddy aunt comin' after me?"

"Yes." Then her eyes widened, and she looked at Adam.

He gave her a weak wave. "Hi."

"He's the loudmouth," Woodson said.

Adam grimaced. "'Loudmouth' is a bit harsh." Nora snorted beside him, and he gave her a quick glare.

"That was you?" the cheerful-looking young man standing next to Woodson said. His mouth quirked up in a smile that Adam couldn't really decipher. He seemed amused maybe. Or possibly impressed.

"All hail the kingmaker...so to speak," the man said.

Woodson rolled his eyes. "Shut up, Sunshine."

The man—Sunshine, apparently—just smiled

bigger. His name definitely suited him.

Adam shook his head. "I didn't make him a gunfighter or king of the gunfighters or whatever. You were the one who got in the gunfight in the first place. And won. Spectacularly, I might add."

Gray's eyes narrowed. "You were the one who blabbed about it to anyone who would listen."

"Well, if you want to nitpick about it."

Woodson sputtered and Adam hurried on. "It's not like I'm the only one who saw what happened. Everyone else was talking, too." Keeping his mouth shut would have been a wiser decision, but...well... again, decisions weren't his strong suit.

Woodson stepped down from the platform, and Adam straightened his backbone. If he was going down, he'd do it with dignity. As much as he could muster anyway. That look Woodson was giving him would give even the bravest man a yellow streak or two.

"Everyone might have been talkin', but *you* were the one who did a whole damn interview with that busybody reporter. I could have just ridden out of there and nobody would've been the wiser. Talk would have died down. Nobody even knew who I was except you, and it could have stayed that way, but you had to go tell everybody my name, and after they ran that cockamamie story, my life was over. I was up on posters all over the place with that ridiculous nickname—"

"I *did* come up with Quick Shot," Adam said to Nora, grinning. She raised her eyebrows, her gaze flashing back to Woodson, and Adam immediately kicked himself. But really, it wasn't every day a person got to name a notorious gunfighter. Who was at that moment glaring daggers at him.

Right. Time to shut up.

"I'm surprised, given your obvious…irritation with the matter," Sunshine said, "that you didn't track him down and…umm…well…" He trailed off and grinned, though his meaning was clear enough.

"Oh, he did," Adam said. "Only took him about a week before he found me and told me to keep quiet or else."

Mrs. Woodson's eyes grew round, and she looked at her husband. "You challenged him?"

Woodson grunted. "No. I threatened him. Then *he* challenged *me*."

All eyes turned toward Adam, who shrugged. "What can I say? I was a naive kid who thought I was invincible."

"So you let him walk away?" Mrs. Woodson asked, looking at her husband like she'd just found out he'd saved a litter of kittens from a rabid fox.

Adam raised his brows. She was either so loyal of a wife that she couldn't believe her husband could ever lose a gunfight, or she knew just how good Woodson was and that no one walked away from him unless he allowed it. Maybe it was both.

Woodson scowled. It seemed to be his default expression. "I told you I've never killed anybody who wasn't tryin' to kill me first."

His wife glanced Adam's way. "And you weren't trying to kill him?"

Adam gave her a sheepish grin. "Oh, no, ma'am, I was definitely trying. But like I said, I was just a kid who didn't know what I was doing. I think ol' Quick

Shot there took pity on me."

The gunslinger in question grimaced, and Adam went back to his explanation. "He did, however, fire a warning shot across my bow, so to speak. I'm pretty sure my bullet at least grazed his arm" — Woodson snorted and Adam ignored him — "but his took my hat clean off my head. I've never harbored any delusions that the bullet couldn't have gone right on through my skull if Mr. Woodson had wanted, and he certainly could have taken a second shot while I was on my butt in the dirt. But whatever his reasoning, he let me walk out of there alive and with the reputation of the only man who'd survived a gunfight with old Quick Shot Woodson."

"Right," Woodson said, glaring at him again. "With the stipulation that you kept your mouth shut and never darkened my door again. Yet here you are."

His wife laid a soothing hand on his arm. "Maybe we should all calm down a bit. I know you've got some…unresolved issues with this gentleman—"

Woodson glowered. "He's no more a gentleman than I am. He told you: he's a gunfighter. And a filthy, dirty one at that. What have you been doing with yourself?" he asked, his nose crinkling. "Rolling around in pigsties?"

"Horse dung," Nora supplied helpfully.

Adam flashed her a glare and then turned back to the group on the platform. "Gambling, mostly. Gunfighting is more of an occasionally unavoidable hobby," Adam said. Not that being a gambler along with being a gunfighter made him any more respectable.

"Another gunfighter, eh?" a buxom, flamboyantly dressed woman said, looking at him with interest. "We don't get many of you. Get our fair share of train robbers and the occasional cattle rustler or two, but gunslingers are fairly rare. Have we heard of you, then?"

Adam returned her smile. "Probably not. I'm not nearly as good as ol' Quick Shot there, reputation as his only survivor notwithstanding. I tried to keep that under my hat as much as possible, and after a few years, people forgot who exactly it was who'd walked away." He flinched a little when Woodson's face darkened a deeper shade of red.

"A courtesy you didn't see fit to extend to me," Woodson bit out through clenched teeth.

"I said sorry," Adam muttered.

Woodson looked about ready to come out of his skin, and his wife patted his arm again.

"Well, whatever your background, you're good enough to still be standin' here," the buxom woman said with a wink.

Adam chuckled. "True." Then he turned back to Woodson, his amusement evaporating. "And I'd really like to keep on standing here, if you can keep from killing me long enough to hear me out."

Woodson scowled. "Hear you out about what?"

Adam took a deep breath and blew it out. "I just want what you seem to have found. Peace and quiet. A safe place to retire."

Woodson was already shaking his head. "No way in hell. You're not staying. Yo—"

"Gray," Mercy said. "We should at least discuss it. You can't just tell him he can't stay."

"Yes I can. I—"

She leaned in and whispered something in his ear, and Adam watched Woodson's anger visibly deflate. Fascinating. Who knew marriage could change a man so much? One of the many reasons why Adam remaining unmarried was his number one rule. He liked himself just as he was, thank you very much.

The sudden realization that rule number one may have just flown the coop hit him in the gut and made his apple breakfast curdle. He glanced at his possible wife again, but Woodson's deep inhalation drew his attention back before he could say anything to her. Not that he had any clue what to say.

Woodson pinned Adam with his nut-withering gaze again. "Fine. We need to get this meeting finished before dealing with any…new business," he said, looking Adam up and down with a gaze so sharp, Adam was surprised there was anything left of him by the time he was done. "So *you*, don't be a nuisance. I'll deal with you in a few minutes."

Then he turned his attention back to the group waiting on him, and Adam released a long breath. He'd survived his first run-in with ol' Quick Shot Woodson and was still breathing. Somewhat. He wouldn't wager too much on his chances just yet. He wasn't a complete fool. But…

Maybe he'd live to see retirement after all.

Though maybe that wasn't a good thing. Because his plans for retirement had never included a wife.

# CHAPTER FOUR

The sheriff turned to address the crowd around them. The ones who hadn't been "lucky" enough to get hitched started grumbling, and the one at Nora's side seemed ready to follow their example. Nora sighed. That was her cue to skedaddle. She'd figure out what to do with her new husband later.

While she hadn't completely intended on going to the tavern to join in the mass marriage ceremony, she had thought she might at least check it out. The last thing she wanted was a husband, but it did solve a rather pressing problem she had. One she hadn't wanted to burden any of her friends with. Adam being there at just the right time might be the first stroke of good luck she'd had in a while.

She turned to head back to her wagon, but Adam's hand shot out and grabbed her arm. "You aren't going anywhere until you explain what the hell is going on."

The grumbling in the crowd had grown so loud that Adam had his mouth almost pressed against her ear to make himself heard. She pulled away so she could look at him. His eyes roved over her face, focusing on her lips long enough that her breath hitched ever so slightly.

She had quite a few male friends in town. Men who would drink or gamble with her, work with her, ride beside her, without hesitation. She was just "one of the boys" to them, and for the most part she liked it that way. Not one of them had ever looked at her with anything but friendship, or if they had, they were very good at hiding it. That look that flashed in Adam's eyes as he gazed at her lips wasn't one she'd ever seen in a man before. And it was gone so quickly, she couldn't be sure she hadn't imagined it.

She opened her mouth to answer him, but before she could, a gunshot went off, and they both ducked for cover. After a few seconds, it was obvious no more shots were coming, and she raised a cautious head to see who'd pulled a gun.

Jason Sunshine, the sheriff's deputy, was putting his back in the holster while the poor sheriff scrubbed a hand over his face before looking out at the crowd. He was obviously about at the end of his limited patience. Nora could almost see him counting to ten in his head.

"I wonder if he's even aware that his hands keep straying toward his empty gun holsters. Or if that's just a nervous tic," Mr. Brady said. "Why *are* his holsters empty?"

She ignored the question and focused on the implied insult. "Our sheriff does *not* get nervous."

He held up his hands. "I meant no offense. I'm just glad I'm not in the line of fire. Yet," he added on with a mumble.

"All right," the sheriff thundered, holding his hands up to quiet everyone down again. "Enough discussion. If you didn't get picked, you didn't get picked. Get a job. It won't kill you. But the rules stay the same. Thirty days to get a wife or a job or you're out."

"What does he mean, thirty days or you're out?

And job? What job?" Adam said, turning to her again. "What was that bit? Can I pick that option instead?"

Nora snorted and looked him up and down. "Are you qualified for any type of employment?"

He opened his mouth, probably to say of course he was, and then snapped it shut again with a grimace.

"Thought not." Nora smiled and turned to walk away, but Adam stopped her again.

"What?" she said impatiently, pulling her arm from his grasp.

"Shouldn't we talk for a minute?"

Her new husband was starting to grate on her nerves. "Don't see why that's necessary." She shrugged and tried to push her way to the edge of the crowd, but there were too many people to get through. This town was growing altogether too crowded for her liking.

"Don't see why…" he repeated, apparently flabbergasted at her statement. "Because apparently we just got hitched."

"Right," she said. "Didn't we already cover this bit?"

He let out a choked cough. "Not really, no! We've got things to discuss."

She pursed her lips. "Don't see why. You wouldn't have been my first choice by any stretch, but it's done, so…" She gave him a lopsided shrug. "I suppose it doesn't matter too much. You wanted to get hitched, and while I wasn't planning on getting married today, it does solve a little problem I've been having, so I suppose you'll do as well as any."

"Except," he said, keeping her from heading off again, "that's where you're wrong. *I* didn't want to get married."

She stopped trying to push through the crowd and looked at him, eyebrows raised and stomach tied in knots. *What?* "Then what were you doing standing in among the fellows who did?"

Adam threw his hands up. "I didn't know that's what they were there for! I just got into town."

She let out a short bark of laughter. "So you just wandered into town and thought it would be a good idea to mingle in with the crowd without knowing why they were congregating in the first place?"

He frowned. "When you put it like that…"

She chuckled again and then turned and continued on her way.

"Wait," he said, chasing after her.

"Don't got time to wait," she said.

"Yes, but…" He pulled her to a stop again. "At least explain to me what just happened."

She blew out an exasperated breath and turned around. "It's real simple. We've had several newcomers find their way to town over the last couple years. Nearly a dozen so far. That's a lot for this kind of town, especially when they are all…your kind of people."

Adam frowned. "*My* kind of people?"

There really wasn't a polite way to expound upon that. "You know, the kind who come with wanted posters."

Adam rolled his eyes. "Rude. But fair, I suppose. Go on."

"Anyway, they don't seem to know how to do

much except cause mischief. So the Town Council instituted some new rules. You want to stay, you get married. The ones who were interested were supposed to meet up this morning in front of the tavern. You get chosen, you get hitched. And since we were both standing in the wrong place at the wrong time and apparently said the right words at the right time...well...congratulations. We're married."

"But..."

"If it makes you feel any better, it's a shock to me, too. Yes, I'd gone to town and thought maybe I'd look over the options. But I didn't have a solid plan of choosing anyone. I got a little tied up with my father—who is still out cold in the back of my wagon, by the way, which is why I really need to go—and I didn't realize they'd started the ceremony, or I would have grabbed someone else. Maybe. I still hadn't really made up my mind. Though..." She looked him up and down. "I really didn't want to marry any of the others who were there, so maybe it's a good thing you wandered into town."

"No it isn't. And I don't get—"

She sighed again. "It's really not that complicated."

"It's hugely complicated!"

She turned and started walking again with him close on her heels. "Look, Mister...Mister..."

"Brady. Adam," he said, looking nonplussed that she didn't remember. Hey, it had been a busy morning. "Really, you want me to believe you are fine with this marriage thing when you can't even remember my name? If we're married, which we're not, it would make it your name, too. What kind of woman can't remember her own name?"

"Fine. I'll work on it. If it makes you feel any better, I don't rightly care what you do with yourself. If you don't want to stick around, I won't complain. In fact, I'd prefer it."

He frowned harder. "I thought you wanted to get married."

"I do, sort of. That doesn't mean I want a husband."

He took his hat off and scratched at his head, his face twisted in confusion so comical, she'd laugh if she had the time or patience for it.

"That doesn't make a lick of sense," he said, clapping his hat back on his head.

She just shrugged and kept picking her way through the crowd but got pulled up short again when the sheriff barked out another order.

"I don't want to hear another word of complaint about it," the sheriff said. "Everyone knew the rules. Everyone agreed."

"Not everyone," Adam grumbled. She rolled her eyes and folded her arms, giving up on pushing through the crowd until the sheriff had said his piece.

"No matter the outcome of today's little matchmakin' contest, the rules have not changed. Especially the first three," the sheriff said. "In case any of you knuckleheads has forgotten how things run in this town, let me remind you. It's one thing to pick up a stray here and there," he said, glancing at Deputy Sunshine, who just gave him a cheerful smile. "But we've had far too many newcomers trickling in. Almost a dozen in the last year or so. At this rate, we're going to be less of a town and more of a retirement community for the infamous and notorious. I don't think any of us wants that."

There were nods of agreement through the crowd. The sheriff looked them over with a stern eye. "So you best not forget, the first rule of Desolation is keep your yaps shut. The last thing we want is for people to go around advertisin' this place. Second, there will be no fightin' in the town limits. You got a disagreement, take it elsewhere. I don't want any part of it, and if the town's peace or, more importantly, *my* peace gets disturbed by havin' to break up more fights, both parties will be fined five hundred dollars and will be spending a week in my jail cells."

"Now, Sheriff," someone started, but the sheriff gave him such a withering look, even Nora shuddered.

Mr. Brady snorted out a laugh. "That's a look that'll shrink a man's balls to the size of raisins."

Nora's mouth dropped open, and Mr. Brady did a double-take look at her and shrugged. "I'm not wrong."

She didn't know whether to laugh or head straight to church and pray for his soul.

"And I can't believe I even have to point this one out," the sheriff said, "but there will be no killin' of anybody under any circumstances."

"Now that's a rule I can get behind," Mr. Brady said, and Nora's lips twitched. With his history with the sheriff, he *would* like that one.

"Killin' another town member is automatic

expulsion from the town, and that's if you ever see the light of day again. For those of you too distracted or just plain stupid to pay attention, let me sum it up for you. No talkin'. No fightin'. No killin'."

"Good rules," Mr. Brady said.

"You break those three, you answer to me. As for the new ones...Mrs. DuVere?" The sheriff stepped back, apparently done with what he had to say.

Mrs. DuVere stepped forward, the beads on her extravagant—just a shade under gaudy—gown flashing.

"Who's that?" Mr. Brady whispered.

"The mayor."

"*She's* the mayor?" he asked, but Nora just shushed him.

"Now, I know some of you are mighty disappointed. Many of our new arrivals weren't taking to retirement all that well to begin with, and this surely won't help those who didn't get matched. But we still expect you to behave yourselves," she said, pinning a few men in the group with a gaze that made them squirm. "As I've said before, men without a purpose tend to get into mischief."

Nora thought about her father in the wagon. If that wasn't the god's honest truth...

"So," she continued. "As was discussed, if you want to stay in this town, you're going to find yourselves some purpose. Those lucky enough to have gotten hitched today, congratulations. The rest of you have thirty days to find yourselves some employment."

The sheriff stepped up again before the grumbling could get too loud.

"This isn't up for discussion. We've discussed it to death as it is, and it wasn't a conversation I wanted to have the first time. There've been too many men who are used to livin' life on the edge comin' into this town thinkin' they want the quiet life and findin' out it doesn't suit them after all. I've had men in and out of my jail like it's got a revolvin' door because none of you have anythin' better to do than stir up trouble. That's not what we're offerin' here. If you got matched up, congratulations. If not, find yourselves something better with which to occupy your time! You want peace, quiet, relative safety? Follow the damn rules! You don't want to do that... you know the way out of town."

There were a few more grumbles, but no one argued too loudly, and the sheriff nodded.

"Now, I realize no one likes someone imposin' rules on them, least of all me. But we all agreed that somethin' had to be done because things were gettin' out of hand, and I didn't take this job so I could spend my days breakin' up petty arguments and managin' mischief makers. I was promised boredom, dammit, and my days lately have been chock-full of diverting occupation, and I won't stand for it!"

The crowd around him muttered again, though this time with more than a few amused laughs quickly disguised. The sheriff waited a few more moments, his eyes roving over the crowd before he gave a sharp nod.

Mr. Brady leaned a bit closer to her. "I actually don't disagree with the Town Council, you know," he said. "Bored men are absolutely apt to get into trouble. And I'm sure most of these men are like me, in that we want to stay in this town to escape that kind of life. Stay out of trouble. *However*. I must state this again. I want no part of matrimony. I've been avoiding it my whole life and have no desire or intention of changing that now. I'd make a horrible husband."

She couldn't help but smile. "Don't worry so much, Mr. Brady. I'll make a terrible wife."

Adam turned to her with an exasperated huff. "Then why do you want to stay married?"

"Didn't we already cover this bit?"

He stared at her like a newborn lamb who had no idea what sort of world it had just been pushed into. She sighed again. "Look, Mister..." She frowned.

"Brady. B-r-a-d-y," he said, spelling it out, then said it again, drawing it out real slowly. "Braaaaady."

She tried not to smile. So easy to get under his skin. "Mr. Brady. Desolation isn't the easiest town to find, and it's certainly not one most people want to stay in. Most who come have secrets that keep them here. I doubt you're much different. You want to stay? You stay hitched."

He blew out a long, frustrated breath and stared at the ground. She almost pitied him. Almost. But now that she'd had a few moments to let it sink in, she realized he was her ticket to a better life for herself, and she wasn't going to pass up the opportunity. She didn't want a husband. But she needed one. At least temporarily. So why go about the trouble of trying to find someone else when she already had one hitched and ready to go?

"So you have no qualms whatsoever about marrying a total stranger?" he asked.

"Nope," she said. Not the total truth, but she didn't know him well enough to trust him with her qualms yet.

"If you don't mind my saying, it seems rather… imprudent to commit such a permanent act when you have no desire to do so, so why are you doing this?"

She swallowed back another sigh. "I got my reasons."

"I've got my reasons, too."

"Then I guess you were standing in the wrong place at the wrong time, stranger."

"Brady!" the sheriff yelled, and Adam jumped a little, drawing another smile from her lips. "Get in here. Nora, you too."

The sheriff and Town Council were moving into the tavern, and Brady glanced at Nora, eyebrows raised. She shrugged and moved to follow them. Now that she had a husband, she could actually put the rest of her previously half-baked plan into motion. And that involved doing whatever she needed to in order to keep their property—*her* property—and more specifically the deed, safe and in her name.

Well, hers upon her thirtieth birthday or her marriage, whichever came first. And she didn't trust her father not to lose, sell, or completely destroy the place she loved more than any other before she turned thirty in five years. Hence, her need for a husband. Now that she had one, all she needed was two witnesses to the marriage—not a problem there, as most of the town had been in attendance—and the deed was hers. Technically it would belong to her husband, but what he didn't know wouldn't hurt him.

She'd meant what she'd said. Now that they were hitched, she didn't care where he went or what he did. In fact, her purposes would be better served if he decided Desolation wasn't the town for him after all and left.

"You two, sit," the sheriff said to them.

Nora perched on the edge of her seat, trying not to squirm. She'd never been the focus of the sheriff's displeasure before. The sheriff was a good man, but he did tend to be a bit of a curmudgeon. He was even grouchy with his deputy, Jason Sunshine, and it was damn near impossible to be grouchy around Mr. Sunshine.

"Preacher says that you two were one of the pairs who just got hitched. That true?"

"Yes," she said, at the same time that Adam said, "Not really."

The sheriff raised his eyebrows. "Well, which is it?"

Nora glanced at her new husband, her own eyebrows raised. Adam groaned and rubbed a hand over his face.

"All right, yes, I suppose we are. But…" He opened and closed his mouth a few times as if he just couldn't make himself say the words, then rubbed two hands over his face before getting up to pace in front of their table.

"Of all the things I thought might happen when I rode into town this morning, this was not something that was even in my wildest realm of possibilities. I mean…" He paced again and Nora watched him, not sure if she was amused or offended or both.

He finally stopped in front of her, his face a picture of nonplussed exasperation. "Do you have any idea what you've done?"

"What do you mean, what *I've* done?" she said, also getting to her feet. "You were standing right in the middle of the marriage mart and yelled 'I do' at the top of your lungs. Don't blame this on me."

"I swear I'm doomed," he muttered.

"What do you mean, doomed?" she said, scowling.

He just shook his head, both of them oblivious to their audience. "I only have two hard-and-fast rules I live by, Miss…what the hell is your name anyway?"

"Schumacher," she said through gritted teeth. "Nora Schumacher."

"Miss Schumacher. I have two rules. Avoid life-threatening situations at all costs, which can also be translated into never crossing Gray Woodson again. And never under any circumstances get married. Two rules! That's it! I've been avoiding *that* man for half my life," he said, flinging a finger out at the sheriff, "and I've been avoiding matrimony even longer than that. And somehow within fifteen minutes of setting foot in this town *and meeting you*, I've broken both of the rules I live my life by. So yes, I say doomed. What would you call it?"

"Lucky?" she said with a grin, hoping to bring levity to the conversation. Because his horror at their spontaneous marriage was starting to sting.

Adam's jaw dropped. She was pretty sure she'd struck him totally speechless. *Finally*. She'd never met a man who loved to hear himself talk so much.

"Nora," Preacher said, frowning down at her,

"did you want to be wed?"

Nora's cheeks heated, but she kept her chin up. "I...I didn't necessarily wish to be wed, but I have my reasons for needing a husband. So...yes. I came to the gathering today intending to...explore a few options, let's say. He's not exactly what I was hoping for but..." She looked him up and down and shrugged. "He'll do, I suppose."

"I will absolutely *not* do," he said, stepping away like she was riddled with plague and aiming for a kiss. "The last thing in the world I want is a wife."

Martha Clifford, the woman who ran the general store, leaned forward. "Then why were you standing in with all the other men hoping to get hitched?"

"I didn't know I was! I'd just ridden into town." He turned back to Nora. "Why didn't *you* say anything?"

"I would have if I'd noticed they had started the ceremony. Unfortunately, I had my hands full with a right jackass at that exact moment."

"Sheriff Woodson, sir," a voice said from the back, and they all turned to see the boy who'd been trying to get them to sign something push his way forward.

"What is it, Tommy?" the sheriff asked.

"Well, sir, they was standing with the other couples and I heard them both say 'I do,' clear as day. But they didn't sign the form, sir."

Nora and Adam turned to each other with a frown and then turned back to the boy. "What form?" Nora asked.

The boy looked at Preacher, who frowned down at them. "The marriage license. And if you didn't sign it, then it would seem that while you might be married in the eyes of the church, it's not quite legal yet."

Nora's stomach dropped. She *needed* it to be legal. It's the only thing she *did* need from this travesty of a marriage.

"So…we aren't married?" Adam asked, his face creased with confusion.

Preacher's frown deepened. "I suppose it depends on who you ask. I have the legal and religious authority to marry couples. In my eyes, and in the eyes of God, you are married. I'll record it in the church registry. Sometimes that will suffice for legal reasons, or at least it did in the past. But more likely…the state of Colorado would not consider you wed until the proper paperwork is filed. Paperwork which you haven't signed."

Nora's head spun. "I'm sorry, Preacher, but what the hell does that all mean?"

"What she said," Adam piped in. "Are we married or not?"

Preacher let out a deep sigh. "It means you're in a sort of limbo, I suppose. You either get an annulment through the church and go your separate ways or sign the paperwork and make it legal."

Nora and Adam turned to each other and spoke at the same time.

"Are you going to sign?"

"Are you going to annul me?"

"No!" they both answered.

Adam turned back to the Council, his hand thrown out to gesture at her. "Can you imagine us stuck together? I mean…you can't expect to hold me to a wedding I didn't even know was happening. Surely something can be done. I can't be—"

"You can't be what?" Martha said, lurching to her feet, her usually pleasant features screwed up into such a perfect mask of fury that Adam took another step back. "Nora Schumacher is one of the best people I know. You could do a lot worse than the likes of her, but you'll never find better. Of all the rude, arrogant, ignorant men I've seen come through this town, you are the worst. I'll have you know—"

Doc Fairbanks, the town doctor and final member of the Town Council, wrapped an arm around her waist and pulled her back when she looked about ready to climb over the table to defend Nora's honor and clobber Adam. If that didn't just warm Nora right down to her oversize toes, she didn't know what did. That Martha was such a sweetheart.

"It's all right, Martha," Nora said, straightening to her full height and looking down her nose at the jackass in question. It was one thing to be taken aback by a surprise wedding. But this man…this man acted like being tied to her was worse than death. In front of everyone in town. Not being chosen, by anyone, not once in her life was bad enough. Being so outrightly rejected in front of everyone…

She wouldn't let them see how badly it hurt. She pasted the most disdainful look she could muster on her face and looked at Mr. Adam Brady with as much contempt as she could.

"I have no desire to be stuck with this cretin, either. Preacher, do what needs doin' to make this all go away," she said, waving a dismissive hand at Adam. "If you'll excuse me," she said to the Council,

"I've got chores that need tending."

Nora turned her back on them all and pushed her way out of the overflowing tavern before the tears that were clogging her throat erupted. She wouldn't let any of them see how his rejection had hurt. She knew she wasn't everyone's cup of tea. It was why Adam would be so perfect. A stranger in town. Someone who didn't seem to want to attract attention. Someone who might not be staying long. Someone who might help her get what she needed and then disappear before he became too much of a nuisance.

All the other men in town wanted an actual wife. Permanently. And none of them would have wanted her even if she'd been amenable. She was one of the boys. Not one of the boys' wives. In a town with a serious female shortage, the fact that she was still single into her mid-twenties spoke for itself.

But Adam had made it so…so personal. In front of everyone. It was bad enough they all knew she'd wanted to get married, but to be rejected in such a fashion…

She took a deep breath and blew it out through her nose while hopping up into her rig. Her father let out a grunt and a fart and immediately started snoring again, and she closed her eyes, praying for peace.

The temptation to unhitch the wagon and ride out of town to find a life for herself elsewhere was strong. But she wouldn't give any of them the satisfaction. She'd stick it out. Find another solution to keep her property safe until she turned thirty.

Adam Brady be damned.

# CHAPTER FIVE

Adam stared after Nora as she sashayed a rather sweet backside out the door, her head held high. An unfamiliar twinge of guilt curdled his belly. He'd hurt her. She'd tried hard to hide it, but he could see that quick flash of pain in her eyes. Dammit, he hadn't meant to do that. But he was the last thing she or any woman needed. She would have found that out quickly enough. Better to find it out before she'd gotten hurt any worse than a momentary sting of embarrassment.

He turned back to Woodson and the Town Council to find matching glares on all their faces.

Wonderful. Just what he needed. More enemies.

"You better hope you can find, and keep, a viable job, Brady," Woodson said, his voice terrifyingly quiet. "Because aside from a handful of children and schoolgirls, there are only two unmarried and unattached women left in this town. One is only seventeen years old. And you just made a lifelong enemy of the other."

Of course he had. Adam closed his eyes briefly and blew out a long breath. "I can find a job," he said, putting more conviction into the words than he felt.

He had no idea what sort of work he'd be able to find. He'd always made his living at the card tables and kept what he had with the occasional, unavoidable gunfight. He wasn't qualified to do anything but gamble or shoot at people, and he'd really been hoping to retire from both of those…occupations. Without the usual prerequisite of a funeral. A prospect he'd never hoped to consider before and that now he could not dismiss. He *needed* to stay. Even if it *was* Woodson's territory.

The gambling he could probably keep doing recreationally, but it certainly wasn't a profession the Town Council would approve of, and it wasn't really one he could do and remain in the same place for long. A man could only beat the same people at cards for so long before his presence wasn't welcome anymore. So that was out. As for his other skill… even if he wanted to keep gunfighting, Woodson and the Town Council had just made it abundantly clear that wouldn't be tolerated. Which was good because he was pretty sure Nora would be the first in line to call him out if duels were allowed.

Deservedly so.

"Sit," Woodson ordered.

Adam did so, glancing around the table at everyone sitting there, waiting for Woodson—or someone—to make introductions. But Woodson didn't do anything but glower at him, his eyes narrowed like he was trying to pull all Adam's secrets from his mind. Adam wasn't all that sure the man couldn't do it.

*All right, then.* He cleared his throat and smiled at the group. "I know I've gotten off on the wrong foot with everyone. My apologies."

Most of the people around the table nodded, their expressions lightening somewhat. Except Woodson's, of course, though that was no surprise.

Adam cleared his throat. "Well, you already know my background. But I didn't formally introduce myself. Since the sheriff doesn't want to do the honors, I'm Adam Brady. Gambler. Gunfighter. Retired, hopefully."

The woman beside the sheriff gave him a tentative smile. "Mercy Woodson. And this is Gray's deputy, Jason Sunshine." The pleasant-looking young man with the cheery perma-smile next to Woodson grinned and tipped his hat to Adam. "Mrs. DuVere is our mayor and owns the tavern and new boarding-house that's being built."

"Pleased to make your acquaintance, honey," she said, giving him a warm smile. "You see me when this little meet-and-greet is done and we'll get you fixed up with a room."

Adam smiled gratefully, hiding his surprise that the town's mayor was not only female but from all appearances most likely owned the brothel. Or... parlor house, since he wanted to be polite. "That would be wonderful, thank you."

She nodded, and Mercy motioned toward two men sitting on Mrs. DuVere's other side. "This is Doctor Harrison Fairbanks—everyone calls him Doc—and our pastor, Reverend Samuel Connelly. Most around here just call him Preacher."

Both men nodded civilly but watched him with enough suspicion that Adam actually relaxed a little. He'd been starting to think the town just accepted anyone who walked in and, while he definitely wanted them to accept *him*, there were more than a few men who would come to Desolation under the guise of retirement who shouldn't be allowed in. It was good to know they were at least a little discerning.

Mercy gestured to a young woman on the other side of her. "And this is Martha Clifford. She and her grandparents own the general store."

"Pleased to meet you, Miss," he said, tipping his hat to her with a smile.

She glowered at him but nodded. That was fair. Nora was obviously her friend. It was good to have friends who had your back. So he'd heard.

Woodson scowled. "Against my better judgment, I've been persuaded to allow you to stay."

More like it was pointed out that he didn't have a cause to banish him, but Adam didn't feel it wise to poke at his luck too much, so he just gave Woodson a quick nod. "Thank you."

"*But.*"

Adam's eyebrow rose. He should have known there was a *but*.

"You heard the rules," Woodson stated.

Adam nodded again.

"You will abide by those rules, just like everyone else."

"I expected nothing less." He didn't like it. But he *had* expected it. So, abide by it he would. "I'm willing to find employment."

Woodson looked him over skeptically, but instead of questioning Adam's nonexistent skills, he asked something Adam had really been hoping to avoid.

"Why do you want to stay here?"

He didn't ask it angrily or even suspiciously but like he genuinely wanted to know. However, it wasn't something Adam was going to share with him. Not yet anyway.

His lips pinched together, his jaw working silently for a second. Finally, he answered. "I heard tales that Desolation was a place where people are accepted…" He looked Woodson in the eye. "No questions asked."

Woodson's frown deepened, and Adam could see the questions ready to burst from him. His brow creased, but instead of interrogating Adam further, he jerked his head in a nod. "People are welcome to their secrets here. But…"

Adam cocked an eyebrow again. Woodson really liked his *buts*.

"Your past better not be something that puts this town in danger. And you better keep out of trouble."

Adam shifted in his chair, but he nodded. He had no intention of getting into trouble—he never did, it just sort of seemed to find him anyway. This morning was a prime example of that. But he'd do his damn level best to steer clear of it. As for his past…well, as long as it didn't find him—and staying put in Desolation would decrease those odds greatly—he, and the town, would be just fine.

"Good!" Mrs. DuVere said, standing with a flourish. "Now that all of that is settled, why don't you come along with me, and we'll get you set up with a place to stay."

Adam rose gratefully and followed her from the tavern, conscious of the eyes that followed him. But hey, no one had chased him out of town with guns drawn or pitchforks at the ready (it was truly astounding what people would chase a man with when they were riled enough) so he counted it a win and left with a smile on his face.

Adam retrieved his saddlebags, and Mrs. DuVere sent a boy standing near the horses with Barnaby to the town's stables and then chattered companionably while she and Adam picked their way to the half-finished boardinghouse. The first floor with its multiple sitting rooms, large dining room, and kitchen was complete and decorated with simple but luxurious taste. The second floor, though, was little more than studs dividing the space into what would be eight small bedrooms. Four of them had sheets strung on ropes to give the occupants some degree of privacy.

"It's not much just yet, but it'll give you a place to lay your head," Mrs. DuVere said, leading him to one of the open rooms. There wasn't a bed yet, but there was a small dresser with a basin and a pitcher full of water.

"There're some sheets there on the dresser you can hang up for privacy. Hopefully we'll have walls in the next week or so. Outhouse is down the little path out back."

"This will do nicely, thank you, Mrs. DuVere." Who was he to complain? It was certainly better than bunking with Barnaby in the stables.

"Now, you're looking for work?" she asked, and Adam nodded. "Good. As you can tell, we've got plenty to do around here. You ever swing a hammer before?"

Adam grimaced. "No, but I'm willing to swing anything you want me to."

Mrs. DuVere chuckled. "We'll start with the

hammer and go from there. My builder's down a few men, so things have been slow going. I'm sure he'd be thrilled to hire you. I'll have a word with him in the morning."

"I'm much obliged, ma'am," Adam said, genuinely touched that she was putting herself out to help him.

"No thanks necessary, honey. I need this place finished. Plus," she added with a grin, "having you around livens the place up. Gets the sheriff's blood moving. It's good for him."

Adam chuckled. "You've got a bit of a mischievous streak, I think."

She shrugged and winked at him before swinging her skirts through his empty doorway. "Can't say I'm happy about what happened with Nora. She's a sweet girl. That's a mess you better clean up with as little fuss as possible. No one in this town will be happy to see her hurt."

"Understood," he said.

She regarded him for a second and then gave him a sharp nod and turned to go. "Supper is at six," she called over her shoulder.

"I'll be there!"

She waved in his direction without turning back around, and he was alone. Well, alone as a man could be with only a sheet separating him from the other tenants.

He sighed. "Might as well get settled in," he muttered.

Though that wouldn't take long. In fact, until he had more than a sheet protecting his things from anyone who happened to be wandering by, he'd just as soon keep everything stowed in his saddlebags. So, aside from setting up his sleep roll, there wasn't much more to be done. Unfortunately, there were quite a few hours of daylight left. But he was suddenly so bone-tired he couldn't fathom doing much else but lying down and sleeping for a few days.

Might as well.

First things first, though. He went to the dresser and filled the plain white basin with water from the matching pitcher and then did what he could to de-grime himself. What he'd really like was a nice, hot bath, but considering his current accommodations didn't even have walls, an actual bathtub wasn't something he'd hope for. He'd have to ask if there was a bathhouse in town. And a laundry. The state of his poor clothing was truly tragic.

Once he was relatively clean and had changed into a fresh shirt, he settled on his sleep roll and pulled his hat over his eyes. He'd procured a place to sleep and had a job lined up for the next morning, which would keep him in town. Which he needed, since hopefully that annulment would be coming through shortly. He'd survived his first run-in with Woodson unscathed. Mostly. The whole annulment thing wasn't going to help him, and he had some fences to mend regarding Nora if he wanted to make friends in town.

And he did. Because if his past caught up with him—and going by his luck lately, it would—he was going to need them.

# CHAPTER SIX

Nora kept her backbone rigid until she made it through the door of her house. And then she closed it and slumped against it, closing her eyes against the tears that wanted to fall.

Despite the futility of letting his rejection get to her, she couldn't stop the familiar spear of aching pain that lanced through her. She didn't even know the man. He wasn't actually rejecting her so much as the situation. She knew that. Didn't even blame him. Hell, he hadn't known the rules when he'd been standing in that square, so the remote possibility that he'd end up with a wife hadn't even occurred to him. *Of course* he was going to object.

Yet still…

She slid down the door until she hit the floor and rested her head on her knees.

Indulging in her hurt feelings was pointless. It did nothing but prolong the whole unpleasant experience. Unfortunately, shoving the pain back inside that dark corner of her heart where she kept it was easier said than done.

She wasn't even completely sure why it hurt so much. She didn't want to be stuck with some stranger as a husband, either, and it had been just as big of a shock to her. But she was always one to find the best in every situation, and they could have both benefited greatly, even if their marriage had stayed a business arrangement. The man only had thirty days to find a job or he'd have to leave. And whatever else he wanted, it had been obvious how much he wanted to stay. Men outnumbered women ten to one in Desolation. He didn't have any other options. She would have been a guaranteed ticket.

And still he'd said no. Ridiculous or not, that *hurt*.

*All right*. She sucked in a deep breath and slowly let it out again, forcing back all the tears, every ounce of hurt, one tiny shard at a time. No more wallowing.

She lifted her head, took another cleansing breath, and wiped impatiently at her face, then pushed off the floor. There were chores to do, her garden and the animals to tend, and a dress commission to work on. She'd let herself hope for a brief moment…but that was done with. Mr. Brady could go tango with a tumbleweed for all she cared.

A *thump* and a muffled curse came from the direction of her father's office…well, her office, really. He didn't do much in it anymore but drink and fall asleep in front of the fireplace. But he was in there now. And that could only mean one thing.

Her stomach lurched as she hurried down the hall and threw open the door, pausing to take in the chaotic scene. Her father stood behind his desk. Every drawer was open, and he was rummaging through one of them. Open books and papers were scattered about. She didn't need to ask what he was searching for. But she did anyway, hoping that forcing him to say it to her face would instill a little shame. She didn't bother hoping it would be enough to deter him, but she wanted him to at least acknowledge what he was doing.

"What are you looking for, Pa?"

He glanced up, his red-rimmed eyes barely skimming over her before turning back to the desk.

"Where'd you put it this time?" he asked, his voice gruff and impatient.

"Put what?"

He slammed the drawer closed and started riffling through another one. "You know what."

She just folded her arms and raised a brow, waiting for him to come out and ask. He slammed another drawer with a growl and finally looked directly at her.

"Where's the paperwork on the property? I've got a buyer lined up—"

"You're not selling my proper—"

"It's not yours yet," he said.

Panic clawed its way up her throat, and she forced herself to get a grip on it. Being overly emotional would only set him off, and that was the last thing she wanted to do.

"Pa," she said, trying to keep her voice steady, sweet. "You can't sell off our property. It's all we have. Where will we go if—"

"Calm yourself," he said, waving a hand at her like her concerns didn't matter.

She clenched her fists and dug her nails into her palms to keep from screaming at him.

"I'm not selling off everything, just a couple acres from the back."

*Breathe, breathe, breathe…*

"Pa, we only have three acres left. If you sell that—"

He glared at her. "I said I won't sell it all. I'll keep an acre back. We don't need more than that. It's already too much to take care of."

"No, it's not," she snapped, her anxiety too strong to keep under wraps. "I need that land so I can expand planting for my herb sales and still have enough land for the animals to graze."

"Then maybe you should get rid of the animals. I'm sure my buyer would be glad of them, and it'll increase our profits on the sale," he said, his eyes already gleaming. "And you've been jabberin' on about expanding that little garden of yours for years and haven't done it. The land is just going to waste."

"It is not going to waste!" she said, her patience at an end. "My plants and the eggs and milk and wool we get from the animals are the only things keeping this roof over our heads. You sell off the land, we won't even have that anymore. And the only reason I haven't expanded my planting yet is because I've been too busy running everything else around here. You certainly don't help anymore. If you did, then maybe I could do what I needed—"

"Don't you take that tone with me, girl! You certainly have a high opinion of yourself, but I'm still your father. You don't get to tell me what I ca—"

"Ma is buried back there!" she yelled, her voice cracking.

Her father went stone-still, all emotion draining from his pasty face. Nora tried not to flinch at that vacant look. Her father had taken her mother's death hard. It's why he'd started drinking and stopped caring for everything else. Even her.

She understood…to a point. She loved her mother, too. Missed her so much sometimes it physically hurt. But while she'd buried herself in work, her father had done whatever he could to numb the pain, drinking and gambling their money and land away. He seemed determined to drive himself into an early grave. But she couldn't— wouldn't—let him take her with him.

She tried again, keeping her voice as calm and quiet as she could. "The family cemetery where Ma and her parents are buried is on that land," she reminded him again. "If you sell it off, they are gone. If you just need money…"

She strode to a small box that she'd tucked away on the top of the bookshelf in the corner of the room and pulled out a small leather pouch. "Here," she said, dropping it on the desk in front of him. "That's everything I've been able to save for the last few months. Take that. The land is not for sale."

He remained stiff, unseeing, unyielding. Long enough that, for a second, she thought he might refuse the money.

But after a few moments, he finally unfroze, grabbed the bag, and marched from the room. She shouldn't have allowed herself the hope that he'd do the decent thing and not steal from his own child. From himself, really. That money was all that stood between them and disaster.

The front door closed, and after a few more minutes, she heard him ride off, and she dropped into the chair behind the desk and laid her head on her folded arms.

That was too close. The loss of the money hurt,

but as long as nothing too catastrophic happened, she could weather it. Make it up. But if he'd found the deed to the property…

She reached under the desk, her fingers feeling for the latch to the small hidden drawer that her father didn't know existed. The button clicked beneath her finger, and the drawer sprang open. The weathered paper of the deed still lay folded and safe in the drawer.

She let out a trembling breath and closed the drawer. There was no way she could do this for five more years. Which meant, objections or no, Mr. Brady was going to have to accept their marriage. It would be much easier if she could just tell him why she needed his name on that marriage license.

But she didn't know the man. Couldn't trust him. A wife's property didn't belong to her. And the last thing she was going to do was get the deed from her father just to turn it over to her husband. The property was hers, and she'd be damned if she was going to allow anyone other than herself to claim it.

And since Mr. Brady didn't seem amenable to marriage—she tried very hard to not let her mind wonder why…she'd had enough men laugh at the thought of her as a romantic companion to not venture into that territory again—she was just going to have to convince him, somehow, that he needed this partnership as much as she did.

# CHAPTER SEVEN

By the time supper approached, Adam had managed a few hours of fitful dozing but not much else. Even if Mrs. DuVere hadn't offered to put in a word with her builder, Adam would have volunteered, just to ensure the walls went up on his room as fast as possible. He hadn't been the only one catching an afternoon nap and sleeping on a floor with nothing but sheets separating a bunch of snoring, flatulent men. It made actually getting any rest a bit more difficult than he'd anticipated. He wouldn't be able to take too many nights in the bachelor paradise that was the boardinghouse.

After dinner, Adam headed to the tavern to meet the builder, Mr. Vernice. Mrs. DuVere had indeed had a word with him, and he'd reluctantly agreed to meet with Adam after supper.

Adam tried not to put too much hope into it. The man could say no, after all. However, if Mrs. DuVere was correct, the builder needed workers. Hopefully badly enough he was willing to overlook Adam's not-insignificant shortcomings.

Reggie, the barkeep, pointed him in the direction of Vernice, and Adam nodded his thanks before heading over and sliding onto the barstool beside him.

"Mr. Vernice," he said, giving the man his most charming smile. "I'm Adam Brady. I believe Mrs. DuVere mentioned me?"

Mr. Vernice grunted and went back to his whiskey. Talkative bunch in this town. Luckily, the man's drink was nearly gone.

"How about another for Mr. Vernice?" Adam said to Reggie, who nodded and grabbed the bottle from behind the counter.

"Thanks," Vernice said, taking a healthy sip from his newly refilled glass before leaning on the bar so he could get a look at Adam.

He didn't seem nearly as pleased with the arrangement he'd made with Mrs. DuVere as she and Adam had been. The man looked Adam up and down, his skepticism stamped all over his face.

"You ever done any building before?" Vernice asked.

"No, but I'm willing to do just about anything you need doing."

Vernice grunted. "We'll see."

Adam just grinned, trying his hardest to look strong and capable. Either it worked, or Vernice was more desperate for help than Adam had figured, because he just grunted again.

"Meet me on the walkway in front of the boardinghouse at seven sharp," Vernice said.

"Seven in the morning?" Adam said, quickly trying to hide his dismay behind another smile.

Vernice cocked an eyebrow, and Adam hurried to agree. "Right. Seven o'clock. I'll be there."

Vernice drained his glass and stood, but he only went a few steps before he turned to look back at Adam. "Might want to get some shut-eye," he said. "You're going to need it."

With that, he nodded to Reggie and headed out

the door, chuckling under his breath.

Well…Adam wasn't sure if he should be happy or terrified that he'd apparently gotten the job and settled for both. Happy with a healthy side of caution.

The advice to get some sleep was probably good, but thanks to Adam's nap and the sudden adrenaline rush coursing through his veins at taking the first step on the road to his new life (he'd ignore the whole terror aspect, despite Vernice's chuckle still echoing in his ears), there was no way he'd be able to get some sleep just yet. What he needed was to kick up his boots and relax a little.

He couldn't pick a fight or gamble, but surely he could find *some* amusement.

It didn't take long to realize there was little in the way of amusement to be found that didn't involve cards or the girls from the parlor house. No wonder the single newcomers had been getting into mischief. There wasn't much else to do for a stranger trying to stay out of trouble.

Not that it helped. Trouble found him. As it always did. Except this time, trouble was six foot something of pissed-off sheriff who'd done nothing but sit and glower at him while Adam stared into the glass of whiskey he couldn't quite bring himself to drink. Not that he didn't want it. He did. And it wasn't because of the quality, which was surprisingly good considering the location. But it was hard to drown himself in a good bottle of oblivion when Sheriff Sourpuss scowled at him from his seat at a table a few feet away.

The other men sitting with him seemed more friendly, though Adam wasn't sure how much he could trust that. They *were* the sheriff's men, after all. Doc, Preacher, and Sunshine…if his memory served. *Gee, wonder what they do for a living*, he thought with an inner snort. Churlish of him, maybe, since none of them but Woodson seemed to have anything against him. Still, he'd never been one to trust implicitly. He sighed deeply and took a miniscule sip of his drink. It really wouldn't hurt him to be a little more friendly, though.

So when one of them—Sunshine, the sheriff's deputy, if Adam remembered correctly—waved him over, he gathered up his drink and went, despite his misgivings.

"So how's Desolation treating you so far?" Sunshine asked. "Settling in?"

"As much as I ca—"

"You goin' to tell me why you're really here?" Woodson asked him.

"Now, Sheriff," Doc said, "give the man a chance to take a seat."

Adam nodded his thanks and sat down. His rump had barely hit the chair when Woodson grunted at him again.

"So?"

"I did tell you," Adam said. "I didn't set out to come here. Didn't think it was a real place, to be honest. But since I stumbled across it…" He shrugged. "Word is, this is a place where men like us can hang their hats without having to worry about someone taking a shot at their heads."

Woodson shrugged. "Within reason."

Adam chuckled and then sighed. "I didn't set out to ruin your life, you know."

The older man shrugged again. "Sounds like you don't set out to do much. Doesn't matter, though, does it? If what happens anyway still destroys lives. You already ruined one life of mine. I won't let you do it again."

Adam fixed his gaze at the amber liquid in his glass, wondering if the knot of guilt that had festered in his gut since the day he'd realized just how big a mistake he'd made all those years ago would ever go away.

"You know, sometimes talking through things can be very cathartic," Sunshine prompted, looking at them both.

Doc nodded sagely, giving Adam an encouraging smile. Preacher just grunted, but it sounded like an affirmative grunt. And yes, he'd apologized earlier, but it might not have sounded very sincere. So…all right, here went nothing.

He took a healthy gulp of his whiskey, letting it slowly burn its way down his throat. Then he said, "I was just a kid back then, Woodson. I didn't realize what would come of my actions. I know that's little comfort, but I'm sorry for it. Truly. If that's worth anything to you."

Woodson didn't look at him. "Sometimes I think apologies are more for the people makin' them than the ones they're aimed at."

Adam raised his brows, and Preacher grunted again, a slight smile on his lips so Adam thought he was probably agreeing. Doc looked thoughtful, but Sunshine frowned. "I don't know if that's true."

Woodson just swirled the water around in his glass for a moment before speaking again. "An apology won't erase the years I spent being hunted."

"No," Sunshine said, "but now you at least know Mr. Brady here regrets the situation."

Woodson's eyes briefly flicked to his deputy. "Well, while I might appreciate the sentiment—if I were a better man," he said with a slight smile that was more than Adam had thought the man capable of, "it still doesn't do me much good."

Adam frowned, but Woodson waved at him to let it go. "You've got bigger problems to worry about than whether or not I'll ever forgive you. Figure out what to do about your little situation yet? Ready to beg Nora to keep you?"

Adam recoiled in horror, only half feigning it. "Perish the thought."

Woodson made a noise that might have been a laugh. "Employment, then? The clock is tickin'."

"As a matter of fact, I was just hired by Mr. Vernice, Mrs. DuVere's builder."

Woodson looked him up and down, if anything emphasizing his skepticism rather than bothering to hide it. "You don't seem the buildin' type."

Adam shrugged. "I'm willing to learn. How hard can it be?"

Woodson barked out a laugh. "I'll be amazed if you last the day."

Adam didn't bother to hold in his sigh. "I might surprise you."

"Very few people surprise me."

"Maybe I'll be one of the lucky few," Adam said, still not really believing he was sitting in a tavern, at a table full of men making him chat about his feelings, trading mostly civil words with the bastard he'd been sure would shoot him on sight only a few hours earlier.

Woodson grumbled. "Don't count on it."

"Now, Sheriff, the least we could do is lend him our support," Sunshine said.

"He's still alive," Woodson said with another glower. "That's support enough."

But Doc raised his glass. "Much luck to you, Mr. Brady."

Sunshine followed suit, with a grin that Adam was beginning to realize was his perpetual facial expression. Preacher didn't say anything but raised his glass as well.

"Thanks," Adam said, oddly touched by their well wishes. He raised his glass and gave them a small nod, then took another sip of his whiskey. "Well," he said, blowing out a breath. "If it doesn't work out, I'm sure I'll find something else. I still have time. Three weeks and six days."

Woodson snorted. "You're goin' to need 'em." He drained the rest of his mineral water and clapped his hat on his head. "I think I'll be headin' home to see what my wife has burned for supper."

Woodson nodded at Adam, ignoring his raised brows, and stalked out of the tavern.

Adam groaned into his glass and hazarded another tiny sip. The whiskey singed its way down his throat and hit his stomach like a trail of acid. He released his breath with a hiss. Good stuff.

"Don't worry, Brady. If the building job doesn't work out, I'm sure you'll find something around this town that needs doing," Doc said with an encouraging smile. "If you're sure you don't want to try and patch things up with Nora…"

Brady cocked an eyebrow at him and shook his head. "Trust me, she's better off without me." He'd learned that the hard way, more than once.

"Well, good luck, then," Doc said, draining the last of his drink and standing to take his leave. He tipped his hat at Brady and headed out the door.

"I'll walk over with you, Doc," Sunshine said. He turned to Brady with a big grin. "Welcome to town."

Brady raised his glass to him. "Thanks."

Left alone with Preacher, Brady tried to sit under the man's solemn stare and not squirm.

"You're set on an annulment, then?" Preacher finally asked.

Adam nodded. "It really is for the best."

"If you say so." He shrugged and then frowned. "Well, if you're dead set on it, it'll take me a little time to figure out how to do it."

Adam's brows rose. "You mean you don't know how?"

Preacher shrugged again. "Never had anyone who wanted to annul their marriage before. Out in these parts, you get lucky enough to find a woman who'll marry you, you tend to keep her." He rubbed his finger along his bottom lip, his brow creased in thought. "It'd be easier to divorce…" he muttered. Then his frown deepened. "But you can't divorce if the marriage was never legal. No matter what God may think of the matter." He thought for another moment, then shook his head. "I suppose if you're not a religious man, you could go on your way and consider yourself unwed."

The pastor's grim face said enough about what he thought of that idea.

"However," Preacher continued, "should you wish to marry again in the future—"

"I won't."

*"If,"* Preacher said, his eyes narrowing at the interruption. "It could cause some difficulties, as a case could definitely be made that you are, in fact, already wed."

Adam fingered the cross he wore beneath his shirt. He'd never been one for much religion. His mother, on the other hand, was steadfastly Episcopalian and would absolutely consider him married, whatever the actual law had to say about it. And as sinful as he was, he did endeavor to keep his mother from turning over in her eventual grave. He might be a shit of a human being, but he did try to be a good son. Though he had no doubt he was a huge disappointment to her—and every other woman he'd tried to love. He didn't need to become another woman's biggest regret. Again.

He blew out a breath and downed the rest of his whiskey. "I don't plan on ever indulging in matrimony, Preacher. But I'd prefer to be free from any entanglements, religious or otherwise. So if there's a way to get this marriage, or whatever it is that we're in, dissolved in everyone's eyes, I'd appreciate it."

Preacher nodded, though his expression stayed grim. "I'll work on it. It might take a few weeks, though."

"I understand," Adam said, sighing again before standing. "Good thing I still have a few before

Woodson kicks my hide out of town."

Preacher's lips twitched, and Adam tipped his hat to him before turning to leave. "Thanks for the company."

Woodson hadn't been wrong. Time was short. Adam didn't have the luxury to keep making the mistakes that inevitably derailed his life. This time, he needed to keep things on track. So what if he'd never managed to do it before in his life? First time for everything, right?

He needed to find work and keep it. And avoid accidentally marrying anyone else, though that one didn't seem to be much of an issue considering he'd already made that mistake with the one eligible woman in town. Avoiding her might be prudent, since she was both still angry at him and, for some ungodly reason, wanted to stay married.

A twinge of something he didn't want to identify roiled through his gut at the thought of that mountain of womanly mayhem he'd apparently married. Felt an awful lot like regret. At what, he refused to contemplate.

Instead, he gritted his teeth and wove his way through the tables. There were a couple poker games going on, and Adam itched to join them. But he needed to stay on the good side of everyone in town. Those he hadn't already angered anyway. Some of those men could be potential employers or coworkers. Cleaning them out in a poker game wouldn't help his chances, so he'd be better off remaining a spectator.

Thankfully, he had Mrs. DuVere and her builder. God bless the woman. And since he actually wanted this job to pan out, he gave up on the people watching and headed back to his...room, for lack of a better word. Tent? Area? Whatever it was, his best bet was to lay down in it and try and get some rest.

He was going to need it.

# CHAPTER EIGHT

Nora sank gratefully into the chair Mrs. DuVere offered, glad to be off her feet for a moment. She nodded to Mercy and Martha, then took a long drink from the glass of lemonade Mrs. DuVere had pushed toward her.

"Busy morning?" Mercy asked.

Nora nodded, her bones already starting to relax. They'd begun doing these weekly lunch dates just after Mercy's daughter, Daisy, was born, when Mercy was a harried new mother desperate for a few moments to herself. While Nora had been reluctant to join the women at first, she'd found it a welcome respite from her burdens.

"I had a few sewing orders to finish up, and then I had to wrangle a rabbit out of my garden."

"Oh no," Martha said, her face crumpling in concern. "Did the gate get left open again?"

She meant "did your father leave the gate open again" but was too polite to say it. Nora was never sure if her father was too drunk to remember or just didn't care enough to. Either way, it was more than just a nuisance. The money she made selling her herbs was half their income.

"Yes," Nora said with a sigh. "Luckily, I caught him before he did too much damage."

"I'm just glad it wasn't Lucille," Mercy added with a wry grin.

Nora laughed. "Me too."

Mercy's goat, Lucille, was a diva who thought she owned the town. She was constantly escaping from Mercy's ranch and would gallivant about, demanding treats—or taking them—from every person she came across. Despite her spoiled ways, the townsfolk loved her. She had become something of the town mascot.

Nora, however, preferred the goat stay far away from her garden. Lucille enjoyed munching her herbs far too much. Left unsupervised, the goat could demolish her garden in just a few minutes.

"I'm sorry if the sewing kept you up too late," Mrs. DuVere said, leaning forward to give her hand a pat. "But the new dress you brought is divine! Pearl is going to love it."

She had commissioned Nora to sew a new dress for Pearl's birthday. Pearl was one of Mrs. DuVere's girls, though Mrs. DuVere didn't run a typical parlor house. While her girls did pay her a fee, they were free to come and go as they pleased, though most were so happy there, they'd been with Mrs. DuVere for years.

Nora flushed, ducking her head to nod her thanks. Compliments always sat funny in her gut, squirming about like they didn't belong there. Though she was pleased that Mrs. DuVere was happy with her work.

"And where is little Daisy today?" Mrs. DuVere asked Mercy.

Mercy gave them a mischievous half grin, her eyes twinkling. "She's with her father."

Mrs. DuVere, Martha, and Nora all stared at her for a second and then jumped up to look out the window. Their collective "awww" once they had their faces pressed to the glass had Mercy laughing.

Their fierce sheriff was pacing the length of the walkway in front of the sheriff's office, jostling his nearly two-year-old daughter in an apparent effort to get her to sleep. A pastime in which she seemed disinclined to participate, preferring to try to snag her father's hat from his head.

The women giggled and went back to their lunch.

"What is it about men holding babies?" Martha said with a happy sigh.

Mercy laughed. "Watching those two together makes me start thinking about having another one all over again. And I've already got my hands full enough with Daisy."

Nora nodded with an indulgent smile. Watching men cradling their babies was enough to get even her to briefly muse on babies of her own, even though she had never had a real desire to start a family. She had enough on her plate without adding another helpless being to look after.

"Now, Nora," Mrs. DuVere said, pinning her with that look that said she meant to get to the bottom of something. "What's going on with you and the newcomer?"

Nora's cheeks instantly flushed, but she forced herself to hold Mrs. DuVere's gaze. "Nothing is going on. I haven't spoken with him much since the day he got here."

Martha nibbled on a sandwich, her brow furrowed. "Are you all right after he…after the things he said? About the whole marriage thing?"

"I'm fine, Martha, I promise," she reassured her,

not for the first time.

"I was surprised to see you at the marriage gathering," Mrs. DuVere said. "Marriage had never seemed like anything you were much interested in. A girl after my own heart," she said, patting her hand again.

Nora gave her a weak smile and fiddled with the sandwich on her own plate. This was really not something she wanted to discuss, though she'd known it was going to come up. Besides, these women were her friends. There wouldn't be any judgment here. So she took a deep breath and tried to explain.

"It's not, trust me. The last thing I want is a husband. But," she hurried on before the questions could start again, "I need one. Temporarily, at least. You all know the troubles I have with my father."

They nodded in sympathy, and Nora pressed on. "I can manage most of the time, but his gambling is getting worse. Right now, it's mostly the pocket money he can find. Truthfully, I leave a bit lying around here and there, enough to keep him busy without making us completely destitute. And I think you know that our property was actually Grandfather's. My mother's father. He'd always wanted the property to go to me. Spent my whole childhood walking me over every inch of it, helped me start my first garden. We had so many plans for it. And his will left the property to me in the event of my mother's death."

"Well, that's good, isn't it?" Mercy asked.

"Yes, it's wonderful. The only problem is I can't claim it until I turn thirty or upon my marriage, whichever happens first. My father legally has charge of everything until then. I *had* hoped to wait until my thirtieth birthday. But with things with my father getting so much worse, I'm not sure I can wait another five years. He's already sold off a good portion of the land."

The women around her nodded, each one looking at her with concern.

"So you decided to take advantage of the new marriage rule," Mrs. DuVere said.

"I thought it could be a possible solution, at least," Nora answered, though it hadn't been a question. "But I didn't want a man from town who would expect an actual marriage. Or one who knew me well enough to know my history and might claim my property as my husband. The stranger seemed like the best option."

Martha frowned. "But don't you have the same problem? Once you're married, what's yours belongs to your husband."

"True," Nora said. "But only if he knows about it, at least in my case. A stranger wouldn't. He'd probably assume the property belongs to my father, at least while he's alive. And I certainly wouldn't offer up any information to the contrary. For the deed to transfer to me, I just need two witnesses to the marriage."

"Which you have," Martha said with a grin.

"Exactly. Though I do need the marriage to be legal. But once it is, the two witness signatures are all I need for the deed to transfer to me. And hopefully, once that is all squared away, I could make life unpleasant enough for my so-called husband that he'd be happy to quit me," she said with a mischievous smile. "If he bothered to stick around in the first place," she added with a shrug.

Mrs. DuVere laughed, grasping Nora's chin in her hand and giving her an affectionate little shake. "You devious little beauty, you. So you wanted to marry this man just to get your deed and then make sure he was happy to go on his way, leaving you to live happily ever after with your property safe in your own name."

Nora nodded, and Mrs. DuVere laughed again. "Brilliant."

Mercy gave her a wry smile. "Yes, but even the most brilliant plan can backfire. Remember how my own marriage started out."

The women laughed, chattering for a second about Mercy's own fake marriage gone awry. She'd only meant to pretend that Gray was her fiancé until she got rid of a man who wanted her land at all costs. Of course, the townsfolk didn't know that and threw them a wedding they couldn't refuse. It all turned out all right, though, as Mercy and Gray were hopelessly in love before too long.

That wouldn't happen with Nora and Adam. With Gray Woodson in town, Adam now had two people he desperately wanted to get away from. Her and the sheriff. It shouldn't be too hard to run him off.

Then again, if he wanted to leave, he'd probably be gone already, not trying to find a job that would keep him there. She rolled her lips between her teeth, thoughtfully chewing on them for a second. Oh well. At least he wasn't trying to get her to keep him.

She did, however, need him to stick with her long enough to sign the marriage license so she could get that damn deed in her name.

"Since you have witnesses who will swear you are married, can't you get things settled with the deed now?" Mercy asked.

Nora frowned again. "Possibly. Even with all the signatures, none of this is technically legal until it's filed at the county courthouse. But you know how things work this far out. As long as I've got the paperwork, I'm most likely safe. But if it were ever challenged…" She shook her head. "No. Without a signed marriage license, it's not legal, and I want it all legal so there is no question. No way to challenge it."

Mrs. DuVere leaned forward, her face alight with excitement. "So what you need is for Mr. Brady to need you enough to agree to a brief, but legal, marriage."

Nora nodded. "Essentially."

Martha picked up on Mrs. DuVere's excitement and clapped her hands together. "How can we help?"

"Help?" Nora asked, looking among them.

Mercy grinned. "If Mr. Brady wants to stay in this town, he has to get hitched or get a job before the end of the month."

"Right," Nora said. "But he's already secured a job. And lodgings."

Mrs. DuVere frowned. "Yes, thanks to me and my generous ways."

The women all laughed. Mrs. DuVere could never help but take in whatever strays she could find, no matter what the species.

She slapped her hand lightly on the table and sat back. "No matter. His lodgings are far from comfortable, I assure you. And I can make sure they become even more so. In fact, I had to shoo Tommy out from under Mr. Brady's window last night. He and that friend of his were caterwauling and making all kinds of ruckus chasing one of the stray cats. Next time, perhaps I'll just look the other way. And maybe drop an unsubtle hint or two that he's welcome to make as much noise under that particular window as he wants."

Martha giggled. "There's nowhere else in town to get lodgings, so that means Mr. Brady will be needing a place to stay."

Mercy snorted. "And take it from someone married to a former gunslinger and who has spent a lot of time with his city-bred deputy. These men aren't really equipped to do much else. I don't see Mr. Brady lasting too long as a builder."

The women all grinned, and Mrs. DuVere tapped her finger against her lips. "Very true. And once he fails at that, he'll need another job."

"I could hire him at the store," Martha said. "And make sure it's an experience he can't wait to forget."

"And I'll talk to Gray," Mercy said. "I have no doubt he and Sunshine can find a few unpleasant tasks for Mr. Brady to fail at."

"I'm sure Preacher and Doc will help as well," Mrs. DuVere said. "Martha and I will have a little chat with them."

Martha grinned and nodded enthusiastically.

Nora huffed out a laugh. "I think I'm starting to

pity Mr. Brady."

Mercy waved that off. "Ah, he'll be fine. Once you've got what you need, we'll make sure he lands on his feet."

"*After* he helps you," Martha emphasized.

Nora chewed at her lip again. "You really think it's possible to talk a man who wants to avoid matrimony at all costs to accept our marriage?"

Mrs. DuVere took her hand. "You don't worry about a thing, my dear. Give us a week and we'll make sure Mr. Brady has no other option but to seek you out. If he wants to stay in this town, he's going to need you."

Nora nodded slowly. It could work. Then she could offer him a bargain. Sign the form to make it legal and promise to give him a divorce after a few months. That should be plenty of time to get all the legal stuff squared away with the deed. And once she had that, she wouldn't need the pungent, bedraggled, and yes, maybe handsome but infinitely irritating Mr. Adam Brady anymore.

# CHAPTER NINE

Adam's morning had started off…poorly. He'd stood blinking blearily at Mr. Vernice who just looked him over and muttered something under his breath that Adam probably didn't want to hear.

Frankly, he was just glad he'd managed to get dressed and on the sidewalk in front of the boardinghouse by the correct time. If it wasn't for Mrs. DuVere's hair-stripping coffee, he probably wouldn't have made it. Not that he'd slept in. Sleep was a distant dream with all the racket that had gone on during the night.

Besides all the noises coming from his neighbors, Adam was pretty sure someone had set a cat to yowling right below his window. He hadn't caught sight of anything but the stable boy when he'd stuck his head out to chuck the pitcher at it. But unless someone had paid the kid to make noise under his window, Adam couldn't fathom what else would have been making that noise.

He needed to get some actual glass in his window and walls up as soon as possible. Too many more nights like the one he'd just had, and his naturally cheery disposition was going to suffer.

"All right, Brady," Mr. Vernice said. "Seeing as how you've got no experience at building, we'll start you off slow."

He pointed at a large stack of lumber that was piled on the street beside the building. "Get all that up the stairs and then we'll see how you do with a hammer."

Adam nodded and turned toward the stack of wood. Hauling lumber didn't sound fun, but it was definitely something he could handle.

It took him less than twenty minutes to discover just how wrong he was.

Sure, hauling boards up a few stairs seemed simple enough. But there were a couple of things he neglected to take into consideration. One, wood was *heavy*. His muscles were screaming before he'd made it back for his second load. How he was going to do the entire stack without dropping it in the street, he had no idea.

And two, long, heavy boards weren't the most manageable items to carry anywhere, let alone up a staircase. He learned very quickly that trying to turn while holding a board over one's shoulder was a surefire way to remove the head of the person standing behind him. He'd have to remember to buy George a drink that evening to make up for the goose egg on his forehead.

Not to mention, wood boards weren't made to bend. So if the staircase had a landing that turned, a man couldn't just turn the corner without some fancy finagling of the board in order to get it around the corner as well.

By lunchtime, Adam was about ready to beg Nora to take him back just to get out of hauling any more wood. Well, maybe not anything that drastic. But a nice broken leg or arm sounded pretty good at that point.

Vernice must have sensed Adam's lagging spirit, or perhaps he just got sick of Adam sweating all over his wood, because once they ate a quick meal, Vernice handed him a hammer and bucket of nails, quickly showed him what to do, and left him to help a couple other men in getting the outside walls up in one of the rooms. Unfortunately, not his.

Adam squinted at the board he was supposed to hammer to the wall studs. "Can't be that hard," he said under his breath.

He grabbed a nail and held it to the spot he thought it should go, then swung the hammer down. Right on his thumb.

He dropped the hammer—which landed on his toe—and clasped his aching thumb with his other hand, his eyes watering, hopping on one foot. The other men roared with laughter, but one of them came over and retrieved his hammer for him.

"Give it a few taps first," he said, demonstrating with another nail. Once the nail had been tapped in enough, it stayed fairly well without being held, and the man gave it a good whack or two and it was in. "Got it?"

Adam shook his hand but took the hammer back and tried again. He did get the nail to go in this time, though the last whack bent the head instead of hammering it all the way in. But still, he counted it as a victory. The man who'd helped him shook his head but didn't say anything, so Adam carried on.

All went well…for about an hour. His nails weren't the straightest, and more were bent than hammered in straight, but his wall was up, and he only managed to hit his thumb three more times. A victory, all in all.

A woman's voice called out a goodbye to Mrs.

DuVere, and Adam looked out the window.

Nora.

She glanced up just as he hung his head out the window, and he gave her a jaunty little smile and wave. Forgetting that he still held a hammer, and his small bucket of nails was sitting on the makeshift windowsill, his arm bumped the bucket and sent it flying.

"Watch out!" he called, helpless to do anything but watch the nails rain down on whoever might be standing beneath them.

He was afraid to look, but the shouts and curses filtering up from the street didn't bode well. He glanced back at Nora, who gazed at him with wide, horrified eyes…and twitching lips. Yeah. He knew the feeling. Laughing wasn't going to buy him any goodwill, though, so he kept it mostly under control as he ran down the steps to see what damage he'd caused.

And promptly wished he'd stayed upstairs.

Mrs. DuVere stood on the sidewalk below the window, nails spread in a circle around her.

He opened his mouth, but nothing came out as she picked a nail out of the blessedly thick hair coiled on the top of her head and glanced up at him.

"How's the construction job working out for you?" she asked, her lips pulling into a wry smile.

He chuckled and shook his head, thanking his for-once lucky stars that no one had been hurt.

"I'm sure Mr. Vernice will be promoting me any day now," he said.

Mr. Vernice glowered at him and held out his hand. Adam sighed and handed over his hammer. "I'll always treasure our time together," he said.

Mr. Vernice stared at him like a dog trying to get a fox out of a hole before shaking his head and walking away.

Mrs. DuVere laughed. "I suppose I should be thankful you dropped a few nails and not the hammer."

He grinned. "I don't know. The hammer might have missed you. A whole shower of nails spread out a bit more."

She picked another nail from her bun. "Hmm, true." Then she let out a sigh and put her hands on her hips while she surveyed him. "Apparently, you are still in need of employment."

"Guilty."

"Out of curiosity, did you drop the bucket by accident or sheer incompetence?"

"Accident," he said, giving her another sheepish grin. "I was, uh…a bit distracted."

His gaze flickered to Nora, who still stood gaping at him from across the street.

Mrs. DuVere's eyes widened a bit. "Are you sure you wouldn't rather go down the matrimony route?"

He shuddered. "Believe me when I tell you that I'm doing womankind, and Miss Schumacher in particular, a favor by taking myself off the marriage market. I think I'm more than any woman would be willing to put up with."

Mrs. DuVere snorted. "I don't think you know women as well as you think you do. But, your choice, of course. Why don't you come to the tavern after breakfast tomorrow? I'm sure Reggie could use a hand."

"Mrs. DuVere," he said, taking her arm so he

could lean in and kiss her cheek, "you are a saint."

"Get on with you," she said, playfully slapping his arm. "Just be a dear and get the rest of these nails picked up, would you?"

"Yes, ma'am," he said, a little overwhelmed at her kindness.

He bent to scoop up the nails, glancing up when a pair of boots and shapely, trouser-clad legs stopped beside him, briefly blocking out the sun.

His gaze traveled up her long, nicely muscled legs, her ample backside scandalously encased in the trousers, past the hint of a bosom that was covered by a too-large man's shirt, up to a pair of amusement-filled eyes. "Miss Schumacher."

"Husband," Nora said, gazing down at him with a raised brow.

He glowered a bit at that and stood. "I'm not your husband."

"I'm hoping if I say it enough, you'll get used to the idea." His snort brought another smile to her lips. "Having a good day?" she asked, her eyes twinkling.

"The best."

"Hmm, your definition of 'the best' must differ from mine."

"I don't know. I spent the day tossing about hammers and sharp metal spikes and managed not to maim anyone. Though it was a close call, I'll admit," he said with a half grin.

She tilted her head and regarded him for a second. "You like to make jokes, don't you?"

"About damn near everything, yes, ma'am."

Her lips twitched again. "Why is that?"

"Why not?" He shrugged. "I'm not going to get out of this life alive…might as well enjoy myself while I can. I'd be pretty miserable if all I did was mope about my situation. Especially since my situations are almost always worthy of excessive moping."

She folded her arms and regarded him a moment. "That's annoyingly optimistic of you."

He laughed. "That's one of the nicer ways of putting it."

"Ready to admit we're married yet and sign the papers?"

He took a step back. "My day wasn't *that* bad."

"All evidence to the contrary, husband," she said, shaking her head. But he saw a smile peeking out before she turned away. "Have a good rest of your day, Mr. Shady. Try not to maim anyone else."

"Brady!" he called after her.

"Whatever," she replied, waving him off over her shoulder. He rolled his eyes, though his lips tugged into another smile. Damnable woman.

He stared after her until she passed the sheriff's office on the other side of the street, and he noticed Woodson standing on the porch, watching him. They stared at each other for a second. Then Woodson pulled the pocket watch from his vest, looked at it, and sent a cold grin Adam's way.

*Yeah, yeah. Tick tock.* Time was running out.

He dumped the nails he was holding into the bucket and turned on his heel toward the tavern. Maybe Reggie could find some work for him right away.

Time—and Woodson—waited for no man. Particularly him.

# CHAPTER TEN

Nora loaded her basket into the back of the wagon and turned to thank Martha, but the young woman was busy smiling in the direction of Doc, who'd come out to chat with the sheriff across the street.

"How are things going with you two?" she asked her.

Martha blushed prettily. "Good. I think."

Nora tilted her head, trying to read her friend's expression. "You could always marry one of the newcomers if you don't think it will work out with him."

"I suppose. Though…" Martha shrugged and then glanced behind her before leaning closer. "I don't want to marry just anyone. And Harrison is… well." She blushed again.

Nora nodded. Doc was indeed blush-worthy.

Martha sighed. "I don't think he's quite ready for marriage. In fact, if it hadn't been for the Town Council's new rules, I don't think he'd have expressed an interest in me. Not yet anyway. But with all the newcomers needing wives by the end of the month…"

"Ah," Nora said, pursing her lips. "You're worried that his hand was a bit forced, unless he wanted to watch you get snapped up by someone else."

"Yes. And while I'm glad we are finally courting, I don't want it to be just because he didn't have any other option."

"Understandable. Though truly," Nora said, leaning in with a conspiratorial smile, "the man has been making eyes at you for months. Longer even."

"You think so?"

"I know so."

Martha chewed her bottom lip, her gaze straying back over to where the handsome doctor laughed at something the sheriff said. "I hope you're right. I've always been afraid…"

"Of what?" Nora prompted when her friend paused.

Martha let out a long sigh. "That I'm just some sort of consolation prize now that he can't have Mercy."

"Oh, Martha, no," she hurried to reassure her. "He may have been interested in her once, but that was years ago. You are no one's consolation prize."

The hesitant smile that pulled at Martha's lips grew stronger when Doc caught sight of her. He tipped his hat with a slow grin that had Nora feeling like she should turn away and give them some privacy.

She laughed. "That man is definitely interested in you."

Martha ducked her head, her brilliant smile warming Nora's heart.

Then Martha sighed again. "Truth be told, even if he proposed tomorrow, I'm not sure how it would work. It's difficult, with my grandparents…"

"Ah," Nora said, nodding. Martha ran the general store with her grandparents and presumably, if she married, she'd leave the nest. Nora saw her dilemma. Her grandparents definitely relied on their granddaughter.

"There probably aren't many men who'd want to move in with his wife's elderly grandparents and run their business. Harrison already has his practice, so he wouldn't be able to help with the store. And while I don't think he'd object to me continuing to work here, it might be difficult if we had children."

"Doc might not be able to help much at the store with the responsibilities he has with his patients. But if you were married, you'd be close enough to help care for your grandparents still. And I'm sure you'd be able to work out something that would allow you to keep helping at the store and be a wife and mother as well."

Martha let out a wistful sigh. "I hope so. I do like him," she added, her cheeks pinkening again. She tore her gaze from Doc and turned back to Nora.

"And what of you? Any luck getting that husband of yours to admit you're married?"

Nora snorted. "Not yet. I haven't seen much of him for a couple days. But that's all right. I can be patient…for a little while longer, at least. Preacher told him that he's still trying to work out the whole issue with annulling a marriage that isn't legal anyway. At one time, I suppose it would have gone through some ecclesiastical court, but we don't have one of those here."

She frowned and shrugged. "Honestly, it's probably as easy as just scratching out the record of the marriage in the church register. As long as we don't consummate the marriage, which would be rather difficult considering the man avoids me at every turn," she said with an amused half grin.

Martha chuckled, and Nora patted her horse.

"We've got a few more weeks until the end of the month. Our plan still has time to work."

"You could always abandon that ship and make an arrangement with one of the other newcomers. I'd love to see you happy and settled down."

Nora grimaced at the thought. To Martha, being settled with a man was a requirement of womanly fulfillment. Not a notion Nora agreed with. "So far, the men I've met are all looking for an actual wife. That is not something I have any desire to be."

Not that any man had ever looked at *her* as a wifely possibility, but she wasn't going to point that out.

Martha still looked concerned, and Nora laughed. "Don't fret," she said, patting Martha's hand. "I'm perfectly happy with the way things are. The last thing I need is another man to look after. I just need a temporary man until the deed is settled. Then I will be more than happy on my own."

Martha didn't look entirely convinced but thankfully didn't push the issue.

"So, will you be needing an extra bushel of thyme for your next order, or is—"

*CRASH!*

Nora and Martha both jumped as the sound of breaking bottles echoed from the tavern, and then they hurried over to see what had happened.

Adam stumbled out the door, dripping wet and reeking of liquor. He pulled up short when he saw them.

"Good afternoon, ladies," he said, nodding at them and acting for all the world like he didn't look like a cat who'd just taken a swim in the whiskey barrel.

"Husband," Nora said, smiling at his grimace while Martha just gaped at him. "Busy day?"

He wiped a hand across his eyes and licked his lips. "Reggie has decided he is better off without my services," he said, clapping his hat on his head and sending a stream of liquid cascading down his face.

"I see," Nora said faintly, biting her lip to keep her laughter inside. Going by the squeak that emanated from Martha, she was having similar difficulties.

"Is there a bathhouse or perhaps a water barrel or stream nearby?" he asked.

Nora didn't know how he was still standing. The fumes coming off him alone were making her head spin.

"At the end of the street, just around the corner, there's a bathhouse."

"Thank you," he said, tipping his hat. "Good day."

He sloshed off, pausing after a few steps to remove a boot and empty it of several ounces of amber liquid.

Nora clapped her hand over her mouth, unable to keep her laughter at bay any longer, and Martha devolved into peeling giggles at her side.

"For the love of heaven, that man is a walking menace," Martha said. "He's making our job easier than I ever expected."

They both laughed again, and Martha put a hand to her chest. "Did you know he sent a whole bucket of nails onto Mrs. DuVere's head the other day?"

Nora took a shaky breath, trying to rein it in, but Martha's reminder of the bucket of nails set her laughing again. "I did. I was there. I don't know how he didn't turn her into a walking pincushion."

Martha snorted. "If her hair were any thinner, he would have." She shook her head. "He sure is handsome, though. Not as striking as Harrison, of course, but if I weren't already spoken for, I might be willing to risk injury for the likes of him."

Nora glanced after his retreating form. She didn't disagree. In fact, his handsome face had been featuring prominently in her dreams every night since he'd shown up in town. But she didn't see any need to share that tidbit with Martha.

"Thank you for holding that fabric for me," Nora said, climbing onto the wagon bench. "My father has been in need of a new shirt or two. It will work perfectly."

"I'm so glad," Martha said, standing back to wave. "And yes on the thyme. An extra bushel would be wonderful if you have it."

"I should. I'll bring it by later."

"Thank you," Martha said, waving goodbye.

Nora clicked at the horses, trying to resist the urge to follow the wet trail Adam had left down the middle of the dirt road. It was just sheer, morbid curiosity as to what that man might get up to next. It had nothing at all to do with the fact that if she did follow the trail, she might find him naked and fully submerged in a bath of hot water.

Nothing at all.

Then again…meeting him in the bathhouse might just solve all her problems. She knew she wasn't what most men found attractive. She was too tall, too sturdy, too…independent for most of them to glance at her twice. They wanted someone small and soft, someone who needed them. That was *not* Nora.

But she'd caught Adam's gaze lingering on her more than once. And not in the way any other man had ever looked at her. She wasn't entirely sure what that meant, but he had to be at least a *little* curious. If nothing else, he was a man. He would be there, naked. A naked man presented with a willing woman probably wouldn't turn her away.

Though, *was* she willing? Was this something she really wanted to do?

It would solve the whole marriage problem, certainly. Preacher wouldn't annul a marriage that had been consummated. And while she had no desire to be a wife, that didn't mean she didn't have the desire to indulge in a few wifely benefits. She would like to know what it felt like to be touched by a man she desired. To be kissed and caressed. To be wanted in that way, in any way, even if it was for a short time. And while she didn't want Adam as a permanent husband, he did…intrigue her in other ways. In all the ways that counted for this particular plan.

If she could seduce her wayward husband, she'd get to feel all that. It would be nice to experience it at least once. And, more importantly, with annulment off the table, Adam would surely see reason and grant her a temporary marriage.

Not that she had any earthly idea how to go about seducing someone. But one thing was for certain. She couldn't do anything from where she was. Maybe if she went to the bathhouse and just talked to him. Saw how things went…and then took the seduction plan from there. It couldn't be that difficult, could it?

She sat for a few more seconds, her eyes fixated on the rapidly approaching fork in the road. She did *not* want to follow him.

Half a heartbeat later, she sighed. Even she didn't believe herself anymore.

She snapped the reins to get the horses moving faster, guiding them away from home. And toward the bathhouse.

# CHAPTER ELEVEN

Adam groaned, letting the heat seep into his weary bones as he sank farther beneath the water. It had cost him extra money he couldn't afford to spend to get a full bath of hot, clean water, but it was so worth it.

He hadn't properly bathed since arriving in this godforsaken town, and remnants of his pathetic "disguise" lingered, no matter how he tried to scrub during his sponge baths. Add in manual labor he was not used to performing and his recent bath in liquor strong enough to make his eyes water, and yeah…he desperately needed a good, long soak. Even better, at this time of day, when most other men were out actually working, he had the place to himself. Or this particular room, in any case. And he fully intended on wringing every last penny's worth of the time he'd paid for out of this bath.

He thoroughly scrubbed his body and washed his hair, twice, and then settled back to enjoy just soaking until the heat ran out.

Nothing about Desolation was turning out like he'd expected. But he was at least relatively sure Woodson wouldn't be demanding to meet him with guns drawn any time soon.

No, he had a more pressing problem. Miss Nora Schumacher. The woman who would be his wife. Or who already was his wife.

He frowned. He had no idea how he should think

of her. His overly religious mother would consider them wed, to be sure. Just the thought of telling his mother about the whole situation had him squirming like he was a child facing her stern reprimands again. But legally, at least, he did *not* currently have a wife. And that's the way he wanted to keep it.

He'd tried the whole love-and-marriage thing a time or two in the past. It had worked out about as well as anything else in his life. The first one had carved a hole out of his heart that would probably never heal, and the second had damn near succeeded in carving a hole out of his hide. Or shooting a hole through his hide, to be more accurate. Women, on the whole, were beautiful, amazing creatures... but he'd be a complete imbecile to even attempt to trust another one.

Not that the woman in question wasn't intriguing. In fact, just the thought of her long, long legs and those flashing eyes had parts of him mightily intrigued. The part in question stirred beneath the water and he shifted, trying to ignore it. Dwelling on the enigmatic Miss Schumacher—and all the interesting things they could get up to if they were, in fact, married—led nowhere good. Matrimony was not a part of his future, and the sooner she understood that, the better. How he was going to convince her of that fact was another question entirely.

"You know, it can be dangerous to doze off in a bath," a voice said behind him, and he nearly jumped from the tub with a strangled gasp.

He twisted to look around. Nora stood in the doorway, whisps of steam capturing a few of the stray tendrils of hair that had escaped her braid and making them adorably frizzy.

"What are you doing in here?" he asked, properly scandalized.

She walked farther into the room, and he slapped his hands into the water, covering all his important bits as she perched on the tub next to him.

"I wanted to talk to you," she said.

"And it couldn't have waited? How did you get in here anyway?"

"I'm friends with the owner."

"Is there anyone you aren't friends with?"

She shrugged. "Not really. And besides, we're married. There's nothing improper about it."

"I'm going to have to beg to differ." He rubbed a hand over his face, jerking it back into the water when he remembered what he was trying not to expose.

Nora just grinned and crossed her legs, swinging the foot that dangled from her other knee. She leaned an elbow on her knee and propped her chin in her hands. And just…watched him.

"Is there something I can help you with?" he asked, and she raised her brows.

"I thought I made it clear there is something I can help *you* with, if you'd stop being so stubborn. It's just a tiny little paper that needs one itty-bitty little signature. There's really no need to keep torturing yourself with jobs you obviously aren't equipped to perform when you have a perfectly good wife sitting right here."

He groaned and slid farther into the water. "I don't know how many other ways I can say this.

Thanks, but no thanks. Appreciate the offer, but I decline. Thanks for thinking of me, but stop."

Her brows drew together as she glowered down at him. "Well, you needn't be rude about it."

"All evidence to the contrary," he muttered and then sighed at the daggers her eyes were throwing at him. "Look, I understand you're hankering after a husba—"

She held up a hand. "Stop right there."

He blinked innocently, trying to keep a grin from escaping. Purposely riling her up wasn't going to do him any favors in the long run, but he just couldn't seem to help himself. She made it too easy.

"I am not now, nor will I *ever* hanker after anybody." She pursed her lips for a second before continuing with a grumble. "I may need a husband temporarily, but there is no hankering involved."

He lifted one shoulder from the water with a shrug. "So you say."

The look she shot him was such a perfect blend of scandalized shock and sheer angry frustration that he couldn't help but chuckle. "Oh, come now. You say there's no hankering, yet every time I turn around, there you are, trying to entice me, purloin my virtue."

"Purl—what?" she nearly screeched. Her jaw dropped, and she slapped a hand to her chest, indignantly horrified. He beamed at her. The woman had no boundaries whatsoever and was becoming a right nuisance, but he was certainly never bored in her presence.

"I have n-never tried to entice you," she sputtered, "so if you've been enticed, that is your own fault. And I've certainly never *purloined* anything, let alone your nonexistent virtue. I am simply trying to do you a favor. And yes," she said before he could respond, "it would be helping me out as well. But let's not pretend you are doing so wonderfully on your own. You've been in town nearly a week now, which means your time is ticking down. And in that time, you've already managed to lose two jobs. Your horse could probably do better."

Adam snorted. "You don't know my horse very well. He barely manages to haul me around without falling over. And those jobs are harder than they look," he said, grumbling.

She cocked an eyebrow, obviously not buying it. "Be that as it may," she said, thankfully not arguing his dubious point, "you are down to a little more than three weeks before you hit your thirty days. Seems to me it would be a lot easier on everyone if you would just accept the marriage and sign the papers. It doesn't have to be forever. Just think of it as…a temporary solution to both our problems."

He really didn't appreciate her making sense and tempting him with logic and an easy way out.

"First of all, marriage isn't a temporary anything. It's a forever kind of thing. Which is why I avoid it at all costs. I'm not a forever kind of man. Besides, if I ever went and got a divorce, my sainted mother would turn in her grave."

Nora's expression immediately melted into one of sympathy. "I'm so sorry."

"For what?" he asked, frowning at the interruption to his train of thought.

"For…your mother. Losing her. How long has it

been since she died?"

"Oh, she's not dead, but this whole situation will absolutely kill her."

Nora gasped and sputtered some mostly incoherent and decidedly colorful language at him before leaning forward to swipe a fistful of water in his face. He lifted his hands to guard his face with a laugh, and then *he* gasped, slamming his hands back into the water to cover himself.

"Why do you want me to sign those papers so badly?" he asked, staring at her like he could pull the information directly from her brain, since she didn't seem inclined to offer it up. "You said yourself you don't want a husband, so why shackle yourself with one? Especially one who does not want to be one."

Her eyes narrowed. "I said I have my reasons."

He opened his mouth to ask yet again what those were, but she pushed on before he could. "Look, despite how it seems, I get why you're asking. I'd be asking, too. But it's not really something I can share right now. All you really need to know is that this marriage solves your problem just as well as it solves mine. You get what you need—your ticket to staying in town. Heck, you'll even earn a place to stay, since it would be mighty odd if my husband were living in the boardinghouse rather than with me."

Adam slowly sat up, though he took care to keep his hands beneath the water. He let his gaze rove over her still-bouncing foot and up her tightly muscled body before finally locking on her eyes.

Her foot stopped bouncing, and she straightened, watching him like he was a predator stalking her in the grass. Rich, considering she was the one with all the indecent proposals. Then again…he let his gaze skate over her again. This time her eyes narrowed, but he didn't miss the fine tremor that went through her body at his obvious interest.

"I'll admit, there are certain aspects of what you're proposing that I might be on board with," he said, giving her a slow grin that had her cheeks flaming.

She held up a hand to stop him again. "I didn't propose anything of the sort."

"Of what sort?" He'd said nothing untoward. Oh, he'd meant it, and the look he was giving her said much more than his lips needed to, and they both knew it. But if the brazen filly thought she could just waltz in and stare at him while he was buck-ass naked in the tub, he was damn well going to make her say it.

"Of a…a physical sort," she said, and his grin widened. Her bravado slipped a little when sex was on the table. She really needed to stop making his life so interesting. Saying no to her was getting more and more difficult.

"Isn't that what you're offering?" he asked.

She closed her eyes briefly and let out a long-suffering sigh. Yeah. He tended to have that effect on people.

"I offered lodgings," she insisted.

"Yes. In *your* home."

She swallowed hard and shifted on her perch so she was a little farther away from him. "My *house*. Not my bed."

"Ah. Well, that's too bad, then."

Her scowl had him chuckling. "Don't pretend

you'd be running to sign the papers if I was offering something more," she said.

He shrugged. "I guess we'll never know."

As a gambling man, he really shouldn't try and call her bluff. It wouldn't be the first time he'd been wrong. The last time he'd gambled on a woman's heart, they'd both barely survived. And if she suddenly said, "Okay, let's go," he wasn't all that sure what he'd do.

Well, that's not true. He had no doubt he'd be out of the tub and halfway down the street in search of the preacher and a pen with nothing but a towel wrapped around his waist before he came to his senses. But he also had no doubt he *would* come to his senses before it was too late. Probably.

She watched him, her eyes narrowed to slits for a moment, and then something in her demeanor changed. The look in her eyes was less wary and more...speculative. Her features softened, and she gave him a sweet smile that had him frowning and hunkering back down in the rapidly cooling water. Nothing he had learned about this woman so far made him trust that innocently sweet smile on her face.

"You know, I suppose you are right," she said, leaning forward before leaving her perch altogether and moving over to the edge of his tub.

"I am?" Did his voice just squeak?

"Mm-hmm." She nodded and leaned a little closer, perusing him over one coquettishly arched shoulder.

"There are other advantages to marriage that I hadn't really considered before."

No, no, no, no. She was just bluffing, right? She had to be. Totally bluffing. Stone-cold poker-face bluffing. Right?

"Are there?" He forced the words out, even though his mouth suddenly felt like he'd been licking the dirt road out front, and pressed himself back against the side of the tub as far away from her as he could get. Which wasn't all that far.

"So I've heard, at least. Having a wife presents a man with certain…comforts he can't get on his own."

"Comforts?"

She bit her lip and nodded, and he was pretty sure if she did that again, the water he sat in would start boiling just from the heat rushing through his veins.

She leaned over him, reaching across to the other side of the tub, and he sank down in the water up to his chin. She grasped the bar of soap and held it up.

"Do you mind?"

"Mind?" he echoed, his voice barely audible. He managed to shake his head, and she smiled again, sinking her hand beneath the water to start rubbing the soap across his chest.

He froze, afraid if he moved, her hand would slip lower where he desperately wanted—no, *didn't*, didn't want it to go. "What are you doing?"

"Bathing you," she said with a little giggle. "Just like a good wife would."

All right, who was this woman and what had she done with Nora? The Nora he knew, and yes, he realized he didn't know her all that well yet, but the Nora he knew would never make that tittering little sound that passed for a laugh.

Some of the tension bled out of him. Well, most of him. She was good. But two could play at this little game.

"You would bathe me?" he said, sitting up to give her better access. He watched her hand move across his chest with a sort of morbid curiosity. How far was she going to take this bluff of hers? Because she *had* to be bluffing. There was no way she'd had that fast a change of heart. Sure, he presented a rather stunning specimen lounging in the water as he was, but he wasn't *that* tempting.

She shrugged, continuing her movements, though she didn't delve lower than his chest. "I'm sure I could on occasion. I would also launder your clothes so you wouldn't have to pay to have it done the next time you take a swim in a vat of whiskey."

He pursed his lips. "Funny," he said.

She gave him a little grin and let her hand sink just a little bit lower. Enough that he sucked in a breath, and everything south of the waterline stood at attention.

"There'd be a home-cooked meal every night," she continued, her hand moving leisurely across his skin like she had all the time in the world and nowhere else she'd rather be. "A nice, warm bed to sleep in, not just your saddle roll in an unfinished boarding room."

He slapped his hand over hers, keeping his other pressed firmly to his groin where his cock was now straining to break itself free from the prison in which he kept it trapped.

"While all those things sound wonderful," he said, "they all hinge on agreeing to the one thing I want least in the world." He grabbed her wrist and pulled her forward enough that she was inches from his face and had to grab the side of the tub to keep from toppling in. *"A wife,"* he whispered, his breath mingling with hers.

She scowled at him, and he let her go with a chuckle.

"Fine," she said, standing up. "Have it your way. You keep trying to find a job that you can hold on to for longer than a day, and I will keep watching that clock tick your days away. You let me know when you're ready to take me up on my offer."

She turned to leave but spun back around. "Here. You better take this," she said, raising her hand, her nose crinkling. "You stink."

She tossed the bar of soap at him, and he caught it just before it hit his chest, both hands raising in reflex to grab it. Her eyes trailed down, her lips pulling into a smug grin. "I don't think you're quite as opposed to the idea as you think you are, Mr. Grady."

He grimaced, his hands jerking back down to cover his misbehaving appendage. "Brady. The name is Brady."

She smirked. "See you around, *husband*."

Nora turned and sashayed out of the bathhouse, her laughter following her through the door.

Adam let out a long, frustrated breath and slid beneath the water, blowing bubbles as the now-tepid water blocked out everything else around him. But he couldn't erase the image of those laughing eyes and full, kissable lips a breath away from his.

He was never going to survive the next three weeks.

# CHAPTER TWELVE

As soon as she was through the doorway, Nora picked up her speed, putting as much distance between herself and her naked husband as she could. What had she been thinking? She'd meant to go in and knock him off his game, and instead all she'd managed to do was rile herself up. Well, she'd riled him up a bit, too, if what he'd been sporting beneath the water was any indication. And sweet mother of mercy had he been sporting mighty plenty.

There had been a moment there when her lips had been oh so close to his. All she'd had to do was lean the tiniest bit forward and she would've been kissing him, and the fact that that thought didn't absolutely terrify her…well, absolutely terrified her. She shoved her trembling hands in her pockets and marched as quickly as she could back to where she'd left her horse and wagon.

The only good thing that had come out of that whole debacle was that she had definitely gotten a little more under his skin. She wouldn't dwell on how much he was under *hers*. Whether or not it was enough to convince him to abandon his protests and just make it legal already would remain to be seen. Somehow, she doubted it. The man was a lot more stubborn than he'd looked when she'd first seen him.

She closed her eyes to take a deep breath, but that only made it worse, because the instant her eyes were closed, the image of his long, hard lines only partially obscured by the soapy water flooded her mind. She'd probably dream of the stubborn man every time she—

Someone shouted, a horse screeched, and Nora's eyes flew open as she jerked her horse to a stop with a gasp. It took her a moment wrestling with the reins, getting her horse under control after a near collision with a worried Preacher.

"Miss Nora," he said, his brows drawing into a frown as he looked her over. "Is everything all right?"

"Yes," she said, pressing a hand over her chest to keep her thundering heart from escaping. "Sorry. I…I guess I wasn't really paying attention to where I was going."

Preacher dismounted and straightened his hat. "Why don't you come in and sit a spell?" he said, gesturing to the church she hadn't even noticed she was in front of.

She frowned but couldn't really think of a good reason to say no. And honestly, sitting in the quiet, private church for a moment to collect her thoughts sounded like a good idea.

"Sure, thank you."

He tied his horse out front beside hers and preceded her, opening the doors to let her enter first. She nodded as she passed him and stepped inside, slipping into the first pew that she came to.

Preacher closed the doors and sat beside her. "Are you doing all right? I know the last week or so has been a bit strange."

Nora lightly snorted. "Yes, it has been. But it's

hard to complain too loudly when the situation is one of my own making."

Preacher gave her a wry grin. "I suppose that may be true of most situations. But I've found that doesn't make them any less difficult to navigate."

Nora smiled back. Preacher, like most folks in town, had some sort of past that he was running from. She didn't know what it was, nor would she pry. But if he had been a stranger on the street somewhere, without his starched white collar, she never would've guessed the man was a preacher.

He was a considerate man but tended to be a bit gruff. Quiet. Always seemed somewhat on the rough side, his hair just a fraction too long, his face not quite clean-shaven. She'd always sensed a dangerous air about him. Not one that she feared, though. Preacher was a good man. He'd never been anything but kind to her and everybody else in town that she knew of. One day, whatever that was, whatever had happened in the past to drive him to a town like Desolation, would erupt. And she wouldn't want to be on the wrong side of it when it happened.

But right now, she looked up into his kind, warm eyes and was grateful that she had him as a friend.

"I'll be fine," she said again. "Once we get everything squared away."

Preacher nodded, but the concerned frown stayed stamped on his face. "I can probably drag this out a little while longer. Mr. Brady hasn't outright asked me why I can't just dissolve the marriage. Since there was no intent and no consummation, there truly *isn't* a marriage, I suppose. I've never come across this situation before...usually people who say 'I do' in front of me mean to do it," he said, his lips pulling into a half grin. "But first time for everything. I probably don't need to do much more than strike it from the church record, since the church is the only entity recognizing the marriage. But I can delay doing that a bit longer. I've written to a colleague in Boston asking for his guidance. I will do nothing until I get his reply."

"Thank you, Preacher. I truly do appreciate the help."

He patted her hand where it rested on her thigh. "I'm glad to do what I can. I know your circumstances haven't always been the easiest. If we can make this work for you so you can put your mind to rest, well, what are friends for?"

She gritted her teeth against the anxious twisting in her gut. Asking for help was not something that came easily to her. Accepting it, especially when she *hadn't* asked, was even more difficult. She appreciated what her friends were doing for her, more than she could express. But it still made her feel…unsettled. The whole situation seemed to be getting further and further out of her control, and for the thousandth time, she wished there was a solution that would allow her to just take care of everything on her own so she didn't have to be a bother to anyone else.

Despite her inner turmoil, she gave Preacher a grateful smile and then took a deep breath before standing. "Thanks for letting me borrow your church for a moment," she said. "I better get back to work."

"The door's always open if you need it."

She nodded and walked back out, squinting into

the sun. If that husband of hers kept resisting her offers, she might need to avail herself of Preacher's offer in the not-too-distant future and find herself another man who would marry her and then skedaddle.

But the image of Adam stretching out in the hot water assailed her mind again, and for the first time, it occurred to her that they might have a few new problems if he ever did take her up on her offer. They didn't need to consummate the marriage to make it legal, so she could still get what she needed and send him on his way if they behaved themselves. If they didn't, getting rid of him after he signed the license would be much more difficult. Because Preacher wouldn't annul a marriage that had been consummated.

And the more she saw of Mr. Brady, the more consummating seemed like a mighty fine idea.

# CHAPTER THIRTEEN

Adam shuffled out the door of the boardinghouse, letting loose a yawn so wide, it cracked his jaw. He rubbed a hand over his face and groaned. He'd gotten little to no sleep the night before. And the night before that. It was almost as though someone was paying the men surrounding him to be as loud and obnoxious as possible. And that yowling cat kept coming back around. All. Night. Long.

Between the snoring, farting, drunken laughing, and fighting of his bunkmates; the construction on the boardinghouse starting the second the sun rose; the squalling cat; and the disturbingly erotic dreams of a certain statuesque woman that plagued him every time he did manage to fall asleep, Adam was ready to marry the first woman who crossed his path, as long as she came with a quiet bed. Well, almost. He would do a few other unspeakable acts to get a few hours of sleep, though.

But instead of finding a quiet corner of town to nap in, he had to go find employment. Again.

The town wasn't large, but he was too tired to wander around on foot. He'd let Barnaby earn all that grain he was eating in the stables and haul him around for a few hours. Only when he got to the stables, Barnaby wasn't inside. Nor was he out back. And definitely not tied out front.

"Hey," Adam said, grabbing one of the stable boys who ran by. "Where is my horse?"

The boy pulled out of his grasp. "Which horse is yours?"

"Barnaby. The old pain in the ass who has his face shoved in a feed bag all day."

"Oh, him," the boy said, a grin breaking out on his freckly face. "Dunno."

He tried to run off again, but Adam snagged the back of his shirt.

"What do you mean, you don't know? It's your job to know."

"It's my job to take care of the horses who are in the stables," he said, pulling out of Adam's grasp again. "Your horse isn't in the stables."

"Well, that's where I left him," Adam said, trying to keep a rein on his irritation. But the kid was making that extremely difficult.

The boy huffed like he'd never heard anything so unreasonable. "Oy, Willy," he said, hailing another boy who ambled by with a shovel. "You seen that old stallion we were feeding last night?"

"Sure," Willy said. And then kept on walking.

Adam gritted his teeth. "Where is he?" he asked, though at this point it seemed easier to just let the matter go, say his silent goodbyes, and move on with his life.

"He wandered off this morning," Willy said.

Adam threw his hands up. "Why didn't you stop him?" Was it murder if you were goaded into it through sheer frustration? Surely a judge would side with him this once.

Willy shrugged. "He was following Birdie."

Adam briefly closed his eyes. *Count to three, murder is bad, Woodson specifically said* No Killin', *deep breaths.*

He gave Willy what he hoped was a nice smile, but judging by the confused and slightly horrified expression on the young man's face, Adam wasn't pulling it off. "You're saying that like it answers all my questions. That doesn't answer any of my questions. Who is Birdie and why didn't you stop her from taking my horse?"

Willy eyed him like he was speaking a foreign language. "Birdie is the sheriff's horse. She pretty much does what she wants. She got friendly when she passed by earlier, and your horse just followed her on out. I've been keeping an eye on him, but he'll be fine. Birdie always naps for a few hours in the morning. No one can get her moving if she's napping. Your horse is right over there." He pointed to the sheriff's office and then took off before Adam could grab him again.

Adam rubbed his hand over his face again. "Women are running around marrying men willy-nilly, horses are horse-napping other horses, and a goat named Lucille apparently runs the town. What kind of place is this?" he muttered.

He took a long, cleansing breath that did nothing whatsoever to steady him, then headed over to the sheriff's office to retrieve his horse.

"Sherriff, I—" he started, trying, and failing, to keep his voice at a non-angry level.

Woodson spun around. "Shh," he said, cutting him off before he could get more than two words out.

Adam opened his mouth to protest, but his jaw was too busy dropping to form words.

Woodson patted the back of the baby strapped to his chest and bounced a bit. The little girl snuggled into his chest, let out a sigh, and settled back to sleep.

Adam looked back and forth between Woodson and the baby a few times. Woodson just raised a brow, a faint smile on his stern lips. Adam finally shook his head. Everything else about this town was stranger than a cat swimming circles in a lake; why should the fact that the sheriff was strapped with a baby instead of his firearms be any different?

"Why did you take my horse?" Adam asked, though he was careful to keep his voice down.

Woodson frowned. "I didn't take your horse."

Adam flung out an arm, pointing to where the horse in question stood beside the sheriff's own horse. "Then what is he doing here in front of your office instead of at the stables where I left him?"

The men were getting closer, their voices more heated, though they still kept them low, whisper-shouting at each other just loudly enough for the other to make out the words.

"Ask him," Woodson said, jerking his head at Barnaby. "He just showed up here earlier, seems to have taken a liking to Birdie."

Adam just stared at him, not sure how to respond. "Does your horse often pick up strays when wandering about town?"

Woodson shrugged. "Occasionally."

Well, that…wasn't the answer he was expecting as he'd been half joking. "Did it not occur to you to return him, or send word, or—"

Woodson let out an irritated sigh that Adam felt

down to his soul. "Your horse was in no danger. He wasn't far from where you'd left him. Anyone in town you cared to ask would have pointed you in this direction, so trying to hunt you down to tell you your horse was perfectly fine seemed unnecessary."

A flood of responses flew through Adam's mind, but each one seemed more likely than the last to get him shot, so he just kept his mouth shut.

"Besides," Woodson continued, "it's the first time I've seen her awake for this long of a stretch in years. She must return his affections."

Adam stared at the horses, who were now nuzzling. Wonderful. His horse was courting. *Traitor.* "I…" He sighed and shook his head. "Never mind."

"Mr. Brady," Doc said as he and Preacher stepped onto the walkway in front of the sheriff's office. "How are you this fine day?"

Adam opened his mouth to answer but got distracted when Deputy Sunshine popped out of the office door and pinned them all with a cheerful smile.

"Want me to lay her down now, Sheriff?" he asked.

Woodson nodded and carefully disengaged himself from his daughter. When Sunshine had her and went through the door again, Adam caught sight of a small baby's cot inside the office. His brows hit his hairline at the surprising domestic turn the country's most notorious gunslinger had taken. But all it took was one glance at those hard, unyielding eyes for Adam to know that Gray Woodson could still be a very dangerous man when he wanted to be.

"Mr. Brady?" Doc asked again, and Adam gave

himself a little shake.

"Apologies, Dr. Fairbanks."

"No worries at all, Mr. Brady. And call me Doc. Everyone else around these parts does."

Adam gave the friendly man a sincere smile. "Doc. I'm…well, not great, to tell the truth. I've lost two jobs already. Just can't seem to shake this bad luck of mine."

Woodson aimed an amused grin his way. "Two jobs already and one whole week gone."

"Yes, I know. My time is ticking," Adam said before Gray could rub it in.

"If you're looking for work, I could use some help in my office," Doc said.

Woodson's gaze shot to him, and his eyes narrowed slightly, but he didn't say anything. Was he annoyed that his friend had offered Adam a job? Oh, Adam would take it regardless, but if he could needle Woodson a bit while doing it, all the better.

"Do you have any experience with doctoring?" Doc asked.

Adam shook his head. Gunslingers didn't tend to be the ones patching people up. They were more likely to be the reason people needed patching, if not a grave.

"That's no matter," Doc said. "As long as you have a strong back…and stomach," he added after a second of thought, "you'll be all right."

Adam hesitated. A strong back, sure. He could lift, haul, carry whatever the doc needed him to. Stomach…that might be a different story. He'd probably be fine. But then he'd never really put that to the test. He'd seen plenty of injuries in his time, of course. Caused more than a few as well. But seeing them and having them actively smeared all over his freshly laundered shirt were two entirely different things. He'd try to hold it together, but if blood, pus, or any other bodily fluid stained his custom-made clothing, he very well might disgrace himself in any number of undignified ways.

Still. It was employment, and it beat giving in to the whole matrimony thing, so he nodded. "I'm your man for whatever you need, Doc."

"Excellent! Come by the clinic later this afternoon, and I'll give you a quick rundown of what I'll need you to do. Then you can start first thing in the morning."

"That'll be great, Doc, thanks," Adam said, reaching out to shake his hand.

Doc turned to leave, but not before exchanging a look with a sour-faced Woodson that had Adam's curiosity hackles up. Woodson just shook his head when Doc smiled and walked away. Preacher looked back and forth between Woodson and Adam but didn't say anything. Just nodded to them both before going about his business.

"Looks like I'm employed again," Adam said.

Woodson gave him that half grin that somehow both conveyed subtle amusement and sent a shiver of apprehension down Adam's spine. "I'm not worried." Then he turned to head into his office.

Adam frowned at his back. Woodson wasn't worried because he didn't think Adam could hack being a doctor's assistant. To be fair, Adam wasn't all that sure himself. But he was still willing to give it a shot.

He shoved his hands in his pockets and looked over at his horse, who was now snoozing peacefully beside his new lady love. Adam sighed. Actually, a nap wasn't a bad idea. Surely he could find someplace in this wretched town where he could catch a few minutes of uninterrupted sleep. He'd go back to the bathhouse if he wasn't afraid of falling asleep in the tub and drowning. Or having his would-be wife track him down again to continue whatever game she'd started with that bar of soap. She'd damn near won last time. He couldn't afford to give her another crack at it. Hell, if she cornered him naked again, he'd probably be on his knees worshipping her before she so much as batted her eyes at him.

He stepped off the walkway and just started walking, letting his mind wander along with his body. Adam had thought about ol' Quick Shot many times over the years. How could he not when their fight had set him on the path that had led him to this town in the first place?

But never once, even in his wildest, most uninhibited moments, had Adam ever imagined that Gray Woodson would be an obviously happily married father and a sheriff to boot. Oh, the man was still a grouch, no doubt about it. But there was no mistaking that tender look in his eyes when he gazed at his daughter. Or the devotion that shone from him when he looked at his wife. The way his friends spoke of him, and the way he talked with them... He still grumbled, sure. But they all seemed to care about and respect one another.

Adam had never had that. He'd never been able

to trust anyone that much. A fact he'd learned the hard way. And for the first time in a long time, it looked really nice. Watching the people of Desolation interact with one another, it wasn't hard to start imagining what it would be like to have people at his back like that. To have…a family like that.

He still had his mother, and he loved her dearly. But he hadn't seen her in years. They'd always been so different. She hadn't understood his desire to go west, to carve out his own life. She preferred her comfortable life back east. She'd always wanted him to be a banker or someone…respectable. Successful. With the perfect job, the perfect life. The perfect wife.

He couldn't help but smile at the thought of his mother meeting Nora. She'd have a fainting spell over Nora's penchant for wearing men's trousers. But for the most part…his mother would probably like her. A lot. She was impossible not to like, frankly, as aggravating as she was.

But the last thing he wanted was to let someone else in his life down. Or worse, let them in only to be betrayed again. Or even worse yet, drag someone he cared about into danger. His enemies were not the type of people to spare a man because of his attachments. Loved ones were nothing more than leverage at best. Cannon fodder at worst.

Better to just continue to steer clear. No matter how much he was starting to wish otherwise.

He'd left the main street and continued to wander past a few homes that were just on the edge of town. The one at the end of the lane made him stop and smile. The small white house was a bit shabby, but the yard was neat, what he could see of the garden and back acreage looked well-tended, and the whole place exuded an air of cozy homliness. And sported a tree that looked like the perfect place for a nap.

Until the back door opened and Nora descended the stairs. Adam froze like a deer in the crosshairs and then turned on his heel and double-timed it back to town. A nap could wait. The last thing he wanted was to draw the attention of his so-called wife. And he'd keep repeating that thought until his body started listening.

He found himself in front of Doc's again without really realizing how exactly he'd gotten there. So much for keeping that wife he refused to think of from distracting him.

"Mr. Brady, back already?" Doc stuck his head out the door with a face-splitting grin. "Come on in and I'll show you where we keep everything. We can start with the bedpans."

Adam closed his eyes, fighting the urge to run as fast as he could for the town border. But he knew what awaited him out there. His choices if he stayed in Desolation might not be great, but he'd at least be alive to make them. So, time to choose. Bedpans or marriage?

He took a deep breath and slowly let it out. *All right, then.* There was really only one option that didn't make his stomach twist into nautical knots.

Bedpans it was.

He squared his shoulders and marched into the clinic, praying the bedpans in question were empty. Judging by Doc's smile…he wouldn't bet his last dollar on it.

# CHAPTER FOURTEEN

Adam dropped onto his bedroll, his body aching for sleep. Doc's quick tour of the clinic had turned into a full inventory and reorganization afternoon. If Adam saw one more roll of bandages, he'd have to shove them in his mouth just to keep the scream in.

He rubbed his hand over his face, scrubbing at his burning eyes. For once, he was actually tired enough he might even sleep through the cacophony of sounds being produced by his neighbors.

A feminine giggle drifted to him through the open hole of his window, and he sat up so he could peer down to the street below. So much for sleeping. Two young women were huddled just below his window, one of them growing increasingly more agitated as the other tried to shoo her off.

"Calm yourself, Annie. It's going to work."

The other girl, Annie, he presumed, huffed and folded her arms. "You don't know that. And even if it does, you don't know what kind of man you'll be getting."

That perked Adam right up. He shimmied as close to the window as he could get without being seen.

"I'll get a man—that's enough for me."

Annie tried again. "You don't need to do it this way, Sally. You heard the rules. All the single men in town have to get hitched if they want to stay. You could have your pick!"

Sally snorted. "The best ones were spoken for long before the sheriff got involved. The ones who are left are either too old or too good at avoiding me. Until this new one rode into town."

Adam's heart thudded. *He* was the new one. What did the little schemer want with him? Well, never mind. He could guess. Why she thought he'd go along with it was a better question.

"Yeah, but he was with all the couples who got hitched. Him and Nora. You saw it."

There was a soft, feminine grunt and the sound of something large being dragged and then a sigh. "Yes, but I told you, Mrs. DuVere said they didn't actually do it. Or they did, but not really."

The other girl let out a frustrated groan. "That doesn't make any sense. They are either married or they aren't."

"I don't know all the specifics, Annie. All I know is that whatever they did, it didn't take, so he's up for grabs."

What? No he wasn't. A knot of dread settled in his gut as more scraping sounds filtered up to him.

"You know Pa'll be furious. He says you're still too young."

"Yes, well, once I'm married, he won't be able to say a thing about it. And I'm not much younger than Ma was when she married him, so that argument isn't a very good one."

"Well, fine then, why do we have to go sneaking in the window in the middle of the night? I heard he'd been fired from three jobs already, so he's gotta be desperate for a wife if he wants to stay. Just let him know you're interested. I bet he'd be thrilled."

He quietly snorted. She'd lose that bet. And what did she mean, three jobs? It had only been two. So far.

The thought of what new ungodly surprises might await him at Doc's the next day set his stomach churning again, and he tried very hard to put that out of his head for the moment. He had a bigger problem at hand—two apparently very young women who seemed set on whatever wild scheme they were hatching.

Sally scoffed. "Why dawdle around with courtin' and all that nonsense when this is so much easier?"

*This?* Adam frowned. *What is this?* He risked another peek out the window.

Sally put a foot on the ladder that still leaned against the wall from earlier in the day, but Annie grabbed her leg.

"Sally," she hissed. "This will never work. Come back down."

Sally shook her off. "Of course it'll work. But only if I get up there before Pa shows up. Once he finds me with my 'beau,' he and his shotgun will make sure I'm married before sunup."

And that was all Adam needed to hear. He grabbed his saddlebags and was reaching for his bedroll when the ladder clapped against the outside of his window. He dove through the sheet separating his room from the one next to it, abandoning his bed gear. It was replaceable; his bachelorhood was not.

What was with the women in this town? And he used that term lightly, because if he remembered correctly, the only other marriageable woman in town was barely seventeen years old. Did they not know how regular folk courted? It certainly did not involve tricking a man into matrimony or forcing him into it at gunpoint!

He froze as a half-dressed man sleepily staggered in through the nonexistent doorway.

The man glanced at him, frowned in confusion, and scratched at his chest. "Sorry, pal. All these rooms look alike without a door and walls."

Then he turned with a face-cracking yawn and stumbled in the direction of Adam's room. His snores filled the air before Adam could draw a full breath. He didn't spare a second to pity the poor man who was about to find himself in front of an irate father and a preacher. He was probably better off. He looked like a nice enough fellow, young enough to make Sally happy, even had all his teeth from what Adam could tell from that yawn. The devious Miss Sally could certainly do worse.

Adam slung his saddlebags over his shoulder and scurried down the stairs. He'd just made it to the parlor when the front door burst open and an older gentleman with wild eyes and what Adam presumed to be a fully loaded shotgun barged inside. A startled, girlish squeal emanated from above their heads, and the man who'd just come in roared something incoherent and ran for the stairs. Adam wasn't too sure if the scream had come from Sally or the poor sod she'd found in his bed, but her father didn't seem inclined to wait to find out. Adam had never seen an old man move so quickly.

He didn't stick around to see what became of sweet Sally and her soon-to-be husband. Instead, he hightailed it down the street just as fast as he could.

To the last place he'd ever thought he'd willingly go. But he'd just run out of options. It was far too dangerous for a single man on the streets of Desolation. He just hoped he could find the place in the dark. He'd only been past it the once, when he'd wandered about town in search of a good nap. But it wasn't too far from the center of town.

It only took him a few minutes and one wrong turn before he was standing in front of Nora's neat little homestead. The white house shone slightly in the moonlight, and though the shutters were in need of repair, and the fence line could use a few nails and some paint, it didn't look quite as bedraggled as it had during the day.

The yard was neat and tidy with its flower beds and trimmed bushes. And what he'd seen of the back of the house looked like most of the land had been put to gardening, though there was a decent-size barn and a chicken coop that was a bit worse for wear.

He took a deep breath, girding his loins, steeling his nerves, bracing his ship for impact…

Who knew how long he'd have stood there gathering his courage, because before he could hesitate any longer, the door opened, releasing a beam of warm light into the night.

"Well, well, well," Nora said, her voice thick with amusement. "If it isn't the prodigal husband."

# CHAPTER FIFTEEN

Nora folded her arms and watched Adam until he reached her porch. He dropped his saddlebags at his feet and looked up at her.

She raised an eyebrow. "Come to sign the papers, then?"

His eyes widened, though he couldn't possibly be surprised that she was asking.

"No, but—"

"Then good night." She slammed the door in his face before he had a second to say anything else, and she didn't feel a lick of guilt about it. Well…maybe a little lick. A nibble.

He knocked again, and she shook her head. She hadn't really thought slamming the door would work, but there was no way she was going to just happily invite him into her home unless he agreed to her terms.

She opened the door again. "Yes?"

"You know, you were a lot nicer to me at the bathhouse."

Her cheeks burned at the reminder of her brazen display. She clenched her hands against the memory of how his wet skin had felt beneath her fingers and stood straighter, determined not to let him see her squirm.

"Yes, well, that was earlier. It's been a very long week."

"I completely agree. And in the spirit of that, I'd

hoped you'd feel some Christian compassion and take in a poor stranger who needs a place to rest his weary head."

She cocked her eyebrow. "But you aren't a poor stranger. You're my husband."

He sighed. "Can't we just agree to disagree on that point?"

She pursed her lips, her eyes boring into his, but he held her gaze until she took a deep breath and pasted on her most insincere smile. "Fine. I agree that I disagree with you. Good night."

She slammed the door again.

He sighed so loudly, she could hear it through the door. "That's not what I meant. And I'm not going away, Miss Schumacher."

She waited a few more seconds and then opened the door again. "Are you going to sign the papers?"

"No, but—"

She tried to close the door again, except this time, he shoved his foot in over the threshold before the door closed.

"Ow!" He grunted in pain.

She glanced down, then back up, her eyebrows softly raised. "Did you stub your toe?"

"What? No! You slammed it in the door."

"Ah, yes. Well, that has a tendency to happen when you shove your foot where it's not wanted. Now, if you don't want it happening again, I suggest you move it."

He held out a hand, pushing against the door just hard enough to keep it open, but not so hard that he forced the issue. Though she had no doubt he could if he wanted.

"I wasn't asking for, or expecting, a welcome. But as I said, I do need a place to stay, so I was hoping we could just discuss matters. Maybe come to an arrangement, at least for the night. I'll try to make it as painless as possible," he added with that half grin that kept doing a thing or two to her insides. The second she got around the man, it was as if her body completely rebelled, wanting to rub itself all over him like an overgrown kitten.

As it was, she couldn't tear her focus from his exceptionally chiseled jawline, though she hadn't quite decided if it was because of the aforementioned affected insides or because she really wanted to plant her fist across it.

She was leaning toward the fist. He *did* seem to enjoy aggravating her. Then again, she quite enjoyed returning the favor, too, so it really wasn't fair to complain.

Nora sucked in several deep breaths, trying in vain to think of an argument that would get him to leave. Or cave and make their marriage official. Since neither seemed likely, she sighed and stepped back. He moved inside, watching her warily. As well he should. He looked around the place, and she gritted her teeth again, waiting for some disdainful comment about their shabby, badly in-need-of-repair surroundings.

She did her best to keep things up, though most of her attention went to the small sitting room where she met with customers. And no one could fault the cleanliness of her home. But she'd basically been on her own for quite a while, and there was only so much she could do in a day.

Adam merely nodded, a faint smile on his lips as he looked around. "It's cozy, homey. I like it."

"I'm so glad you approve," she drawled, laying the sarcasm on thick. He either didn't notice or chose to ignore it. She pursed her lips. "So, what did you want to discuss that we haven't already discussed, Mr. Brady?" she asked, sitting gingerly on the edge of the sofa.

"I've asked you before to call me Adam."

"And I've asked you to sign the papers or leave. We don't always get what we ask for, apparently."

"That, I've found, is very true." Instead of being offended, he grinned and sank into the armchair across from her with a weary exhale. "I do think we need to discuss our little issue, since Preacher doesn't seem able, or willing, to handle matters in an expeditious fashion. But I'll be honest, I'm not sure I'm up to verbally sparring with you tonight, much as I enjoy it under normal circumstances. However, I do need a place to stay. The boardinghouse was…" He paused, then snorted. "Let's just say it wasn't the safest place for me to be."

Her eyebrow rose. "You were in danger?"

He grinned again. "Yeah, of some papa's loaded shotgun." She frowned, her brow crinkling with confusion, and he shrugged. "Apparently there are a few matrimony-minded females in town who are no longer content to wait for me to show an interest. Especially since that was never going to happen. One climbed in my bedroom window with her daddy hot on her heels less than an hour ago."

"Sally?"

Adam nodded.

"My goodness," Nora said, her lips twitching. "Very resourceful, I suppose."

"If you say so," he muttered. "Anyway, between all the assorted noise from my neighbors and dodging ill-fated marriage attempts, this just seemed to be the safest place for me to be."

She gave him a slow, steady smile. "Is it? And what makes you think *I* won't be aiming a shotgun at you in your sleep, Mr. Brady?"

"Adam," he said. "And if you did, at least I've given you more cause than I ever gave Sally's daddy. Dying unprovoked is so uncivilized. But you seem to need me too much to remove me permanently." He shrugged. "Though if you do, at least it solves the whole question of marriage. It *is* until death do we part, after all."

Her eyes widened. "You'd rather end up dead than married?"

"Yes, ma'am," he said without hesitation.

"Interesting. Not that I blame you, mind. I feel much the same way about it myself. Though I don't know if I'd choose death over marriage. I suppose it would depend on who was doing the proposing." She looked him over, making no secret of the fact that she was referring to him.

He chuckled, and she held aloof for a moment longer, then gave up and slumped back in her chair, lacing her fingers over her stomach.

"Look, Mr. Brady—Adam," she said, before he could correct her again. "I do feel for your current situation."

He pursed his lips and pinned her with a pointed, and disbelieving, gaze. "Somewhat," she clarified.

"But if you have no intention of signing the papers to make our marriage legal, then I'm not sure why you're here. You can hardly stay in my home, with me. I'd never live down the scandal."

"Your father still lives here, does he not?"

She couldn't shy away from his perfectly reasonable question, but she frowned all the same. "He does. For the most part."

"Then people shouldn't question the arrangement overly much."

She sat up and glared at him, not sure if he was being purposely obtuse or if it was just a natural talent. "They absolutely would, and you know it."

"Hmm, perhaps." He rubbed his finger along his bottom lip, watching her until she grimaced.

"His presence isn't exactly…reliable. In fact, he's been gone for the last several days, and I have no idea when he'll return. A fact known by most of the town," she muttered.

"All right, Miss Schumacher. We obviously have more to figure out than we are going to tonight. But I'm throwing myself at your mercy. I have to get some sleep. I'm starting work with Doc tomorrow, and I am woefully ill-prepared as it is. So I'm going to do something I've never done with anyone before in my life. And beg."

He sat forward in his chair, leaning toward her with his eyes locked on hers. "Please let me stay. Just for tonight. For now. We can discuss any further arrangements tomorrow. But for tonight…" His voice changed, grew deeper, softer. It sounded as she imagined it would first thing in the morning after waking. A bedroom voice. "Let me stay."

She trembled beneath his gaze, her pulse jumping in her throat. Men didn't speak to her that way. They didn't think of her that way. But the way Adam's voice lowered made it sound like he wanted her. No man's eyes had ever raked over her before, stripping her bare without ever touching her. No man had ever begged to stay beneath her roof. For any reason.

And here he was, a man who seemed to maybe want her. Want *her*. Not just what he could get from her, because aside from this exact moment, he'd made it clear he wanted nothing from her.

Would it be so terrible to be married to such a man? She might never get the chance again.

Of course, despite the way he was looking at her, he hadn't been shy about insisting he wanted nothing to do with marriage to anyone. And she wouldn't stoop to forcing a man to stay married to her when he didn't want to be. Not permanently, anyway. Just for a little longer.

No matter how much she was starting to want him to stay.

"Nora," he murmured. "Let me stay with you."

It was the *with you* that did her in. And her name falling from those full lips. She gripped the arms of her chair and tried to force her body to calm.

It didn't work.

"You'll leave tomorrow if I wish?"

He nodded. "You have my word. Though I hope you'll let me try and convince you that we can come up with an arrangement that saves your reputation without putting me on the street."

"Very well, then. If I have your word that you

will leave tomorrow if I ask…" He nodded again, and against her better judgment, she believed him. Then again, a man's word was all he had in this world. Even gunslinging gamblers had to keep their word if they wanted people to respect them.

Besides, just because she'd agreed to let him stay didn't mean they actually had to share the same roof. In fact, him having nowhere else to go could work perfectly to her advantage. What better way to ensure he was miserable enough to agree to sign the papers? She needed to get this marriage legal and get that deed in her name. After that, she didn't think it would take much encouragement to send her reluctant husband running for the hills.

She stamped down the twinge of regret at that thought. "If you stay, I have a few rules."

"As I expected."

She frowned slightly, not sure if he was mocking her or not, but he seemed to just be listening with polite interest, so she pushed on.

"Don't go wandering about the house or property at night. I sleep with my shotgun, and if you startle me in the middle of the night, you're liable to get shot before I realize who you are."

"No wandering. Got it."

"My father…" She paused, her brow creasing before she sighed. "He tends to come and go. He won't be happy when he returns to find you here, I'm sure. So…just keep an eye out and try to avoid him if possible. I will explain the situation to him, but if he finds you before I can…"

"I'll do my best to stay out of his way."

Truthfully, she wasn't all that confident she could

convince her father to let him stay on their property. But she'd worry about that when, or if, her father ever decided to return home.

She nodded. "And most importantly, never leave the garden gate unlatched."

His forehead crinkled in confusion. "That's the most important rule?"

"It may seem like a small thing, Mr. Brady—"

"Adam."

She ignored that. "But a good portion of my income comes from that garden, so it is a priority to keep it safe. Mercy does her best to keep Lucille at home, but that goat has a mind of her own and tends to go where she pleases. And she'd love to get into my garden."

"Ah. Point taken. Garden gate will stay firmly latched."

"Good." She nodded, feeling like she should say something else. Impose more rules. Surely there should be something else. But she only muttered "good" again and took a deep breath, letting it out slowly before she extended her hand.

"All right, Mr. Brady. If you agree to all that… you have a deal."

His hand wrapped around hers, so warm she sucked in a breath. His fingers squeezed hers, and he gave her a slow, steady smile.

Why did it feel like she'd just made a deal with the devil?

# CHAPTER SIXTEEN

Adam stood staring down at the pile of hay in the barn for a moment before turning to Nora.

"We're in the barn."

"I'm aware."

"Why are we in the barn?"

She tilted her head, her lips twitching. "This is where you're going to sleep."

Deliciously devious woman. She was having fun with him now. He stared at her, just blinking, while he tried to think of an argument that would get her to let him sleep in the nice, clean house.

She cleared her throat, schooling her features into a less amused expression, or at least she tried, and pushed the quilt she'd taken from the house into his arms. "It may not be what you had in mind, Mr. Brady, but if you won't agree to make our marriage legal, then I can hardly allow you to sleep under the same roof, can I?"

"I don't see why not," he said with a shrug. Then he looked down at her, keeping her gaze captive. "Who would know?"

With his voice lowered, his head bending toward hers, he'd made that sound like some forbidden secret they were keeping between them. And the barely audible gasp that escaped her throat made it clear that whether he'd intended it or not, they were now both thinking of things they had no business to be thinking.

She swallowed hard, but she didn't step away from him. Her gaze dropped to his lips. She dragged her bottom lip through her teeth, and he nearly expired on the spot. Oh, she was good. Much better than he'd given her credit for. And he was pretty sure she didn't even know what she was doing. Had no idea what she did to him.

"I would know," she finally said. "And believe me, this is a very small town. Everyone knows everyone's business. The fact that you are living with me will be common knowledge by lunchtime tomorrow. At least this way, I have some small claim to propriety."

His eyes raked over her, and he knew the smile he was giving her was full of wicked temptation. "Now, where's the fun in that?"

She sucked in another breath. "It may not be as fun," she murmured, licking her lips until he had to bite back a groan. "But it is safer."

He glanced around the barn. And the dozen or so chickens roosting in the corner. "I don't know. I think I'd be much safer in the house with you."

She laughed, and the sound made things tighten low in his belly.

"Then I'd say you don't know me very well, Mr. Brady."

No, he didn't. But he'd like to—and that terrified him.

He gripped the quilt tighter to keep from reaching for her. He didn't know if it was residual desire from her help in the bath, or whether it was because it was nighttime, and they were standing alone in the dark together...or maybe it was just *her*.

The woman did something to him. She made him want to throw all caution away. Turn his back on the rules that had governed his life. Leave behind everything he'd thought he wanted for himself.

And he'd only known her a week. Hadn't even kissed her yet.

What was he thinking? *Yet?* There was no scenario in which kissing Nora Schumacher ended well for either of them.

That wasn't to say it wouldn't *end* well, because he had no doubt the two of them together would be explosive. The tension between them was palpable, and they'd barely touched. And still, the fire that was slowly stoking between them seemed enough to burn down the barn in which they stood.

But after it was said and done…that's when they'd have to pay the price.

She stepped a fraction of an inch closer, her breath hitching when her gaze strayed to his lips. "Sign the papers, Adam, and we can go back inside."

His name on her tongue nearly had him reaching for the first available pen to sign whatever damn papers she wanted. Even if she didn't mean what she seemed to be implying, it would almost be worth it just for the possibility.

But he couldn't give in.

Maybe someday, when his past had caught up to him and done with him what it would. Maybe then.

Though, she'd made it clear enough that she didn't want him, not permanently. Whatever her reasoning for marrying him, she didn't want him to stay with her forever. Even if he could offer her forever. But he couldn't even offer her for now.

He sighed and stepped away. She was right. Unless they wanted this marriage between them to stick, they would be better off keeping their distance. And if that meant sleeping in the barn with a brood of clucking chickens instead of the nice, warm, clean house, so be it.

• • •

Adam was beginning to think getting a good night's sleep had been a mistake. At least if he'd been overly tired, he wouldn't be so aware of every detail of what was going on around him now in Doc's patient room. Instead, he was awake and alert. And...was going to be sick again.

He darted out the back door for the third time that morning. The eggs and bacon that Nora had made him in a surprisingly generous gesture had left his stomach long ago, and there wasn't much left to do but dry heave over the bushes in Doc's back garden.

"Are you all right, Mr. Brady?" Doc called out the door.

"Just fine," he said with a groan.

Doc gave him an amused grin, though there was nothing mocking about it, for which Adam was very grateful.

"I've got the abscess in Mr. Terletter's toe drained. If you feel you're up to it, I could use some help while I bandage him up."

Adam nodded and took several shallow breaths, trying to force back a new wave of nausea. "I'll be right there."

"Good man," Doc said with another grin.

The door to the front of the clinic slammed, and someone called "Doc!"

"Damn," Doc said, shooting Adam a glance that, while sympathetic, also suggested he'd greatly appreciate it if Adam could pull himself together.

Adam took a deep breath, swallowed hard against the urge to vomit again, and headed back inside to see what other fresh hell awaited him.

He should have stayed outside.

Mr. Vernice sat on a chair, his foot propped up in front of him. Sticking out of his foot, boot and all, was a nail that the poor man had apparently stepped on during construction.

Doc was finishing up wrapping Mr. Terletter's toe, apparently having decided it was easier to just do it himself, especially with a worse patient waiting to be seen.

"Adam, I need you to grab me a few things." He rattled off a list of items that he'd need to re-move the nail and properly cleanse and patch Mr. Vernice's foot.

Adam rushed about the clinic, trying to grab everything in one go as time seemed to be of the essence. And of course, the last item needed was on the top shelf of the small storeroom in the back. Not an issue for him normally. But with his hands full... Perhaps he should have taken the few extra seconds to deposit everything he'd already been carrying before reaching for the bottle of alcohol that Doc kept to cleanse wounds.

"Hey there," said a voice behind him. A voice he'd know anywhere.

Startled, his hand jerked as he grabbed the bottle, juggling it a bit before getting a solid grip. But he knocked into the bottle next to the alcohol on the shelf, and he watched it in horror as it teetered for half a breath before crashing to the floor.

He closed his eyes, biting his lips against the groan of frustration that clawed its way up his throat.

"Nora," he said, turning to face her.

"Oops." She looked at the mess on the floor. "Didn't mean to startle you. I just wanted to…" Her nose wrinkled, and she put her hand to it to block the fumes coming off the floor. "What exactly is that?" she asked, nodding to it.

He frowned down at the broken bottle. "I'm not sure."

"What happened?" Doc's voice came from the clinic. "What's that smell? Is that ether?" His voice held a hint of panic that had Adam's heart pounding.

Nora's gaze flew to the shards of glass on the ground, then widened when she looked back to the shelf. Where a sputtering lamp was lit.

Doc appeared in the doorway just as Adam dropped the supplies in his arms and made a grab for the lamp.

"Everyone out!" Doc shouted. He turned on his heels and ran, grabbing Mr. Vernice around the waist so he could haul him out.

Adam snagged the lamp, grabbed Nora's wrist, and dragged her out behind him through the back door. They ran to the front of the clinic, where Doc's shouting had drawn a crowd. Wonderful. The whole town could witness yet another epic failure on his part. He sighed, released Nora, and extinguished the lamp.

Doc's gaze darted around the crowd, his body relaxing just a hair when he caught sight of them. He rushed over. "Did you manage to get— Oh. Thank God," he said when he noticed the lamp Adam still held.

He sucked in a huge breath and let it out slowly. "Mr. Brady…"

Adam sighed. That tone of voice never ended well. He held up a hand to stop Doc before he could continue.

"You don't have to say it."

Doc nodded. "I'm truly sorry, Adam."

"That's kind of you, Doc. But I spent the morning cleaning up my own vomit instead of your patients' because I apparently do not have the stomach for even the smallest medical emergency, and I nearly blew up your clinic. Trust me, I have been fired for far less."

Doc smiled. "I wish you luck, then." He paused and then added, "Far away from my clinic."

Adam laughed and shook Doc's hand. "I'll do my best."

Doc left to open all the doors and windows to the clinic to air out the highly flammable vapor Adam had let loose when the ether spilled. It would take a while and a considerable amount of care to soak up the spilled liquid and air the vapors out of the cloths used so they could be safely burned and disposed of. Without causing an explosion, hopefully.

Adam turned to Nora, who had the grace to give him a sheepish smile.

"Sorry?"

He glowered at her, blowing out his frustration with a hissing breath when she gave him another tentative grin. He took her arm and pulled her with him behind the sheriff's office.

"Where are we going?" she asked, though she made no move to extract herself from his grasp.

As soon as they rounded the corner, he spun her so her back was to the wall and caged her with his arms. She sucked in a breath but, again, didn't fight him.

"Did you show up this morning just to try and get me fired?" he asked.

"No," she said with a slight gasp. "I was passing by and thought I'd stop in and see how things were going. I didn't mean to cause any trouble."

"Hmm." His gaze bore into hers as he tried to read the truth of her words.

He was fairly certain she spoke the truth. But he was also fairly certain if she hadn't been actively trying to get him fired, the fact that it had happened again was definitely a perk for her.

He brought his hand up to cup her face, letting his thumb trail along her bottom lip. Her mouth opened with a little sigh that nearly dropped him to his knees. He leaned in closer, and she sucked in an almost imperceptible breath. His body screamed at him to close the distance between them, to taste those lips. Instead, he leaned his forehead against hers with a sigh that sounded more like a groan.

"I'm not going to marry you, Nora."

She jerked slightly, but her lips curved into a smile beneath his still-caressing thumb. "You already did, Adam."

He shook his head, though his own lips pulled into a slow smile. His hand bracketed her chin, and he leaned in—

"Nora?" a feminine voice called from around the building.

Adam released her and took a large step back just as Martha bustled around the corner.

"Nor— Ah, there you are." She stopped short, her gaze darting back and forth between them. "Sorry, I didn't mean to interrupt anything," she said, her eyes shining with amusement.

"You didn't," Adam said, stepping back farther. Nora just watched him, a mixture of emotions flitting across her face. Confusion. Frustration. *Hunger*.

He knew exactly how she felt.

"If you ladies will excuse me," he said, nodding at each of them, "it appears I have another job to find."

Martha bit her lip, but if she meant to keep her smile in check, it didn't work. Not that he could blame her for laughing. Really, at this point, his situation was nothing short of ridiculous. He spared one last glance for Nora, who looked like she wasn't sure if she wanted to become one with the wall or chase after him.

He spared her the decision and hightailed it out of there.

What had he been thinking, pulling her aside like that? Touching her like that? He'd only meant to talk to her, but the moment he'd had her alone, her eyes locked on his, her clean, woodsy scent invading his senses, the only thought in his head had been how badly he wanted to kiss her.

Her words echoed in his mind. *You already did.* And for a split second, he'd wanted to give in. Agree. Sign whatever she wanted, then drag his wife back to her house and show her what being married entailed.

What had she done to him?

One week. One week was all it had taken for her to do the impossible and make matrimony seem tempting. And now he was living under her roof...well, sort of. Close enough. With a woman who apparently had no qualms whatsoever about convincing him to give in, using any means necessary. And he was growing less and less capable of fighting her.

Fighting her? Hell, he'd damn near kissed her not three minutes ago, and it had been entirely his fault.

He needed to go see Preacher and see what he could do to move the annulment along. Because he wasn't sure he would survive another week dodging his growing attraction to the tantalizing Miss Nora.

# CHAPTER SEVENTEEN

"Ow!"

Nora jerked her bleeding thumb away from the fence railing and pressed it to her lips.

Adam hurried over, concern stamped on his face. "What happened?"

"Nothing," she muttered, glaring at her thumb. There was definitely something stuck in it. Probably a splinter. Lovely.

"Let me see it." He pulled her thumb from her lips and brought it close to his face to inspect. So close his breath danced over the skin of her hand, sending a delicious shiver down her spine.

She didn't fight him when he brought her hand even nearer, though she weakly protested, "It's fine, really."

"Hmm," he murmured, his thumb rubbing across the soft skin of her inner wrist and up to the base of her thumb. "Looks like you have a nice splinter in there. Do you have something to treat this? Bandages?"

She nodded, though she knew she was frowning at him. She tried to school her features into a disinterested mask. But that was impossible to do with Adam's thumb leaving tingles in its wake where it still moved softly over her skin.

She led him inside to where her small basket of medical supplies sat and let him deposit her in a chair while he went to rummage for what he needed.

"I can take care of it," she said, though a large part of her wanted to keep her mouth shut. Still, she didn't want him to think she was taking advantage of him or putting on an act. She'd been taking care of herself for quite some time. She was certainly capable of bandaging one nicked thumb.

"I'm sure you can," he said, dropping to his knees before her. "But it wouldn't kill you to let someone take care of you for a change."

She opened her mouth, but not a sound came out. He moved closer, giving her that slow, sweet smile that melted her insides and turned her heart into a gooey pile of mush.

He pulled a rather large knife from a sheath near his gun holsters and brought it to her finger, and she let out a little squeak of protest.

"Shush," he said, concentrating on her thumb. "This won't hurt. Much."

He made quick work of it, using just the tip of the knife to cut away the top layer of skin above the splinter. Once the splinter was revealed, she expected him to use the knife again to lift it from her flesh. Or maybe pull it out with his fingers.

Instead, he raised her thumb to his lips and drew it into his mouth. She sucked in a breath, not bothering to pretend she wasn't affected when his gaze locked onto hers and he sucked on her thumb. Hard.

A line of heat shot straight to her core, tightening the muscles low in her belly and leaving her fighting the sudden haze of pure desire burning through her veins.

Adam slowly drew back, finally releasing her

thumb from the wet heat of his mouth. She stared at him, trembling, her breath coming in strangled gasps that she tried in vain to control. He gave her that slow, sensual grin and then stuck out his tongue and plucked the splinter off it.

She tried to swallow past the desert her mouth had become. "You could have just pulled it out," she managed to say.

He grinned. "Where's the fun in that?"

Her mouth dropped open, but he held up a finger. "Don't move."

He took a piece of linen and doused it with alcohol, murmuring soothing nonsense when she hissed against the sting. Once the wound was disinfected, he made quick work of a rudimentary bandage and then sat back to admire his handiwork.

"Where did you learn all that?" she asked, her voice still fainter than she'd like.

"Doc." He raised a shoulder in a lopsided shrug. "Apparently I picked up a few things before nearly burning the place down."

She barked out a laugh and slapped her hand over her mouth. "I'm sorry, I didn't mean to laugh, it's just…"

He raised a brow, which just made her laugh harder. "My employment woes are funny to you?" he asked, though there was no heat behind the words.

"Of course not," she protested. Then added, "Well, maybe a little."

He glowered at her, and she laughed again until he placed a hand on the armrests on either side of her and leaned in. "Maybe if someone didn't insist on distracting me, these little mishaps wouldn't keep happening."

Her breath hitched in her throat again. "I'm distracting?"

He leaned in closer, until their breath mingled, and his eyes started to blur when she stared at him. "You have no idea," he murmured, leaning in more. Giving her plenty of time to pull away if she wanted.

But...she *didn't* want to. She'd never distracted anyone before. Not in the way he implied. Annoyed, yes. Badgered, yes. Amused even, yes. But distracted? Never. Only he seemed to see her as something more than "another one of the guys." Someone to be desired. She enjoyed being part of the gang. Enjoyed the freedom being "one of the boys" had lent her. The safety. But she'd longed for someone to look at her the way Adam was looking at her now. Like he wanted to devour her.

And heaven help her, she wanted to let him.

Her heart pounded furiously the closer he got. And when he gently brushed his lips across hers, the touch so light she wasn't sure if she imagined it, her heart nearly stopped altogether.

"Adam," she breathed.

"Hmm?" he murmured, brushing another barely there kiss across her lips.

"What are—"

A loud *crack* and sudden, furious bleating had them jerking apart. They frowned at each other, but it didn't take more than a second for Nora to realize what was going on.

"Oh no. Lucille!" She jumped up and ran for the yard.

• • •

Lucille? How had she gotten into the—

A heavy ball of dread dropped into Adam's gut, and he jumped up to follow Nora. When he'd heard her cry out, he hadn't had a thought in his head but getting to her, finding out what was wrong, fixing it. And in his haste, he must have left the garden gate open. The number one most important thing to her in the world. And he'd let her down.

*Shit!*

He ran outside just as Nora chased Lucille off, sending her running back through town, the blue ribbons around her neck fluttering in the wind as she went. Then Nora turned to her garden, her hands to both cheeks. Her trampled mess of half-eaten garden.

"No, no, no," she muttered before letting loose a string of curses that would have made any sailor proud.

The garden wasn't a total loss. Most of the damage seemed to be contained to one particular bed, so Lucille didn't seem to have been in there too long. Probably just while… He sighed. While they were inside and he was distracting her, flirting and playing at a seduction he shouldn't have been engaging in. Yet again, he'd managed to screw up a good thing. Make the absolute worst choice possible. And he'd managed to hurt someone else in the process. Again. This time someone he…someone he was starting to care very much about.

He took his hat off and jammed his fingers

through his hair. "Nora, I'm so sorry. I—"

"Don't," she said, holding up her hand. "Just…I don't want to hear it right now."

She bent and started to clean up the mess the goat had left, setting things to rights as much as possible. There were a few plants that could be salvaged that she started to tuck back into spots in the dirt. He squatted down to help her.

"Nora," he tried again. "I didn't mean—"

"You gave me your word," she said, tossing aside a bundle of half-eaten herbs. "I asked one thing of you, something so simple even a child could have followed it, and in less than twenty-four hours, you managed to completely destroy everything I've been working for."

"It's not completely destroyed," he said, trying to bring a little levity into the situation. Going by her glare, she didn't appreciate it.

"I'm sorry, Nora. Truly."

She sighed and paused what she was doing long enough to rub the back of her hand across her brow. "I know, Adam. I know you didn't do this on purpose. At least I hope not." She pinned him with a gaze that rivaled the sheriff's, and he bit his lip to keep from smiling at the comparison. She was so ardent, so fierce. She was absolutely magnificent.

And it was absolutely the wrong time to be noticing that.

"No, I didn't do this on purpose. I just have an unfortunate tendency to make the utterly worst decisions in any given situation. If there is a way to ruin something, hurt someone…I'll find a way to do it. And it seems like the harder I try to keep bad things from happening, the worse things get."

She tilted her head, watching him as he tried to shove some escaping dirt back into the raised planter. "No one's luck is that bad."

He snorted. "I used to think that, too. But welcome to my life. I'm still running from the last time I tried to right a wrong I committed. You think I'd learn by now to do the opposite of whatever my instincts are. Or maybe I should just remove myself from society altogether. Everyone would probably be a lot safer."

He chuckled, but she looked at him with an expression that seemed an awful lot like pity. And that was the last thing he wanted from anyone.

He let out a deep sigh and took the plant she was trying to replant from her hand. "Let me."

"I can do—"

"I'm aware of how capable you are," he said. "That doesn't mean you have to do everything on your own. Especially when it isn't your mess to clean up. Besides, you're getting your bandage dirty. I don't want that finger to get infected."

She sat back on her heels and glanced down at her bandaged hand. "And what would you do if it did get dirty?" she asked, her voice hardly more than a whisper. "Would you suck it clean again?"

Her soft question sent a heated bolt of desire straight to his gut, and he gripped the planter box so tightly, he wouldn't have been surprised if the wood drew blood. He focused on breathing and fighting against the urge to toss her over his shoulder. It was a battle he really didn't want to win.

He stood and moved toward her, slowly enough

that she could stop him. She didn't. When he reached her side of the planter box, he held out his hand. Barely a heartbeat passed before she slipped her hand into his and let him draw her up.

He gently brushed off the dirt that clung to her injured hand. "Would you like me to?" He brought her hand to his mouth, pressing a kiss to her palm.

Her hand trembled in his, and he nipped at the soft pad of flesh at the base of her thumb, drawing a gasp from her that had his blood roaring. She stepped willingly into his arms when he tugged on her hand.

"What are you doing, Nora?" he murmured, rubbing his nose along her jawline.

She tilted her head to give him better access to her neck, and he brushed his lips across the sensitive spot just beneath her ear.

"I'm not doing anything," she breathed. "Yet."

"What's stopping you?" he whispered in her ear, his pulse pounding when she shivered in his arms.

She lifted her head and brushed her lips across his cheek in a tentative kiss. "If you would just sign the papers, we—"

He abruptly let go of her, feeling like someone had just doused him in ice water. "I should have known I was making yet another mistake."

# CHAPTER EIGHTEEN

Nora staggered back. "What? What's wrong?"

"What's wrong?" Adam repeated, not bothering to keep his anger from his voice. He turned and started toward the barn. "I just keep walking right into your traps, don't I?" he said over his shoulder.

"Where are you going?"

"To my room!"

"To your…" Right. The barn. "Would you stop?"

"No."

She threw her hands up but kept following him. Then he wheeled around, stopping so abruptly, she nearly ran into him.

"What's wrong is you continuously turning this desire we have between us into some sort of weapon," he said. "Trying to twist it to your advantage."

"What? No! I didn't mean—"

"Didn't you? Every time we've let this…this… attraction we apparently feel for each other get the better of us, you immediately bring up signing the papers."

"Well, yes, but not because… I mean, I do want you to sign them, but I'm not trying to trick you or… or…"

"Seduce me into doing something I have repeatedly said I do not want to do?"

"I'm not trying to seduce you into anything." She stopped. Wasn't she, though? She'd abandoned her ill-thought-out plan from the bathhouse the moment she'd fled his presence, so perhaps she wasn't doing it consciously. But she could see why it might look that way. And…she had, even if briefly, thought of doing exactly what he accused her of. Still…

"If that is how it has seemed to you, then I apologize," she said, though her tone was anything but conciliatory. "But did it ever occur to you that maybe I just want our marriage to be legal before I give up…before I let…before we…"

"If you can't say it, you certainly aren't ready to do it," he said. "And no, that didn't occur to me, because you have been going around town for over a week now, insisting that we are already married." He moved closer, backing her up and wagging his finger at her. If he put it in her face, she was going to break it off. "And if that's the case, then anything further happening between us is just the normal course of action between a husband and wife. A husband, by the way, who you also keep insisting you do not want. So you'll have to pardon me if I'm a bit confused by the muddled messages coming from you."

"The muddled messages coming from *me*? You're one to talk!" She moved even closer, until they were almost nose to nose. "You keep insisting that you don't want to be married at all. You keep insisting that we aren't married, legally or otherwise. So what does it say about you that you are willing to seduce me—"

"I'm not—"

"You seduce, I seduce, what difference does it make?" she said, spinning them around so that now she was the one backing him up. "Either way,

seduction is happening, and if you have no intention
of ever marrying me and have no belief that we are
already married, but you are still trying to get me
into your bed, then—"

"In my defense, I'm just trying to get into *any*
bed that doesn't involve chickens!"

She stared at him for a second and then burst out
laughing. She slapped a hand over her mouth but
couldn't keep it contained. When she accidentally
snorted, his lips started twitching.

He turned, keeping his gaze locked on hers, and
took another step forward. When she backed up, she
bumped against the wall. She hadn't noticed it was
so close. Sneaky little bastard.

Adam didn't say anything for a moment, just
stared down at her before finally sighing and resting
his forehead against hers. "One of these days, it
would be nice to have a conversation with you that
didn't end in us shouting at each other. Or running
away from each other."

She shrugged. "Where's the fun in that?"

He smiled at the echo of one of his favorite
phrases. "I'm not trying to seduce you into something you don't want to do."

"Neither am I."

"Then what are we doing?"

She sucked in a deep breath through her nose
and let it out slowly. "I don't know."

"You're an infuriating woman," he said, though
there was no heat behind the words.

She smiled. "And you are a stubborn, aggravating
man."

He cupped her face, his gaze fixed on her lips. "I

want to kiss you," he said, rubbing the tip of his nose against hers.

Her heart stuttered, and it suddenly felt like she was both breathing too much and not enough at the same time. "Don't you always do what you want?" She slid her hands up his chest, bunching the material in her fists.

"Almost never." He said the words against her mouth, his lips brushing against hers as he spoke.

"Maybe you should work on that."

"Maybe I should."

His lips crushed against hers, moving hungrily, demanding. His hand gripped her chin, keeping her captive, tilting her face so he could more easily plunder her mouth. And she opened beneath his onslaught willingly. Desperately. This was no soft kiss. No tentative caress. This was pent-up passion, aggression, frustration, feelings that neither of them had the willpower or desire to stem finally finding an outlet.

Her fingers threaded into his hair, pulling hard enough it must have hurt, but Adam just groaned and pressed closer. They fit together perfectly, creating sensations she had never felt before. It wasn't the first time she'd been kissed. But it had been when she was younger, young enough not to realize that the boys she was with had no interest in her other than a brief dalliance. When they'd been young enough that most of the boys she knew hadn't yet finished growing, but she had. She'd towered over most of them since she was twelve years old, and few ever caught up to her. And were too immature to ignore that fact or make the experience pleasant for her.

But Adam. His entire intent seemed to be to bring her as much pleasure as possible. For the first time she actually felt...small. Dominated. It felt good to let go and allow someone else to take the reins for once. Someone who would have her sobbing for more if she let him continue for much longer.

She shouldn't. She should stop this. She should...

He pressed his thigh against her core, and she ripped her lips away from his, gasping at the bolt of pure molten heat that shot through her.

She should shut up and just enjoy it.

He grabbed her chin again, bringing her lips back to his, and she moaned, gripping his shirt so she could drag him more fully against her. His hand skimmed down her arm and—

A bucket of cold water sluiced over both of them, and Nora gasped, wiping at her eyes. Adam whirled around, his hand going to his holsters.

"You reach for those guns, and it'll be the last thing you do!"

Nora peered over Adam's shoulder. "Pa?"

• • •

Adam whipped his head around to look at Nora before immediately turning back to face the man who was holding a gun on them. Well, more specifically, on him.

Now that he was a little less occupied, he did recognize the man he'd helped Nora load into the wagon what felt like a lifetime ago.

He gave the man a cautious nod. "Mr. Schum-acher."

"Don't you Mr. Schumacher me when you're in my barn, taking liberties with my daughter," he shouted. He wasn't weaving on his feet, but his words were slightly slurred. Not the best state to be in when handling a loaded weapon.

"Put the gun away, Pa," Nora said, pushing her way out from behind Adam.

Adam frowned. He didn't want her in the line of fire if her father lost control, but short of physically shoving her back behind him, he didn't think he would get her out of the way.

"I'm not putting nothing away until this no-good sidewinder gets offa my property."

"I said he could be here, Pa. It's my property and—"

"Not yet, it's not. And yer still my daughter and will do as you're told. Now get in the house. You should be ashamed of yourself, out rutting in the barn like a cat in heat. I've never been so ashamed in my life. I have half a mind to—"

Adam opened his mouth to lay into the man, but Nora beat him to it. "You're ashamed of *me*? Did you really just say that? Do you know the first time you met Adam you were dead-cold drunk, and he had to haul you into the back of the wagon just so I could get you home? And you have the nerve to say you're ashamed of *me*? I'm a grown woman, I can make my own decisions, and you have no right to say one word about it when I'm the only reason we still have a roof over our heads."

Her voice cracked, and Adam reached for her,

but she pushed away from him, arms folded tightly across her chest. She glared at her father as if she were trying to find the right words, but she just shook her head and muttered something about getting changed before she stomped out of the barn.

Adam made to follow her, but her father swung the gun around again. Unfortunately for him, he wasn't nearly sober enough to be threatening anyone. Let alone someone with Adam's expertise. All it took was one quick step forward and Adam was able to wrest the gun from the man's hands.

Mr. Schumacher grabbed his shoulder when Adam tried to move past him. "Don't think just because my daughter let you take liberties that I'll stand by and—"

Adam gripped the older man's wrist until he let go. He didn't want to hurt the man. He wasn't in his right mind, and he was Nora's father. Regardless of how she might be feeling about him at the moment, she wouldn't want harm to come to him.

However…

"The only reason I'm not soundly beating you for the words you just said to your daughter is out of respect for her. But if I ever hear you say such vile things about her again, I will make you eat the words, whether she would approve or not. And then I'll make sure you never step foot near her again."

"Don't you threaten me, boy. My daughter wouldn't know the right end of a snake if it bit her. She needs me around to—"

"She doesn't need anyone," Adam said, "least of all you. That woman is more than capable of fighting her own battles and is definitely more than capable of taking care of herself. And anyone else who comes along."

Like himself, for instance, though he didn't bother pointing that out.

Her father looked like he was about to argue again, so Adam stepped closer. "Nora is by far the most intelligent, capable woman I have ever met. From what I've seen, she's kept this place from falling down around your ears while running two businesses, keeping food on your table, and making sure you are dragged home every night. Without her, you'd probably be lying in a ditch somewhere. So when you speak of her, you will do so with the respect she has earned. You owe her that much."

"I'm still her father, and you have no right to put your hands on my daughter."

Adam took a second to get his anger under control. The man had just walked in on Adam mere seconds from stripping his daughter from her clothes and having his way with her in a haystack. Any man would take exception to that. So rather than tell this man what he could do with his opinions, he'd hold his tongue. Mostly.

"With all due respect, sir," he said, "Nora is the only one who has the right to decide that."

The man still had his dander up, but most of the fight seemed to have gone out of him.

Adam bent to retrieve Mr. Schumacher's gun and emptied it of ammunition before handing it back to him.

Then he turned toward the house. He needed to get out of these wet clothes. With Mr. Schumacher back home, Adam would definitely be sleeping in the barn again tonight. The chickens would be happy. They probably missed him. More importantly, though, he needed to see how Nora was doing.

Because no matter how strong that woman was, her father was obviously a weak spot for her. And he'd said some horrible things.

Adam wouldn't be able to rest until he was sure Nora knew not a single thing her father had said was true.

And then he'd go find a few chickens to cuddle with for the night.

# CHAPTER NINETEEN

Nora stomped into the house, letting the door slam shut behind her. Her father had angered her before, but this time her blood pounded in her ears with the vehemence of it.

*How dare he! How* dare *he!*

She stood seething in the middle of the kitchen until she finally sucked in a deep breath, went to the bucket of water she'd left on the counter that morning, and grabbed the cloth that was drying on the sink. The counter already gleamed, but it could always use another wash.

She didn't even pay attention to what she was washing down as her mind careened from one thought to another, too furious to settle on any particular thing. Her throat ached with tears that she tried to keep at bay, but they spilled down her cheeks anyway. She batted them away angrily and kept on scrubbing.

Her father had been this way for years now. But somehow, today felt so much worse. She closed her eyes and let out a tortured breath, her chest aching. She knew why it was different. Why it felt so much more…horrible. Humiliating.

This time, Adam had seen. He'd heard how her father had spoken to her. The things he'd said. He'd seen her father's red-rimmed eyes, seen the shake in his hand, heard the contempt he had for her in his voice.

Everyone knew the demons her father fought. Hell, they saw it often enough, since her father spent most of his free time in the tavern. Even Adam had seen that his first day here. Dealt with it even. But… that had been before. It hadn't been so personal then. And now…

The private part of her life that she kept hidden from everyone had just been ripped open and laid bare at Adam's feet, at the exact moment he'd torn down her defenses and…

His arms came around her from behind, and she sucked in a breath. She hadn't heard him come in. Her body went rigid, and she squeezed her eyes tight, fighting to get herself under control before she disgraced herself even more in front of him.

He plucked the rag from her hands and then wrapped his arms around her, pulling her in again until her back was tight to his chest. He rested his chin on her shoulder and just held her, not saying a word, until she slowly relaxed and sank against him, bringing her arms up to rest on top of his.

After a few minutes, she took a deep breath and let it back out. "Where is he?"

"He rode off after I came in, toward town."

Nora nodded. He was probably headed back to the tavern. She should care, but at the moment, she was just glad he wasn't still at home.

"Why do you stay?" Adam asked, his voice quiet, sincere.

A small, sad smile played on her lips, and she gently pulled away but didn't turn to look at him. The reason she stayed…the answer wasn't simple. Her fingers trailed along the wooden counter, tracing the apples and blossoms that were carved into the border.

"My grandfather carved these into the counter when I was five. He knew how much I loved apples. They're carved into most of the surfaces around the house."

She leaned forward and touched the lace curtains at the window above the sink. "My grandmother made these for my mother's birthday one year. I helped her wrap them with the prettiest blue ribbon. It was the last birthday my grandmother celebrated with her."

Adam leaned against the counter, and she could feel him watching her as she moved to the small table in the corner and ran a finger along the back of a chair. "I made this. It was the first thing my grandfather taught me to make. I was ten," she said with a fond smile. "It took a few tries to get right and it's still a little lopsided. But he was so proud."

Then she walked to the door and looked out. "I planted my first flower in that box near the window. I helped deliver every one of the goats in the barn. We built that fence together, my grandfather, my father, and me." She swallowed hard against the emotion gathering in her throat, and Adam came to stand beside her. "He was different back then, before my mother died. I wish you could have known him. Sometimes…sometimes I think I still see the man he used to be in there. But when my mother died…" She bit her lip and finally looked up to meet Adam's eyes. "Something in him just died along with her. But…"

She looked around the warm, cozy kitchen that

had always been a place of refuge for her. Just the smell of the polish on the wood, the faint, familiar thumping of the one shutter outside the window that never quite stayed latched… She took a deep breath and let it out slowly.

"It's my home. How could I ever leave it?"

. . .

Adam brushed his thumb across her cheek. "I understand."

"Do you?" Nora asked, her brow furrowed.

He smiled, trying to put as much comfort as he could in the expression, since he wasn't sure how much she'd continue to take from him if he tried to hug her again. He was more than a little surprised she'd allowed what she had already. His hands dropped to her shoulders, and he gave them a squeeze before settling them around her upper arms, holding her loosely enough she could pull away if she chose.

"Yes, I think I do. I've never had something like this," he said, glancing around the warm kitchen and then out the door to the yard beyond. "I have nostalgic memories of the home I grew up in. But I don't feel any strong ties to the place. More to the people there. But this place…there are little touches of the people you love in every corner, aren't there?"

"Yes," she said, giving him a gentle smile that stole his breath. "And I suppose I could start over somewhere else. It wouldn't be easy, but it would be possible. But I know this land. I know where I need to plant each specific herb and flower for it to flourish. I know which corner of the paddock floods every spring and which side of the barn provides the best shelter when the wind is strong. I've already spent my whole life building this place into a business that sustains us and would thrive if I could put more time into it. Starting from scratch somewhere else…"

"Is unthinkable," he finished for her.

She nodded, her eyes lighting up at his understanding.

And he did understand, which made everything so much more difficult. This place was a part of her. She'd do anything for it, including marrying someone she neither knew nor loved. Her devotion to the place and his growing fondness for her—he refused to think it was anything other than that—was almost enough for him to agree to the marriage if doing so would keep it secure for her.

But all it did was make him more determined to never sign that paper. Desolation seemed like the safe haven he'd been searching for. Hopefully it remained that way. But there was still someone out there hunting him. And while the chances of Spurlock ever finding him in Desolation were slim, there was still a possibility. Marriage did nothing but put someone else in danger. Spurlock wasn't the most scrupulous lawman. He'd once torched a barn to smoke out his quarry—without any care for who else was in there. Just the thought of something like that happening to Nora and the home she loved so much was enough to put Adam in a cold sweat.

He pulled her into his arms again and kissed the top of her head. There was much he'd do for her. But the top of that list was keeping her and everything she held dear safe. And that meant he'd continue to avoid that damn paper and whatever this was that was blossoming between them. He'd already been responsible for ruining the life of one woman he'd cared for. More than one, most likely. There was no outrunning his past. It always caught up with him. And when it did, he wasn't the only one who got hurt.

He wouldn't do that to her. No matter how much she hated him for it.

# CHAPTER TWENTY

Adam had been keeping his distance from Nora in the days following their kiss. A circumstance that irked her more as each day passed even though she knew it was for the best. When she could finally take it no longer, she saddled up her horse, Teddy, and went to seek him out. At least she knew where he'd been spending his time. Preacher had hired him as a handyman around the church. A truly charitable act, since no one was under any delusions that Adam was remotely handy. At anything.

Nora rode up to the church and dismounted. Following the sounds coming from behind the church, she headed around the back to where the church's graveyard sat. Preacher stood toward the back of the yard, arms crossed as he surveyed a hole. Every few seconds a spray of dirt would come flying out to land in a haphazard pile near the edge.

She stopped beside Preacher, who glanced at her with a nod before turning back to watch the hole.

She peered down but couldn't see much from her angle. "Adam down there?" she asked.

Preacher nodded.

"What's he doing?"

"Digging a grave," Preacher said, his lips pulling into a smile.

"Has someone died?"

"Yes." His smile grew bigger.

Her lips twitched, and she glanced around at the

six freshly dug graves that lay open and waiting nearby. "How many people died?"

"Just the one. Old Mrs. Johnson."

"Ah. And the others?"

Preacher shrugged. "They'll be needed at some point. Always good to be prepared."

She sucked her lips in and bit down. "You mean to tell me that for the last three days you've had him digging graves for people who aren't even dead yet?"

Preacher turned to her with a full-blown grin. "Yep."

She covered her mouth with her hand and laughed as quietly as she could. She'd wondered what Preacher had had Adam doing. He'd practically crawled home every night, stayed awake just long enough to swallow some dinner, and then collapsed in his haystack without so much of a whisper of complaint. Completely took the fun out of keeping him out there.

"I'm surprised he's hung in here this long," she said. "I'd have been ready to give up on day one."

Preacher nodded, his smile fading. "He seems determined to keep this job, I'll give him that."

Nora didn't say anything for a moment. Just stood and watched the dirt flying out of the hole.

When she finally did speak, her voice was so low, she could barely hear it. She wasn't all that sure she wanted anyone else to. "Am I truly so undesirable that spending one's days doing backbreaking, ghoulish labor would be preferable to being married to me?"

Preacher turned to her, his brow creased. "Why

do you say that?"

"Because it's pretty evident," she said, waving her hand at the graves. "Since coming to town, he's tried and failed a handful of jobs he isn't remotely suitable for, has no interest in, and in a few cases, actively despises—sorry, but you haven't seen this man clean his nails or hang his clothes up at night—"

"Wait," Preacher said. "And you have?"

Heat rushed to her cheeks, but she ignored it. "My bedroom overlooks the barn," she said, hating to admit that she sometimes spied on her house guest.

"Ah," Preacher said, his grin returning. "Sorry for the interruption."

"Yes, well…you haven't seen how particular he can be about his appearance. The man likes to be clean, neat. Spending his days covered in sweat and dirt, standing in a hole where a dead body will go, can't possibly be his idea of an ideal life. Yet he seems to prefer that to being married to me. What else am I supposed to think?"

On top of the fact that he seemed to be actively avoiding being alone with her, as if kissing her had been a mistake he wanted to avoid making again. Not that she'd say that part out loud. It was painful enough dealing with it reverberating around her own head.

Preacher frowned for a moment, obviously piecing together his thoughts. If it was anyone other than Preacher, she would have assumed they were trying to come up with some lie to tell her to make her feel better. But that was just Preacher's way. He took his time with his words, but he always meant them once they came out.

"I think, perhaps, his reasons for avoiding marriage have less to do with you than they do with him."

She turned back to the hole and took a deep breath, letting it out slowly. "If you say so."

Preacher frowned and lightly grasped her upper arms, turning her to look at him. "I mean what I say. I've seen the way that man looks at you. The way many men look at you."

Her eyes widened and she scoffed. "No men look at me, Preacher. Least of all the one I'm married to."

"Nora…"

"No, it's all right. Truly. I made peace with the fact that I'd probably never wed a long time ago. But then the Town Council made that rule, and I thought…maybe…but even then…"

She stopped herself and took a deep breath, hating the stammering thoughts she couldn't seem to exorcise from her head. "I thought maybe someone would be desperate enough to ask. Even if I wasn't interested, I thought surely…" She shrugged. "But even with the town edict, no one spoke for me."

Preacher rubbed his hands lightly up and down her arms. "Did it ever occur to you that no one spoke for you because they were all your friends? They all knew you and how you felt about marriage. Knew you wouldn't want an arrangement with men who you considered friends when they were looking for someone to call wife."

She looked at him, wanting to believe him. But at the same time… "Some of those men have now left town, Preacher. I don't know about them, but if I harbored secret feelings for someone and was left with the ultimatum that the Council imposed on them, I would have spoken up. Just in case there was a chance. But no one spoke. No one has ever spoken, even before the edict. And now Adam…"

She looked back over at the hole, swallowing past the lump in her throat. The fact that his place in town was in jeopardy didn't force his hand…what else was she supposed to think? Especially now that they'd shared kisses—and then suddenly stopped. And she wasn't so ignorant of men that she couldn't tell he had been very happy to kiss her at the time. Yet still, he refused to claim her as his wife. He hadn't given her so much as a lingering glance since then.

So what was so wrong with her?

"I think you and Adam will have to find your own way through this. But I promise you," he said, giving her a little shake, "he's not as adverse to you as he'd like either one of you to think."

She stared at him for a moment and then swallowed hard, looking down until she had the urge to cry under control. Not that she fooled Preacher for a second.

"It'll work out for the best, I promise," he said.

Then he pulled her to him and gave her a sweet, brotherly kiss on the forehead.

Not a second later, a shovelful of dirt flew through the air and hit Preacher squarely in the face, forcefully enough to knock him on his rear.

Nora's jaw dropped, and she stared at where Preacher sputtered on the ground, trying to wipe dirt out of his eyes. The thundering footfalls that sounded next to her were the only warning she had before Adam was beside her, wrapping a huge arm about her so he could pull her to his side.

"Adam, what are you doing?" she asked, pushing away from him so she could help Preacher off the ground.

"What am I doing? What is *he* doing?" He threw out a finger to point at Preacher. "I'm down there digging yet another grave for who knows what reason, and this so-called man of God is standing mere yards away, kissing my wife!"

Nora's eyebrows hit her hairline. "Your what?"

Adam opened his mouth again and then seemed to realize what he'd just said and snapped it closed, a look of utter confusion on his face. Yeah, well, that made two of them. Did the fact that he seemed jealous that Preacher had kissed her send her heart skittering about her chest like a flat rock on a smooth lake? Yep, it sure as shit did, damn it all. But after spending the last several days ignoring her existence, not to mention the last couple of weeks denying their marriage, he didn't get to act like the aggrieved husband now. Especially to a good man who'd been trying to help her.

"First of all," she said, rounding on him, "Preacher is just a friend, a good friend. I was having a difficult moment, and he was trying to comfort me."

Adam frowned and took a step toward her. "What do you mean? Is everything all right?"

She held up a finger. "Not the point. Second of all, wife? He's kissing your *wife*? Please correct me if

I'm wrong, but you have spent every moment since the second we said *I do* swearing that you didn't mean it and that we aren't married. And now you are assaulting a man of God, of all people, for touching your *wife*?"

"Well, when you describe it like that…"

"How else am I supposed to describe it? You can't have it both ways, Adam. Either you are my husband or you aren't. Either you intend to stay my husband or you don't. You don't get to deny that our marriage is valid, refuse to sign the one tiny form that will make it so, and then act like you have a claim on me."

"Yes, but…"

"No. No buts. You just…shush." She sucked in a big breath and turned to Preacher, who had managed to pick himself off the ground and brush most of the dirt out of his hair. "Preacher, thank you." She leaned over and kissed him on the cheek. "I still disagree with what you said…" She glanced at Adam and frowned. "Well, with most of it…but I do thank you for listening."

"My door is always open, Miss Nora."

She nodded, then glanced over at Adam. "You… just…" She let out a frustrated growl. "You need to figure out what you want and leave me out of it until you do. But you better do it quick, because you only have two weeks left before the decision will be made for you."

She nodded again at Preacher and walked back around to her horse. It was time for tea with the ladies. She could do with getting away from men for a while. One in particular.

Even if there was no way she'd be able to get him out of her mind.

• • •

Adam watched Nora storm off and debated the wisdom of following after her. He knew he'd made a mistake. Yet again. That was no surprise. But he didn't like leaving things with her angry.

"Let her be for now," Preacher said, shaking a bit of dirt out of his ear. "She'll be more inclined to talk once she's calmed down a bit."

Adam gave him a wry grin. "Does she ever calm down? She seems to be fully loaded at all times."

Preacher's lips lifted in a quiet smile. "Her burden is a heavy one. Some days she bears it better than others."

Adam nodded, his heart hurting for her. "I apologize for the dirt," he said, brushing a bit off Preacher's shoulder.

Preacher nodded. "No apology necessary, I understand. But it's appreciated. I will still have to fire you, of course."

"Never thought otherwise," Adam said, handing over his shovel. Truth be told, he was right glad to hand the thing over. He had no aversion to manual labor, but it wouldn't be his first choice. Though it was yet another job falling through. He stifled a sigh, trying to erase the image of Woodson and his damned pocket watch forming in his mind. He was running out of time to find some steady employment.

"Come on," Preacher said, clapping him on the

shoulder. "Let's go get a drink. You look like you could use one."

Adam snorted. "You really are doing the Lord's work. Lead the way."

• • •

When they entered the tavern, Woodson and his deputy were already there with Doc. Adam hesitated at the door, but they'd already seen him. He wouldn't turn tail now.

He sank gratefully into a vacant seat and ordered a cider. He could do with something with a bit more kick, but he was more thirsty than anything and wanted to be able to get out of the tavern on his own two feet.

Deputy Sunshine raised his glass in welcome, and Doc followed suit. Woodson just sat glowering as he typically did. He glanced back and forth between Adam and Preacher.

"Have you two been rollin' around in the dirt?" he asked.

Preacher and Adam glanced at each other with matching grins, and Adam answered, "I have, in a manner of speaking. Preacher here caught a shovelful of it."

Woodson cocked one eyebrow, and Adam sucked down a healthy swallow of his cider before he elaborated. "Let's just say you won't be needing to employ a gravedigger anytime soon."

"And you?" he asked Preacher.

"I was standing in the wrong place at the wrong time," he said with a wry grin.

Woodson looked inclined to pursue the matter but thankfully let it drop. Though Adam should have known that Woodson wasn't done with him entirely.

"Fired him yet?" he asked Preacher.

"Actually, yes. About ten minutes ago."

Adam scowled and Woodson chuckled, shaking his head. "Son, I don't know how you've managed to get yourself fired from nearly every establishment in town. In less than two weeks." He held his glass up and tipped it toward Adam. "But I think I'm impressed."

Frankly, so was Adam. He'd known it was going to be tough, but even he hadn't expected to do quite so poorly.

"No," Sunshine said. "Surely it hasn't been that many."

Adam sighed. "You'd be surprised."

"I know about Mrs. DuVere's builder and Reggie there," Sunshine said, nodding over at the bartender. "And Doc, of course. Who were the others?"

Adam grimaced but Woodson chuckled. "After he'd destroyed half the tavern's new shipment, he tried his luck at the tanner's. You lasted, what…a full day there before ruinin' his whole inventory? Something about scrapin' too aggressively?"

"It wasn't the whole shop, just a few of the hides," Adam said, chugging down more cider. Maybe he should have gotten something a bit stronger.

"After that, I believe he tried the butcher's. Lasted an hour from what I heard. And the barber wouldn't even let him in the door."

"You've been paying attention," Adam muttered. Lucky him.

Woodson shrugged. "This is my town. It's what I do. And it's a bit hard to ignore when someone is goin' through destroying half the establishments."

"*Destroying* is a bit of a stretch."

Woodson snorted. "Not by much." He paused to take a drink, then nodded at Doc. "Then our good doctor here took pity on him and let him play nurse. I'm assumin' that didn't go very well, since it didn't last more than a day."

Adam raised his glass in a salute. "Your assumption would be correct." Might as well embrace his mediocrity.

"You weren't so bad," Doc said, and Adam cocked an eyebrow.

Sunshine laughed. "If you call nearly blowing up your clinic not so bad."

Doc just grinned.

"And now," Woodson continued, "our good reverend is the latest to regret hirin' him."

"I don't regret it," Preacher said. "Though…he wasn't quite as handy as I'd hoped. He does dig a fine hole, though."

"I just need to work on where I deposit the dirt," Adam said, lifting his glass to the preacher, who chuckled into his drink.

Sunshine grinned, probably just happy to see them getting along even if he didn't understand the joke. "So, if you were happy with at least that aspect of his work, why not keep him on?"

Preacher shrugged. "There's only so many graves that need to be dug, and we already have a good number more pre-dug than we need."

"Besides," Adam said, "the last time he gave me a

shovel, I flung a pile of dirt in his face. Actions have consequences, my mother always says."

"Wise woman," Woodson said before turning to Preacher. "I'm surprised you didn't bury him in one of his holes for that."

Preacher shrugged. "They're there if I change my mind."

Adam froze with his glass halfway to his lips until Preacher winked at him. Though something about the man's expression said he'd have no problem following through on his threat if the occasion called for it. Adam definitely should have gotten something stronger than cider.

"There's always the other option, since keepin' a job seems to be too difficult a task for you," Woodson said. "Though what that woman sees in you, I'll never understand."

"You and me both," Adam muttered. "And no, thank you. I'll stick to finding employment. Trust me, she's better off without me. There's more than one reason I swore off marriage."

Woodson shrugged. "Suit yourself. Clock is tickin'. And you're runnin' out of places to work."

Yes, he was. Those who hadn't already fired him were starting to run the other way when they saw him coming. His reputation doth precede him, apparently.

Too bad Nora wouldn't take heed and follow suit. Because she was beginning to wear down his defenses. And if anyone should be running from him, it was her.

# CHAPTER TWENTY-ONE

The moment Nora walked into Mrs. DuVere's, Mercy rushed at her.

"Nora, I'm so sorry. Gray told me what Lucille did to your gardens. I can't believe she did that. Or I can, rather, but I'm absolutely mortified. We are going to pay for everything she damaged. I'm so sorry!"

"It's all right, Mercy, truly. She didn't damage too much, and I was able to salvage a lot of it."

"Thank heavens! I'm so glad. Still, we will pay for whatever she did destroy and whatever damages she did to your property. Gray has money for you over at his office if you'll come with me after our tea."

Nora agreed and hugged her friend, at least some of the weight lifted off her shoulders.

"Wonderful, now that that has been settled," Mrs. DuVere said, happily wiggling in her seat, "tell us all how things are going with that handsome gunslinger you've got living with you."

Nothing got past Mrs. DuVere. She knew everything that went on in this town, even more than the sheriff. Mercy and Martha turned to her with twin expressions of delighted surprise.

"What?" Martha squealed. "When did this happen? Has he agreed to sign the papers? Is he really living with you?"

"It depends on what you mean by *with me*. On my property, yes. With me in my house, no. With me as man and wife, also no."

"So I take it that means he hasn't signed the papers," Mercy said.

"No. I have never met a more stubborn man."

Mercy snorted. "Have you met my husband?"

The ladies all laughed and then turned back to Nora, waiting for more details. She filled them in as best she could. It was hard to get too detailed, though, since she didn't quite understand what was going on, either.

"Does your father know?" Martha asked.

"He does now. He came back the other day and saw us together in the barn and—"

"Wait," Mercy said. "Saw you *together* in the barn?"

Martha's jaw dropped, and Mrs. DuVere looked positively giddy.

"I knew I liked him," she said.

"No, not together like *that*," Nora said, then frowned. "Or, not exactly like that." She waved off a fresh round of squeals. "It was nothing, just a kiss."

"My dear," Mrs. DuVere said, "first of all, a kiss from a man who is theoretically your husband is not nothing, and secondly, even if the first part wasn't true, your face is telling all kinds of different stories."

Nora covered her betraying face in her hands and dropped her forehead to the table with a groan.

She finally sat back up but shook off more questions. "I'm sorry, I really am. But I truly have no idea what is going on with us. One minute we are fighting about nothing and the next he has me against the wall and is kissing me until I can't breathe. And the next," she said, over her friends' exclamations, "my father comes in and tosses a bucket of cold water on us. And…nothing has happened since then. We've barely had a moment to talk."

"Well, if he still hasn't signed the papers, then our original plan is still on," Mercy said. "He's already been fired from nearly every place in town. I've been trying to talk Gray into hiring him to work at the sheriff's office or even to help me out at the ranch if he doesn't want him around. He could mind Daisy for me while I'm doing chores if I can't find anything else for him to do. But Gray hasn't budged."

"That's all right," Martha said. "I've got a few unpleasant tasks at the store that he can do. Leave it to me."

For a moment, Nora felt the tiniest bit sorry for Adam. The men were one thing, and they'd done admirably. Infected toes and grave-digging? Sheer brilliance. But Martha…that adorable, bubbly personality hid a cunning and devious mind.

She couldn't wait to see what her friend had in store for her poor husband.

• • •

Nora returned from a dress fitting the next day already exhausted from the amount of work that awaited her. Not that she wasn't grateful for it. Mrs. Talbot, with her four daughters, was one of Nora's best customers. But she did tend to wait until the last minute to order new dresses and often needed five of them all at once. As she did now, for their annual barn party. The money was much appreciated, but Nora needed a nap just thinking about the hours she'd be putting in on them.

Before she could get started, though, she needed to finish repairing the fence that Lucille had damaged. There were several items in the house that needed fixing as well. The newel post on the staircase rattled every time someone used the stairs. One of the cabinet doors in the kitchen stuck, and there was a drawer she hadn't been able to pull out for months.

But all that would have to wait, as the laundry was a more pressing matter. After the fence. Despite her destructive ways, Nora actually loved Lucille, but that little harridan needed to stay out of her garden.

Nora was going to take Teddy straight to the barn but frowned when she heard hammering. She tied the horse to the post out front and hurried around back, stopping short at the sight that met her. Her garden was fully enclosed once more behind a slightly crooked fence. Not only had the gate been fixed, but other parts of the fence that she'd been meaning to reinforce for years had been repaired. And freshly painted.

She clapped a hand to her mouth, surveying the work. Who? Who had...

Adam stood from where he'd been squatting in the back corner. The broken crossbar that she'd had leaning against the back post now rested a bit haphazardly, but securely, where it belonged.

He glanced up mid-whistle and broke into a grin when he saw her. "Hey there."

"You...you fixed my fence?"

"Yeah." He scratched the back of his neck and looked around at his handiwork. "It's not the best-looking job in the world, but I guarantee it's nice and sturdy. I even tested it out myself—"

Before he could finish, she'd strode across the yard and flung herself at him, squeezing him in a tight hug.

"Hey there, darlin', what's wrong?" he asked, his arms going around her. "I know it's a bit of a mess, but I promise I can clean it up once I get a little better swinging that hammer."

She shook her head with a laugh and stepped back. "It's not that. It looks wonderful. Thank you for fixing it."

Her heart sang at what he'd done for her, but she couldn't help but cringe as well. There shouldn't have been a need for him to do anything. It was all stuff she should have handled on her own long since. "I really appreciate it, truly. But you didn't have to. I could have taken care of it."

He shrugged, though his half grin showed his pleasure at her praise. "It needed doing and I was here. Besides, I picked up a few skills over at the boardinghouse. Before they fired me and took my hammer back. Might as well put them to use." He chuckled, and she laughed along with him.

"Let's go inside," he said. "You've got to be hungry. You've been gone all day."

Her jaw dropped. "You cooked?"

"Don't get too excited," he said, guiding her into the house with his hand on the small of her back. "It's just a simple soup recipe that my mother taught me. I basically took a bunch of ingredients I found lying around and threw them into a pot together. Hopefully it won't kill us. And if we're real lucky, it might taste halfway decent."

She laughed and stepped onto the porch. "Oh, wait. I need to put Teddy away first."

"I'll take care of him," Adam said.

"It's all right, I can do it."

"Nora, let me help," he said, giving her a gentle push into the house. "Go on in."

She frowned slightly. "Are you sure?"

"Yes, go."

She went, but the frown didn't leave her face. What was he up to? Was he wanting to negotiate for better sleeping arrangements and trying to soften her up first? Because honestly, it was working. She was hungry, and whatever he'd put in that pot smelled divine. She'd been planning on just slicing up some bread and cheese for her supper, being too tired to think of making anything else. To come home and have it taken care of…

She didn't know how to feel about it. Though she was embarrassingly close to tears.

Nora walked slowly through the house, putting her sewing supplies away and taking a real look around for the first time in several days. Her father had disappeared again after the incident in the barn. Though she knew he was probably fine, she still couldn't stop the worry. At the same time, not having him there removed a lot of the stress she'd normally feel when she walked in her door.

Something was different about the house that she couldn't quite put her finger on. She walked past the staircase again and suddenly realized the newel post no longer rattled. She grasped it and gave it a good shake, but it didn't budge.

The back door opened, and Adam's heavy footsteps echoed across the kitchen floor as he came farther into the house. He looked around, smiling when he saw her.

"You fixed the newel post?"

He nodded. "I hope you don't mind. I doubt I did it correctly, but that rattle every time I walked past it was starting to get to me."

"Mind?" she asked, completely befuddled by the question. "I think…I think I need to sit down for a moment."

"Well, if you're going to sit, do it at the table so we can eat." He held a hand out to guide her into the kitchen, and she had the sudden desire to laugh.

Here he was, in her home, doing repairs, cooking dinner, inviting her to eat at her own table. And she realized, with a sudden shocking clarity, that she didn't mind at all. She should. He'd overstepped. He'd stuck his nose, and his hammer, into areas where they didn't belong. But she'd been going it alone for so long, it was a welcome relief to not have to do everything for at least a few moments. Despite the lingering embarrassment that she'd allowed things to get so bad in the first place.

She sat at the table and let him serve her a bowl of hot soup and buttered bread.

"Thank you," she murmured, watching while he dished himself up a bowl and took a seat.

She waited, and he raised an eyebrow at her. Then slowly picked up his spoon and took a large bite of soup. "See. Not poisoned."

That startled a laugh out of her. "I didn't think you'd poisoned it. At least I don't think I did," she said, tilting her head. That certainly would have been one way to get away from her insistent demands to sign their marriage license.

She picked up her own spoon and took a cautious bite, then took another, closing her eyes with a happy sigh as the warm broth and savory vegetables slid down her throat.

"This is surprisingly good," she said, her eyes flying to his when she belatedly realized that might not have come across as a compliment.

He laughed. "No, I agree. It is, indeed, a surprise. The bread I can't take credit for, though. I found that in the cupboard."

They ate in companionable silence for several minutes. It was so strange how *not* strange it felt to be sitting in such domestic bliss with him. What did that mean? Did she actually want him to stick around? Even after she had her deed in her name?

Since it was doubtful he'd ever want the same thing, it would be safer to move on to other topics.

"I saw Martha today. She said you start working with her at the store tomorrow."

He nodded. "I know she is a particular friend of yours, so I will do my utmost not to burn, flood, spill, break, or otherwise destroy her store or anything in it."

Nora choked on her soup and grabbed her napkin, coughing into it as she laughed. When she finally got her lungs working properly, she dabbed at her watering eyes. "I'm sure she'll appreciate that."

She stopped the next words from coming out of

her mouth. She didn't want to broach the subject that had been bouncing around in her mind. They'd been having such a lovely evening, and bringing up the glaring situation hanging over their heads never ended well. But she was running out of time to get him to do what she needed.

"If it doesn't work out at the store, you know you can always—"

"I know, Nora," he said, not bothering to hide his exasperation. "Sign the papers."

She dragged her spoon through her soup a few times before finally putting it down. "Why are you so against the idea? And don't say because you don't believe in it or because it's your one big rule or any of the other excuses you've used. I deserve a real answer."

She kept her voice even, calm. She wasn't angry, and the last thing she wanted to do was cause a fight, but she had to know what his reasoning was. His real reasons. Because it was beginning to look as though she'd never be able to convince him, and if that was the case, she needed to make some contingency plans. Probably something she should have been doing all along.

He sighed and put down his spoon as well. "I meant it when I said I wasn't cut out for marriage. I'm not. You've been around me long enough now to see that when I said I always make the worst possible decisions, I wasn't lying. If there is any possible way for me to completely bungle something, I seem to find it. It's been that way my entire life."

"I don't see the universe or God or whoever is

pulling the strings up there making an exception when it comes to marriage. I'll admit I'm not the most selfless creature, but in this instance, I truly am trying to spare whatever poor woman crosses my path the pain and heartache that taking me as her husband would bring."

She watched him for a second but couldn't hold his gaze when she spoke again. "And if she loved you enough to risk it?"

He didn't answer for long enough that she tried looking at him. His eyes locked onto hers, and she could see the sadness and regret there. "All the more reason to make sure she stayed far away. The last thing I would want would be for her to get hurt."

"But…"

"That's not the only reason," he continued, stopping her from whatever argument she'd been about to make.

He wiped his mouth with his napkin and sat back, interlacing his fingers and resting them on his stomach. He sucked in a short, sharp breath through his nostrils and blew it back out. "I'm a gambler and a gunfighter, Nora. Have been since the day I met Quick Shot Woodson in that alleyway. I might have made a name for him, but because of him I made a name for myself as well. And that put a nice, large target on my back."

"I've had someone after me for as long as I've been carrying this gun," he said, slapping the pistol strapped to his hip. "Whenever one would die or give up, another cropped up to take his place. Gunfighters who wanted to make a name taking me out. Gamblers who thought I cheated them of their money. Lawmen who wanted to see me behind bars or strung up. There's always someone."

"Is that why you came to Desolation? You're running from someone again?"

He nodded. "An unusually persistent, but deadly, pain in the ass who won't give up until he's dragged me back to Denver in chains. And he doesn't seem to care much if I'm dead or alive when he does it. So when I stumbled onto this town in the middle of nowhere, a town that might accept a man like myself...albeit with a few strange conditions..." He shrugged. "I took the chance."

"So that's why you won't sign the papers?"

He stared at her for a long moment, his eyes studying her face before his gaze returned to hers. "It's one of the reasons. If I sign those papers, they'll get filed with the county office. There are no records out there with my name on them, nothing other than my birth certificate that showed I was ever on this planet at all. A marriage license...that's a piece of evidence that would not only be dangerous to me but to the woman who was listed on it with me."

She nodded, finally understanding this man who'd been a mystery to her since day one. For a hunted man, a wife was collateral, something his enemies could use against him. There truly was no room in his life for her. Though if he stayed in Desolation, if the ones who were hunting him gave up... The sheriff seemed to be safe enough. Perhaps someday...

What was she thinking? *Someday* didn't help her. She needed a legal husband now. She needed to get that deed in her name before she lost everything.

And not just any husband, but one who wouldn't ask questions and who would preferably agree to divorce her or leave town or in some other way pretend she didn't exist.

She wouldn't dwell for a single second on the thought that maybe it would be nice to find a husband she actually wanted to keep. A husband who wanted her as much as she wanted him. She killed that thought before it could take root in her mind. There wasn't a husband like that out there for her. So she'd take one who could get her what she needed and be on his way.

And Adam had made it more than clear he wasn't that man.

She pushed her chair back from the table and carried her dishes over to the sink, quickly washing them. Adam brought his over, standing silently beside her while he helped. She didn't know if he was as lost in his thoughts as she was in hers or if he was simply giving her space to digest everything he'd just told her. Either way, she was grateful he didn't push for a response.

Because she had no idea what to say when everything she'd been working toward had just come crashing down around her.

# CHAPTER TWENTY-TWO

Adam threw another bolt of cloth over his shoulder and carried it into the back room for storage. It had been about all he'd done all day. Moving bolts of cloth, boxes, supplies, and a myriad of other items for Martha from one place to another.

One bolt, that had to weigh fifty pounds if it weighed anything, she'd had him take from the shelf to the counter and back again all in the space of five minutes. And when she'd realized she'd had him grab the wrong one, he repeated the process with three other bolts. He'd be willing to bet his left nut that she was just making up miserable tasks for him to accomplish.

Then again, he'd proven he couldn't be trusted with more complicated tasks, like actually selling the material to anyone. But really, how was he to have known that a yard of muslin did *not* cost the same as a yard of calico and that measuring it precisely did actually matter? Common sense didn't apply in all matters, despite what Martha thought. So. He was relegated to fetching and carrying. As disillusioning as that was, he couldn't truly blame her.

But once he put this bolt back, he was to join her in the kitchen. To help bake pies, of all things. He'd never admit it to anyone, but he was actually looking forward to the lesson.

After their dinner two nights ago, Nora had been unusually quiet. She hadn't joked with him or even called him "husband" once, despite ample opportunities. Even worse, she'd allowed him to move into the house. He was relegated to a small back room that still served as storage space. But he was inside her home. Without having given her what she'd been after since the moment they'd met. That damn signed marriage license.

He'd wanted her to give up on him, but now that she apparently had, he wanted nothing more than to go back to the way things had been.

She had seemed quite pleased with the work he was doing around the house, though. And she'd nearly cried when he'd put that bowl of soup in front of her. He'd thought it odd until he realized with a sinking feeling in his gut that she had probably never had anyone take care of her like that. And it had been such a simple thing. Just a bowl of soup.

What would she do if he made her a pie?

He watched Martha carefully as she prepared the crust, sliced the apples, and combined them all together in a tin that she popped into the oven to bake. The smell permeating the kitchen was heavenly enough to make him embrace religion again, and his mouth watered every time he took a deep breath.

He watched as Martha made three more pies, each a different flavor than the last, and he was pretty sure he had the process down. Make dough. Slice apples and mix with sugar and spices. Combine together until it looked like a pie. Bake.

Should be simple enough.

Though from the look on Martha's face as she stood with her arms crossed, staring him down, you wouldn't think so.

"Are you sure you can do this?" she asked him for the fourth time.

"Martha, yes. Go. I have been watching you all morning. You have most of the ingredients already prepared and ready to go. All I have to do is combine them and put them in the oven and then pull them back out again before they burn. Even Lucille could figure it out."

"Uh-huh." She watched him for a few more moments, obviously having an epic internal struggle.

It was apparently part of Woodson's employment agreement that Martha provide him lunch every afternoon, and since she and Doc had begun courting, she often went next door to his clinic after dropping off the sheriff's lunch and ate her noon meal with the doctor. But with the Talbots' party coming up, she had several more pies to bake.

"Martha. Go. If I run into any problems, you're just across the street. I promise I will run outside and scream like a wildcat with a stubbed toe if I need your help."

She let out a sigh. "All right. If you're sure you can handle this."

"I'm sure. *Go*."

She hesitated half a second longer before gathering up her baskets and heading across the street.

"Finally," he muttered. He knew his reputation for simple tasks wasn't the greatest, but with all the dough made and the ingredients mixed, all he really had to do was assemble and bake. And as long as he was vigilant and kept his eyes on the pies...what could go wrong?

You'd think by now he'd have learned to stop asking himself that question.

. . .

"Martha?" Nora called out as she poked her head into the store.

The CLOSED sign was up, and Nora knew Martha had to deliver the sheriff his lunch, but when she wasn't eating with Doc, she'd always come back over to have her meal in her own kitchen.

The sound of rattling pots and pans came from the kitchen, along with the mouthwatering smell of freshly baked apple pies, and Nora followed her nose.

She pushed open the kitchen doors and stopped dead, her mouth dropping open.

For a moment, she thought the room was filled with smoke, but that acrid stench that accompanied smoke was absent. She looked down at the fine white dust that was settling on her clothes and realized that there was so much flour floating in the air that it was creating a fog-like haze.

"What's going on?" she asked, pushing farther into the room. And then for the second time in less than a minute, she stopped dead in her tracks.

Adam stood by the kitchen sink, his face and hands liberally smeared with flour. He held his shirt in his hands while he furiously scrubbed at something on it. Which meant he was standing there in nothing but his pants and boots.

The hard-muscled planes of his chest and

stomach had her hands itching to follow every line. She'd felt those muscles beneath the layers of clothing he typically wore around her, plus when she'd run her soapy hands over them in the bathhouse. But somehow her memories of those moments failed to do the sheer masculine beauty of him a lick of justice. Her gaze lingered on every ounce of skin she could see. And then they traveled lower, to the parts that were still hidden from her sight.

It took her far too long to realize that Adam was no longer moving and had turned to face her.

"Nora?"

"Hmm?" she asked, her gaze still riveted to his bare chest.

"Nora. Is everything all right? Were you looking for Martha?"

"Martha?" she asked, blinking at him.

He frowned a little. And she saw the exact moment that he realized what had her so captivated. The slow smile that spread across his lips had her stomach flipping and dipping and her breath strangling in her lungs.

He took a step toward her, and her eyes shot to his.

"Martha. Yes, I, um…I thought maybe she would like to have lunch together."

"Ah," he said, moving closer. She mirrored his movements, taking a step back every time he took one forward as they slowly circled each other. "I'm afraid Martha has gone over to eat with Doc today."

"Oh. Well. That's too bad." She shook her head. "For me. Too bad for me. Not for her. I'm sure she's…enjoying herself immensely. And…um…"

Her back hit the wall she hadn't even noticed was behind her.

Adam came to a stop right in front of her, and she swallowed hard and licked her lips. His eyes tracked the movement of her tongue, and his sharp inhale had her knees quaking. Before she could take another breath, his shirt was on the ground and her lips were molded to his. With the hard wall at her back and the hard man at her front, Nora was well and truly trapped. And had never been so happy about it in her life.

She lost no time in taking advantage of the fact that his shirt had disappeared. And when Adam shuddered beneath her roving hands, she smiled against his lips. She'd had all sorts of fantasies about what it would be like to kiss this man. Not one of them lived up to the real thing. And not one of them had ever included how he would respond to her touch. The power she would feel when he groaned into her mouth, twisted his hand in her hair.

His hands dragged down her sides to her thighs, and then he bent and lifted her, spinning to deposit her on the counter beside them. A cloud of flour poofed out around her when her ass hit the surface, and she wrapped her arms around Adam's shoulders and dragged him back to her.

His fingers skated up her thighs while his lips trailed down her neck. She could do little more than hang on to him and pray she didn't disgrace herself by swooning from the overload of sensations that were careening through her body.

"You know, I've never minded that you often

wear trousers. In fact, I quite like it."

She tilted her head back to give him better access. "Do I sense a but in there?"

He bit her earlobe, and she nearly levitated off the counter. "But," he breathed in her ear, "if you were in skirts right now, I'd already have my hands on your bare skin."

That was it. She was never wearing pants again.

"They say the things you have to work for are that much sweeter in the end," she said, dragging her teeth lightly across his neck.

A low growl rumbled from his throat, and he yanked her shirt out of her pants. His hands brushed against her rib cage, and her head dropped back as she tried to suck air into her suddenly nonfunctioning lungs. He dragged her closer to him, spreading her legs wider to accommodate his hips, and even through their clothing she could feel the hardest part of him pressing against her overheated core.

She whimpered and clung to him, her lips seeking his again. He pressed against her again, his tongue mimicking the action of his hips. The sensations crashed against her, through her, too quickly, built too high, too fast. It was too much and not nearly enough, and she wrapped her legs around him while he ground against her, trying to chase that crest that was just out of her reach.

There was something else there, something familiar that she couldn't quite place through the haze of sheer lust that obscured everything but the sensations this man was creating in her body.

"Adam," she gasped. "What is that?"

"What is what?" His teeth nipped at the juncture

where her shoulder met her neck, and she nearly sobbed at the pulsing jolt that went through her.

But something nagged at her; something was off...

His hand closed over her breast just as he ground against her again and that building pressure broke, cascading through her in wave after wave that had her clinging to him for dear life.

His lips found hers again, and he kissed her until her body stopped trembling against his.

Their gazes locked and Adam smiled softly, holding her while their senses slowly returned. And then their eyes widened in sudden simultaneous horror.

Was that smoke filling the kitchen?

"The pies!" Adam said.

He pushed away from her and rushed to the oven, jerking it open. Flames shot out, and Adam jumped back with a shout. He grabbed his shirt from the floor and waved at the flaming pastries, but that only fanned the flames higher.

Nora tried to get closer to help, but Adam kept her back. "The flames are too big to grab them," he said, pulling her back from the oven.

His eyes darted around the kitchen. "Hand me the broom!"

She grabbed it and handed it to him, then stood back as he used the handle to knock the pies out of the oven. Which removed them from the source of heat that had caused the fire to begin with but might have been a moot point considering they were now their own mini infernos.

The flames licked at the cabinets, and Nora ran to

the door to grab the small rain bucket that Martha kept there for just such an occasion. In her haste, she slopped half the bucket on the floor before she ever got to the pies. But what was left was enough to douse one pie.

The front door burst open, and shouts filled the store. Wonderful. The smoke had alerted the neighbors to the fire, and it sounded like half the town had turned out to help.

She grabbed a small towel and beat at the corner of one of the cabinets that was smoldering. Adam, bless him, used the broom to shove the other still-flaming pie out of the open back door. Once safely outside, he flipped it over in the dirt, finally extinguishing it.

Nora pressed one hand to her mouth, the other to her chest. And slowly realized that most of the town was staring at them, looking back and forth between the half-clad Adam and her own disheveled state.

She'd never been so thankful for a fire in her life.

While it was still a bit odd, to be sure, Adam had obviously been using his shirt to beat at the flames, since it hung from his fingers in rapidly disintegrating shreds. And the fact that she'd likewise been rushing about to put out a fire could account for her less than pristine state.

Though the amused stares of more than one of the people on the street said they weren't fooled for a second.

There was one person most decidedly *not* amused.

Martha pushed her way through everyone and

into the kitchen. Where she stood surveying the damage with open-mouthed horror.

It could have been worse, so much worse. But it still wasn't a pretty sight. The floor and some of the surrounding cabinets were scorched from the flames. There were lumps of a smoldering tar-like substance in the oven that Nora assumed were portions of pie filling. And what wasn't burned was covered in a fine layer of flour and bits of pastry dough from whatever attempts Adam had made at baking a pie before almost burning the kitchen down.

"Martha," Adam said, but Martha just held up a hand as she slowly made her way around the kitchen, taking everything in.

Nora's eye tracked her and then widened in abject mortification when they landed on the counter where she'd sat. Where the print of her rear end was perfectly outlined in the flour.

Her gaze jerked over to Adam, and she tried to show him with her eyes what she'd just seen. He frowned slightly, obviously trying to figure out what she was telling him. She nodded her head over at the counter beside him as subtly as she could, and he finally looked over. His lips twitched, and he glanced up and winked at her.

"I don't know what to say, Martha," he said, grabbing a towel so he could start wiping up. "My humblest apologies." Her butt print disappeared beneath his towel, and some of the tension in her shoulders relaxed. Then another thought occurred to her, and she reached behind her back and tried to wipe away whatever evidence might have remained there as unobtrusively as possible.

"I'll get this all cleaned up," Adam said, making his way over to Nora.

Martha just stared at him, and Adam sighed. "I'm fired, aren't I?"

She snorted. "Yes. Yes, you are."

Adam sighed again, but it really wasn't a surprise. Martha probably would have fired him just from the state of her kitchen *before* it almost burned down.

Adam sidled a little closer, and when no one was looking, he leaned down to whisper in Nora's ear. "Totally worth it."

# CHAPTER TWENTY-THREE

Nora shoved another pile of papers out of the way and yanked open the last drawer in her father's desk, even though she knew what she was looking for wasn't there. A quick rummage proved her right. Her heart bottomed out as she reached beneath the desk to trigger the secret drawer. It popped out.

Empty. Somehow he'd found it.

She stood in the middle of her father's office, hoping there was some other place she could look that she'd missed. But she'd already tried the bookshelf, even going so far as to shake out every one of their few books in case he'd tucked the papers between the pages. She'd searched his desk, under the rug, between the sofa cushions, and through every pile of paper she could find in the entire house.

Her small stash of emergency money was gone. And so was the deed to the property.

The money she could understand. Without that, her father couldn't fund his booze-fueled excursions. But the deed? What did he plan on doing with that?

She didn't really need that question answered. It was perfectly obvious what he'd do with it.

The only other possible explanation for the missing items was if someone else had taken them. Adam had been sleeping in her father's office on the sofa the last several nights. So he'd certainly had opportunity. She just couldn't imagine he'd do that to her. Not after…after what had happened between them in the kitchen.

But she couldn't know that for sure. How well did she really know the man?

Before she could think better of it, she marched out to the barn where Adam had been rebuilding their small chicken coop. She stopped short at the sight of him, her mind emptying of everything but the mouthwateringly handsome man before her. Who had once again removed his shirt.

Why did men do that? It was an unseasonably warm day, granted. But women didn't go around ripping off their clothes in an attempt to cool down. Not that she wouldn't love to. But it just wasn't done.

Then again, neither was a woman traipsing about town in men's trousers, yet there she was. Perhaps she should give Adam a taste of his own medicine and whip off her own shirt in order to cool down. If nothing else, she would love to do it just to see how he'd react. And what he'd do next.

Her mind flooded with images of all the possibilities, and she gave her head a little shake, trying to clear it. She was there for a reason, and it wasn't to seduce her pseudo-husband. She was there to interrogate him.

• • •

Adam hammered one last nail in and then stood back to examine his handiwork. It was…horrible. The angles were all crooked, the door hung slightly off its frame, and not one single line was straight. But it was standing. It would hold the chickens and keep out predators. And at the end of the day, that's all they really needed. Being pretty was optional. It wasn't like the chickens cared much as long as they were warm and fed.

"Adam?"

Nora's voice—Nora's angry voice—floated to him from outside, and he frowned.

"In here," he called out.

She marched inside, her mouth already open to speak, but she stopped mid-stride when she saw the coop. Her mouth snapped shut again.

He frowned and turned to survey it again. "It's not that bad, is it?"

She glanced at him, then back at the coop, then back at him, and he laughed. "All right, I know it is, but look."

He took her hand and guided her over, opening the door of the enclosure so he could pull her inside. Which, admittedly, didn't look any better than the outside. But still, he was proud of what he'd done. Mostly.

"See, I rebuilt the nesting boxes here," he said, pointing to where they were lined up on a shelf along one wall, "and reinforced the shelving, so it shouldn't collapse again no matter how fat the fluffy little cluckers get."

She snorted and followed along behind him as he showed her the new sliding door that would make it easier to let them in and out. Then he pulled her back outside, where he'd crafted a chicken run that ran out through a hole in the barn wall that could be closed off at night.

"And the coop outside has been patched up as

well. But this one will do nicely during the winter when the heavy snow hits."

She took everything in again and nodded, giving him a smile that lit up his whole soul. Nora smiled a lot. She laughed with her friends, cracked jokes, made sarcastic comments, and generally seemed to enjoy life. But he'd come to discover, through way too many hours of watching her when he didn't think she'd notice, that despite her outward show of general joviality, Nora was actually…sad.

Her smiles always seemed to be lacking something. Some inner light that didn't quite reach out. So when she truly, genuinely smiled, as she just had…it was a gift that he'd commit any number of sins to make happen again.

He took her hands in his and brought them to his lips, pressing a kiss to each of them.

"Why were you looking for me?" he asked, pulling her closer.

"Oh. Yes." She frowned and pulled her hands from his grasp. "Did you move any of the papers that were in my father's study?"

His brow creased. "No. Has something gone missing?"

She nodded, chewing at her bottom lip.

"Something valuable?"

She nodded again, and he took a step back from her. "And you assumed it was me."

"No." She rubbed her hand across her forehead. "Not really." She sighed and plopped down on a rickety milking stool. "To be honest, I hoped that it *was* you."

He raised a brow at that. "You hoped that I'd

stolen from you?"

"Yes." She let out a little laugh, though there was no humor behind it. "If it was you, at least you were still here. I could confront you, get everything back, or at least find out what you'd done with everything. The only other explanation is that my father took everything and…"

"Ah," Adam said, squatting down beside her. Mr. Schumacher had disappeared again. He put a hand on her knee and squeezed. "What can I do?"

Her eyes flashed to his. "I accuse you of stealing and you ask how you can help me?" She let out another laugh. "God, I'm truly a horrible person, aren't I?"

He gave her a tender smile, wanting nothing more than to wrap this woman up and carry her off where nothing would ever put that worry in her eyes again. "No, you're not. You are an unimaginably strong woman carrying way more than any one person should ever have to carry on their own, and you've done it with more grace than most people are capable of in a lifetime."

She blinked suddenly shiny eyes, and he drew a finger across her cheek, then dropped his hand and shrugged. "Of course, there is that whole matter of you tricking me into marrying you and hounding me from one end of town to the other about those damn papers, but no one is perfect."

Her jaw dropped, and he grinned at the fire that sparked in her eyes. Anything was better than that aching sadness.

"I did no such thing!" she said, pushing at him. "All right, fine, I'll admit to the hounding about the papers, but I did not trick you into anything. I was just as surprised by that little turn of events as you were."

"Hmm, so you say," he teased.

"I do say." Then she looked at her feet. "Though maybe I wasn't as horrified by it as you were."

She'd spoken so quietly, he almost missed what she'd said, and his heart cracked right down the middle.

He grasped her chin and raised her face so he could meet her gaze. "I told you my reasons. And they have nothing, *nothing*," he said, keeping her face turned to his when she tried to look away, "to do with you. Any man would be lucky to have you."

She let out a little snort and jerked her face out of his grasp. "There's a whole world full of men out there who would disagree with you. Including you, by the way."

She stood and brushed off her pants. "I'll let you get back to whatever you were going to butcher next."

"Nora." He grabbed her hand, pulling her to a stop before she could leave. "What do you mean, including me?"

She huffed out a mirthless laugh. "You're really going to make me say it? Fine. You have me. We're married. Maybe not according to the courts of the state, but in the eyes of God and the rest of the town, we are. And yet, aside from a few moments of ill-advised recklessness, you've made no secret of the fact that you want nothing to do with me. Can't wait to be rid of me. Hell, you've destroyed half the town trying to get away from me."

"I have not destroyed half the town. But while we're on the subject, let me remind you that you've also made no secret of the fact that you can't wait to be rid of me. Yes, you want me to sign the damn papers, though you won't share your reasons. And I've told you why I can't do that. But despite going to truly ludicrous lengths to convince me to make this legal, you've told me repeatedly that you have no desire for a husband. Which makes no damn sense at all, but you refuse to explain."

"There's nothing to explain. It doesn't matter anymore. You can't sign the papers without putting yourself in even more danger. I get it. So it's done. It's over. As soon as Preacher can figure out how to make all this go away, I'll do whatever is necessary to set you free. If I could find someone to take your place, I would. But no one else wants me any more than you do," she said, nearly shouting.

Then she clamped her lips together and wrapped her arms across her waist like she was trying to hold herself together. She took a step backward, away from him. "So. It's fine. It's…whatever. I'll figure out another way."

She took another step, and he reached out and grabbed her, ignoring her surprised squeak as he hauled her to his chest.

"You think I don't want you? Even after what happened at the store?"

She opened her mouth to respond, but he grasped her hips and pulled her against him, letting her feel just how wrong she was.

He kept one hand at the small of her back, keeping her pressed tightly to him, and his other hand snaked up the back of her neck and into her hair. "Any man who says he doesn't want you is either lying to himself or to you," he said, nipping at her bottom lip. "And I'm doing neither. Not anymore."

He gripped the back of her head and crushed his mouth to hers, pouring every ounce of pent-up desire into his kiss. When he finally broke away, they were both breathless. He stared at her, chest heaving, and then nodded, decision made. She yelped but didn't fight him when he bent and tossed her over his shoulder before going into the house.

"What are you doing?" she asked, her hands scrambling at his back. She was probably trying to brace herself, but all she succeeded in doing was grabbing his ass multiple times. He picked up his pace.

"We've got some things to discuss," he said. And they'd *discuss* them until she learned the lesson good and well.

His life was about to get way more complicated than he knew how to handle, but he was going to show this woman exactly how much she was wanted if it was the last thing he did.

# CHAPTER TWENTY-FOUR

Nora didn't know what to think when Adam had tossed her over his shoulder. Well, first of all, she didn't know *how* he'd tossed her over his shoulder. They were nearly the same size, though he did have a good deal more muscle on him than she did. But he managed to carry her into the house and up the stairs to her room without breaking his stride. Giving her a very enticing view of his backside the entire way.

Given their destination, she could work out for herself why he'd brought her here. But she still didn't quite believe it. Or know what to do about it.

He set her on her feet and didn't give her even a second for either of them to catch their breath. The man was apparently fully loaded and ready to ride once he made a decision, because before she could even steady herself, he was on her again, his hands delving into her hair, pulling it loose from her braid, while his lips ravished hers.

"You think I don't want you?" he said, breaking away from her just long enough to pull his shirt from his pants. He didn't bother to unbutton it but yanked at the material, sending buttons flying all over the room.

Then he was back, both hands cupping her face while his mouth moved feverishly over hers.

"Darlin', I've wanted you from the moment you dropped a body at my feet. And I knew you were mine from the moment you tossed that bar of soap at me in the bathhouse, trying to get a look at what I was packing."

She laughed. "That is not why I tossed it at you."

He grinned and kissed her again. "If you say so."

He kissed her until her knees were ready to buckle, and then he sat her down on the bed, bringing his waistband right to her eye level.

"This is how badly I want you," he said, the strain of his trousers leaving no mistake of it. "I want you so badly it hurts. I think of you every waking second of the day and dream about you every time I close my eyes. I've tried to fight it for both our sakes, but nothing I do is going to get you out of my system."

He dropped to his knees in front of her, bracing his arms on either side of her. "Because I don't just want your body. Though make no mistake, I want to worship every beautiful inch of you, and if you let me, then I will spend every damn day thanking the merciful Lord that there are so many of them."

She laughed, though it sounded like more of a sob. It was too good to be true. Like some cruel joke. Any second now he'd jump up and run away laughing.

Instead, he leaned in closer. "But it's not just your beautiful body I want so desperately, Nora. It's your beautiful mind." He pressed a kiss to her temple. "Your beautiful smile." He captured her lips, giving her a lingering kiss so tender, it made her ache. "Your beautiful heart," he whispered, kissing her just below her collarbone.

He looked back into her eyes. "It's you. All of you. Every beautiful, strong, stubborn last inch of you. *I want you.* Need you."

She gazed into his eyes, trying to detect the lie. The angle. The ulterior motive.

Instead, she saw the sincerity, the yearning…and something else she wasn't ready to believe yet. Something *he* probably wasn't ready to believe yet, either.

"Tell me you want me, too," he whispered against her lips.

She brought her hands up to cup his face, her thumbs stroking across his cheeks. "And what if your past catches up to you?"

"Then we'll deal with it." He gave her a one-shouldered shrug. "The sheriff seems to have done all right. He's been left alone. His wife is safe. He even has a child. If Desolation has truly been a haven for him, maybe it could be for me also. But what about you?"

"Me?" Her eyes searched, and he smiled gently.

"Yes, you. Despite your criminal harassment about the license," he said, ignoring her outraged gasp, "you've told me more than once you don't want a husband."

She nodded. "I meant it, too. When I said it."

He cocked an eyebrow. "And now?"

Her heart thundered, screaming out her answer. But her head was more cautious. If she admitted it, put it out there, there was no taking it back. He'd know how she felt. There'd be no denying it. No way to protect herself if he threw it back in her face.

But she'd never been a coward. She took a deep breath. "I want you," she whispered.

His eyes flashed. "Be very sure. If we do this, it

sticks. The marriage, me...it's consummated, permanent, no matter what the courts say. You'll be mine," he said with a growl that had her toes curling. "And I don't leave what's mine."

She gave him a slow smile. "Neither do I."

He didn't wait for her to say it again. He captured her lips with a primal growl that had her clinging to him with a desperation that should have frightened her. But it didn't. It invigorated her. Strengthened her. This man, this mystifying, aggravating, devilishly handsome man wanted her. Claimed her. Just as she claimed him.

She should be nervous. She'd never done this before. Never really gotten close. But with his hands moving over her body, his lips drinking her in, the only thing she felt was a burning desire for *more*.

And he seemed more than happy to give it to her.

She tugged at her clothes. There were too many layers between them. She needed to feel his skin against her own. He seemed to know exactly what she needed, because he pulled away from her just long enough to strip her bare. And then he stood, thunderstruck, staring at her.

For a moment, that doubt creeped back in. All the cruel words that had been hurled at her over the years, the snide comments, even the well-meaning jokes. She was too tall, too big, not womanly enough, no man would want her. It all came rushing back. And she waited, her heart pounding, to see if he'd be the same.

His breath left him in a slow rush, and he stared at her with what looked like...admiration. Awe.

"Adam?" she asked, her voice quiet.

His eyes moved back to hers with a look of utter reverence. "You take my breath away."

She swallowed against the hard lump in her throat. "Let me see you," she said.

The slow, heated smile he gave her as he pulled off his boots and pants had parts of her tingling that she didn't even know could tingle.

The first touch of his skin against her had her sucking in her breath. When his lips joined his hands, her soul damn near left her body. She had never imagined anything like this. Had never known anything could be like this.

She ran tentative hands over his body, exploring the hard angles and planes of him, reveling in the way he groaned beneath her touch until he captured her hands and pinned them above her head so he could return the favor. He left no part of her untouched. He worshipped every inch of her until she was writhing beneath him. When his fingers slipped inside her, testing her, stretching her, she came around them with a cry, her body trembling with the force of it.

He kissed her again as he moved over her, fitted himself against her core. She knew what to expect, though the stretching, burning pain still took her breath away. He held still, letting her become accustomed to him while his lips and hands kept up their onslaught until she was shuddering around him again, her body chasing what only he could give her.

He began to move, and she gasped, the uncomfortable stretching sensation melting into something more primal, desperate. She clung to him, their lips and tongues tangling together as his hand slipped between them and found that bundle of nerves at the apex of her thighs. She cried out, and he smiled against her lips.

"I got you, darlin'. I got you."

Her hips lifted, trying to bring him closer, deeper. The building wave of electric bliss rumbled over her the way storm clouds passed over a mountain, touching everything in their wake, destroying and renewing all at once. Every stroke of his body inside hers changed another piece of her, rewrote the story she'd always thought was her destiny.

Now, there was something new in its place. Something deeper, infinitely more frightening perhaps. But something better, stronger. And irrevocably tied to him.

This time when she came, he was right there with her, their cries mingling, their limbs still tangled. They stayed that way, curled around each other, as their hearts finally slowed.

Adam kissed her temple, then her lips, his body still wrapped around hers.

For the first time in her life, she felt like she belonged to someone. She hadn't realized how truly lonely she'd been until that moment. That despite the wonderful friends she had, there were limits to what she could share with them. Pieces of her that no one else saw that *he* did. Pieces that no one else wanted to see. But *he* had.

And now he was hers. And she was his.

# CHAPTER TWENTY-FIVE

Nora sat beside Mercy in the rockers outside the general store, enjoying a rare moment of relaxation. Under normal circumstances, she'd feel guilty for sitting there when there was work to be done. But, for the first time in a very long time, there wasn't anything that needed to be taken care of right away.

The dresses she'd been commissioned to make were nearly finished, just waiting on some trim to come into the store. Her gardens were thriving, safe behind their new fence. And the rest of the list of things she needed to fix around the house had been taken care of by Adam. Sure, the shutters didn't hang quite straight, and her laundry barrel might still leak a little, but not nearly as badly. Her chickens were happy in their new coop, and Adam was even working on a new fence line for a paddock where she could put a few goats of her own next spring. She hadn't realized how tired she was, how much she'd carried on her shoulders, until someone came along to help carry the load.

And he did enjoy carrying things, that was for sure. Her, especially. Every time she turned around, he was sweeping her into his arms and carrying her up to their room. She'd never known how much she liked being carried and cuddled and coddled until he'd come along. And when all that sweetness preceded and followed round after round of the kind of passionate lovemaking she hadn't even known to fantasize about...

Her body ached in places she hadn't realized could feel pleasure, and every time he touched her, it just made her crave him more.

She searched for him in the group of men across the street until she found him leaning against the wall of the sheriff's office while Deputy Sunshine explained something to him. He was attentively nodding along and then looked up, as if he could feel her gaze. He dragged his bottom lip through his teeth, giving her a slow, sensual smile that had her squirming in her chair.

The goofy smile she couldn't keep from her face spread across her lips again.

"That," Mercy said, leaning forward to look at her. "That smile right there. I know exactly what that means."

"What *what* means?" Martha said, stepping out onto the porch holding a candy stick. She gave Mercy a questioning glance before handing it to Daisy, who promptly stuck it in her mouth with a happy slurp.

"That smile on Nora's face," Mercy said with a smile of her own. "That's the smile of a woman who has been well and thoroughly loved and can't stop thinking about it."

Nora's cheeks flamed, and Martha dropped into a chair, her eyes wide. "Did he sign the papers?"

"No," Nora said, her smile fading. "But we did discuss it. He has his reasons, good ones actually."

"So...what does that mean?" Martha asked.

"I don't know," Nora said with a sigh as she slumped back against her chair. "I guess we'll just figure it out as we go along."

"Yes, but…if the marriage isn't legal, then does it count for the Town Council's rules? He only has a week left until the end of the month."

Nora snorted. "We don't know that, either. I'm sure we could make the argument for it, but he's starting a job working under Deputy Sunshine for right now. If it sticks, then whether or not we are married shouldn't make too much of a difference."

"Um, you might want to let the men know that we don't need them to make life miserable for the poor man, then," Mercy said, nodding across the street where Adam was trying to get Birdie to move from in front of the office.

All three women burst out laughing. Birdie was the most stubborn horse in existence. Even the sheriff's enemies knew that if his horse was sleeping, she wasn't going to move anywhere, for any reason.

"What about the deed?" Mercy asked.

Nora sobered immediately and shook her head. "I don't know," she said quietly. "I'm not sure it even matters anymore. It might be too late already."

"What do you mean?" Martha asked.

Nora sighed and leaned her head back against her chair, letting it slowly rock. "I can't find it. The deed, along with a small stash of cash I kept hidden in the house, is gone. I think my father took it all the last time he came home. He's been gone for several days now. I… He may have already lost it somewhere. Or to someone. Or maybe sold it for the money he could get."

She leaned forward and dropped her face into her hands, trying to keep her rising panic at bay.

"Every time I hear a horse or wagon drive by the house, I stop and wait to see if it'll be a new owner telling me to leave."

"Oh, Nora. I'm so sorry," Martha said, leaning forward to take her hand.

Mercy leaned in also. "If that does happen, you send word to Gray and me right away. We won't let anyone put you out of your home."

She gave her friends a tremulous smile, but before she could say anything else, a shadow blocked out the sun, and she looked up to see Adam hurrying toward her. He strode right up to her and squatted down.

"What's wrong, darlin'?"

She smiled and swallowed against the emotions clogging her throat. "Nothing. I'm all right."

Adam glanced at Mercy and Martha like he wasn't sure if they'd done something to upset her, but he finally seemed satisfied that all was well. He gripped her chin in his fingers and pulled her close for a quick kiss.

"You need me, you just call for me, you hear?"

"I hear," she said, giving him what she hoped was a convincing smile.

"Even if it's just to help bury the body of who-ever got on your bad side," he said with a wink before sauntering off again.

She laughed and watched the tantalizing view his retreating backside presented as he left.

Martha and Mercy turned to her almost in unison and gave her twin grins.

"You're going to keep him, right? Because that right there was keeper behavior," Mercy said, and

Martha nodded enthusiastically.

Nora just smiled. "I'll do what I can."

• • •

Adam stood on Mercy's front porch, his arms full of a squirming child. Mercy was on her knees in her garden, up to her elbows in dirt and vegetables.

"Are you sure the sheriff won't mind me here?" he asked.

"It'll be fine," she said, tossing a pile of weeds into the bucket by her side.

Adam wasn't so sure about that. The sheriff didn't seem at all happy that Adam was even in his town. Let alone at his home, talking to his wife, and minding his daughter. But…he needed the job, so he'd stay…until the sheriff chased him away. Hopefully not at gunpoint.

"So…what should I do with her?" he asked. He hadn't spent much time around children. Actually, he hadn't spent *any* time around children.

Mercy chuckled. "Just play with her. Keep an eye on her. You don't have to hold her the whole time, but if you put her down, make sure you watch her. Children have a tendency to put things in their mouths."

Adam squinted down at the baby. Watch her and don't let her put anything in her mouth. Sounded simple enough.

It wasn't.

After a cursory examination, he made the mistake of thinking there was nothing on the porch she could possibly ingest. He learned very quickly that a two-year-old was astonishingly hard to catch. Within three minutes, he'd pried an old nail, half a leaf, and some sort of wiggling bug from her grasp.

"Where does she find this stuff?" he asked, pulling a rock from her tiny, surprisingly strong hands.

Mercy laughed again. "They are magic. That's all I've been able to work out."

A wagon turned onto the lane leading up to the house, and Mercy stood, brushing off her skirts. She held up a hand to shield her eyes, and then a smile lit up her face.

"Ah, that's Nora. She must have the shirts I ordered for Gray."

Adam's gaze locked onto the wagon, watching it until it pulled into the yard. Nora's eyes widened with surprise when she saw him there, holding the baby no less. He had no idea how he should act or what he should say, so he simply smiled. Her cheeks pinkened, and she ducked her head a bit shyly as she hopped down from the wagon. The sight filled him with a smug sort of male pride that he had affected this woman so much, she could barely look him in the face without blushing. Something seemed wrong about that. And really, really right as well.

If he had a choice, they'd stay in bed all day long, until they'd had their fill of each other. Though he doubted any amount of time would sate him when it came to her.

Nora grabbed a wrapped bundle out of the back of the wagon and brought it to Mercy. They spoke for a minute, laughing with their heads close together, and then Mercy hurried toward the house.

"I'm just going to put these away. I'll be back out in a bit."

Adam nodded, acknowledging what she wasn't saying. He was in charge of the baby now, so he better make sure she was in one piece when Mercy came back out.

Nora made her way over to the porch, smiling down at Daisy and taking one of her hands when she reached them.

"Does the sheriff know you're minding their daughter?" she asked, her smile making it obvious she knew exactly what the sheriff would think of it.

"Not exactly. And it's not a permanent position. Just for the morning. I'm supposed to meet Sunshine again in a few hours."

Her grin grew wider. "Well, if the sheriff shows up unexpectedly, make sure you keep hold of this precious little thing," she said, cooing down at the baby.

"Why's that?" He'd think that putting the baby down would actually be the safer option, certainly for the child.

"Because he won't dare shoot you if you're holding his baby."

"That…is an excellent point. I'll keep that in mind."

He glanced over at where Mercy was working and then turned back to Nora. "Shall we take her for a walk?" he asked, smiling down at Daisy.

Nora addressed her as well. "That would be lovely," she said, grinning as Daisy babbled up at her.

They took her over to a small grove of apple trees and spread out a blanket that Adam had grabbed from the porch rocking chair, plopping her on it. Then they took turns handing her little bits of things to play with.

After a few minutes, their fingers started to overlap as they handed her things. Until they finally stopped the pretense altogether and just sat twining their fingers together over and over.

Adam gave her a slow smile and leaned forward, letting his lips trail up the column of Nora's neck. She shivered delightfully, but she pressed a hand to his chest, gently pushing him away.

"While I'd love to see where those lips of yours planned to go, perhaps we should wait until later."

"I hate waiting. Patience is absolutely not a virtue—I don't care what anyone says."

"At least not one you possess." She laughed and nodded at the little girl. "We have an audience."

He looked down and laughed. "Ah, yes. I'd almost forgotten she was there."

Well, not truly. But Nora was right that they should behave for the moment. He certainly hadn't been paying as much attention as he should have.

"Is it all right that she have that?" he asked, nodding at the apple the child held.

Nora shrugged a shoulder. "I would think so. She certainly can't fit the whole thing in her mouth, and she doesn't have enough teeth to get off a big enough piece to choke on. As long as we watch her carefully, she should be fine for a minute."

He nodded, frowning a bit. It had never occurred to him that children could be so troublesome. Which brought to mind another thought.

"Do you want one?" he asked.

• • •

Nora's eyes flew open. "A baby?" She frowned a little. "I hadn't really thought of it."

That wasn't completely true. She had thought of it. How could she not when that was what women her age typically did? Got married, had kids. But she'd never given it any real consideration because she'd never thought she would ever get married. She liked children and had always thought it would be nice to have them. But it wasn't an opportunity she'd thought she could have.

And she was all right with that. For the most part. So she answered him as truthfully as she could.

"I enjoy playing with my friends' children, and truth be told, it is sometimes nice to play with the children and then go home and let their parents deal with the hard part of raising them."

He chuckled, nodding his agreement.

"I think," she said, "I think, yes. If I had a choice and a willing partner, I'd like children someday. You?" she asked.

"I've never really thought about it, either. The life of a gunslinger isn't really conducive to child-rearing."

She laughed. "I suppose not." Her eyes searched his, trying to read how he really felt about all this. "But…now that you're retired…?"

He thought about it for a moment. "If I could find a place, a good *safe* place, where I knew I could raise my children in peace and not have to worry about always looking over my shoulder, I think it might be nice to have kids. But the last thing I'd want to do is give my enemies any leverage over me. It's one of the reasons I haven't been back to visit my family since I came out west and…well, took up the profession I did."

"You have family somewhere?"

He nodded. "My mother, and a brother and sister. My sister married a banker, lives in New York City the last I heard. My brother is a law clerk. He lives near my mother, takes care of her. I do miss them. But I worry also."

"You don't want to bring your past home to them?"

"It just always seemed safer to keep my distance," he said with a sad smile. "Maybe someday, if that changes, I can think about things like visiting my family. Or starting a new one," he said, bringing their entwined hands up to his lips so he could press a kiss to hers.

She smiled, staring at him for a moment before taking a deep breath and returning her attention to Daisy.

"I think we should get this little one back to her mother. Looks like it may be time for a nap."

Adam smiled down at the little girl who was yawning and rubbing at her eyes. He bent to pick her up and laced his fingers with Nora's as they walked back toward the house. Just before they left the grove of trees, he pulled Nora to a stop and took her chin in his fingers, tilting her face to his for a quick but very thorough kiss that had her lips tingling and her lungs struggling to draw in a breath. The man was criminally good at that.

They continued through to the courtyard just as a man riding a horse approached in the distance. Barnaby turned around and started tossing his head, letting out excited puffs of air.

Nora laughed. "If your horse is anything to go by, I'd say Birdie and the sheriff are about to ride in."

He chuckled at his horse's antics, but a solid thread of worry gnawed at him. One look at the thunderous expression on Woodson's face when he rode into the yard was enough to turn that thread into a lightning bolt. He'd known the sheriff wouldn't be pleased with Adam minding his daughter.

The sheriff came thundering in, jumped down from his horse, strode up to Adam, and plucked Daisy from his arms.

"Why do you have my daughter?"

Mercy came out of the house and gave Gray a kiss. "Because I hired him to mind her for me while I did my chores. So be nice."

The sheriff's eyes narrowed to dangerous slits. "You did what?"

Adam edged toward his horse. "I think I should be going now."

The sheriff glowered at him. "Don't bother coming back. Your services will no longer be required."

Mercy's wide eyes shot to her husband's. "Gray, that's not fair. He was a big help today. I got so much done."

The sheriff's expression softened when he looked at his wife. "If you need help, I will hire you some help. Maybe some more feminine help. Or at least not outlawed help."

Adam snorted. "If you're going to try and find non-outlaw help, you better look in a different town."

The women laughed. Gray kept glowering, looking over his offspring like Adam might have managed to permanently damage her in the short time he'd taken care of her.

"Right. Well, we need to be on our way," he said, jerking his head toward Nora. Thankfully, the woman could take a hint. They said quick goodbyes and then mounted their horses. Though it took some coaxing for Barnaby to leave Birdie's side.

As they got to the lane that would lead back to town, Adam leaned over in his saddle. "I'll race you home."

Nora's eyes gleamed. "You're on!"

And she took off, her laughter ringing out through the countryside.

# CHAPTER TWENTY-SIX

They'd just slowed down as they approached the main street of town—because they didn't want to cause any commotion, of course, not because Nora would have definitely bested him—when Deputy Sunshine waved at them from the sidewalk in front of the sheriff's office.

They reined in and nodded down at him.

"Deputy," Adam said with a smile. It was impossible not to smile at the man.

"Mr. Brady. Mind if I borrow you for a few moments?"

Adam glanced quickly at Nora, who just shrugged. "Have I committed some crime I'm unaware of?" he asked with another grin. Wouldn't be the first time. He was woefully unaware of a lot of things.

Sunshine chuckled. "Not at all. In fact, I've got good news."

Adam's eyebrows hit his hairline. "You're going to officially hire me?" He squinted down at the deputy. "Is the sheriff aware of this?"

Sunshine's smile spread, a mischievous glint flashing in his eyes. "Not yet. But he did give me leave to hire an assistant deputy and didn't specifically say I *couldn't* hire you, so…"

The man shrugged, and Adam laughed, though he'd be lying if he said his stomach didn't clench just a tad at the thought of the sheriff's face when he came face-to-face with his new assistant deputy. Then again, he'd never want to miss that look, either. It was going to be priceless.

Adam dismounted and tied up his horse. While he was partially hidden between the two horses, he caught Nora's hand and gave it a kiss, squeezing gently before he let go. Her cheeks flamed, and he gave her a slow half grin that made them grow even redder.

Nora cleared her throat and shook her head, though her delectable lips were twitching. It was everything he could do not to pull her off that horse and give her a proper goodbye.

"Don't get yourself killed," she said.

Adam grinned up at her. "I'll try."

She snorted and nudged her horse toward home, muttering something about men that he probably didn't want to know about.

Adam turned back to catch Sunshine watching him with a speculative eye.

"Things seem to be going well between the two of you."

Adam's own cheeks grew a little warm. Was he blushing? How the mighty had fallen. He cleared his throat and turned his attention to the street, his gaze roaming casually over the citizens going about their business.

"Things are…good. I think."

Sunshine surprisingly didn't press him on it, just clapped a hand on his shoulder. "Glad to hear it. Come on, Mr. Brady. I'll show you what needs doing."

They turned to go inside, but something flashed

in the corner of Adam's eye, and he stopped, looking back over his shoulder to see what had caught his attention. Nothing seemed to be amiss. People were walking along the sidewalks, going in and out of the businesses that dotted the street. Horses and a few wagons rode up and down. Just a typical day in Desolation.

He frowned, and Sunshine looked around the street before looking back at him. "Is something wrong?"

Adam hesitated and then shook his head. "No. I thought I might have seen something, but I must have been wrong."

He tried to shake off the unease settling in his gut and turned back to the sheriff's office.

Sunshine gave him a tour, not that there was much to see. The office sported a front room with a desk and a few chairs, a potbellied stove with a coffeepot, and that was about it. Aside from the small cot where Daisy took her naps, of course. Two decent-size cells were located in the back of the building, each sporting two cots.

"We have a man who comes in a few days a week to keep things around here tidy and run errands for us. Frank. You'll meet him soon, I'm sure. But it will be nice to have a full-time assistant deputy to help out with the heavy lifting," Sunshine said. "The sheriff likes to keep daytime hours since Daisy came along, and while I don't mind keeping an eye on things at night and when he's not here, especially since I live just upstairs, it would still be nice to have an extra body down here who can relieve us both occasionally."

Adam nodded, but his brow furrowed. "Yes, well, let's wait and see if Woodson actually agrees to this before we make too many plans."

Sunshine just laughed again. "The sheriff really isn't as bad as he'd like everyone to think."

Adam gave him the look that remark deserved, and Sunshine grinned and jerked his head toward the desk. "Have a seat and I'll give you the rundown of how we do things around here."

Thirty minutes later, Adam stepped back into the sun and clapped his ill-fitting hat back on his head. He really needed to find his old hat. Or buy a new one. If he could ever stay at a job long enough to collect some decent pay. Whether or not the sheriff's office would be that job...he didn't want to begin to hope.

Of course, working side by side with Woodson would be interesting. But he hated to admit it, he kind of liked the man. A strange development after spending so many years avoiding the mere mention of him. But he just couldn't help himself. That curmudgeonly old codger was growing on him.

The job itself seemed interesting and more suited to his skills than any of the others he'd tried so far. Woodson ran a tight ship, and Adam wasn't ashamed to admit he was impressed. Though even if he wasn't and it sounded like the worst job in the world, at this point, he'd take it. He was running very low on time, and he had no doubt Woodson would have his backside marched to the town's boundaries the second these thirty days were up.

Things with Nora... He cringed away from examining them too closely. They certainly couldn't go back to pretending there was nothing between them. And he didn't want to. But he also didn't want either one of them to feel rushed into defining what they were to each other because of some ridiculous ticking clock that Woodson and the Town Council had imposed on them. They both deserved the time to decide what their future held. And that couldn't happen if Adam got kicked out of town.

So the best solution for all of them was for *this* job to stick. He was running out of places to destroy…er, work.

Adam went to untie Barnaby when that nagging feeling hit the pit of his stomach again. He stopped and looked around as casually as he could. Something was off. He wasn't quite sure what it was, but his world-is-about-to-go-to-hell intuition was screaming at him.

Instead of mounting his horse, he shoved his hands in his pockets and crossed the street to the general store at a leisurely pace. A man peeled off from behind a group that was chatting near the front of Doc's clinic. Adam paused to look at a selection of pies that Martha had arranged in the window, though his gaze was on the reflection of the stranger who also crossed the street.

Adam's gut twisted. He'd known something was wrong. He continued along the walkway in front of the store and caught the reflection of the man behind him in the store's window, following him from a safe distance. Adam picked up his pace until he reached the tavern. He pushed through the doors and made his way between the tables toward the back, moving quickly but giving his follower enough time to see where he was going.

He darted down the dimly lit back hallway and pressed himself into a corner to wait. A few moments later, his follower turned the corner, and Adam grabbed him by the lapels and slammed him back against the wall.

"Who are you?" he growled at him. "Why are you following me?"

"What? I'm not! I'm nobody—let go!"

The man tried to push him off, but Adam held tight, one arm pressed against the man's throat while his other hand searched through his pockets. The man shoved him off just as Adam snagged a crumpled paper from his pocket. He took off running, ripping the paper out of Adam's hands as he did so, leaving Adam holding just a corner. Adam hurried after him.

The man knocked into a few chairs and drew enough looks, especially when Adam came racing out of the hallway, that they now had the patrons' full attention. Reggie came out from behind the bar, wielding a broomstick, but the stranger had already elbowed his way out the door.

Adam and Reggie jostled their way out after him, but by the time they got to the street, the man had already mounted and was running out of town.

Reggie nodded at his retreating back. "Friend of yours?"

Adam shook his head, frowning deeply. "Never seen him before. Something just seemed off about him."

He was hesitant to share his true fear—that while he hadn't known the man, the man had known exactly who he was. But Reggie didn't press him. Adam gave him a nod of thanks that Reggie returned, and then he went back to his bar.

Adam glanced down at the piece of paper in his hands. It could be anything. It looked to be an advertisement of some sort. Or the corner of a wanted poster.

He swallowed hard, trying to push down the panic that threatened to rise. It was just his own fears tricking his eyes. The shred of paper he held didn't have anything useful on it. No words, no information at all. Just the hint of a border that he'd seen on a poster once. But that didn't necessarily mean anything. Even if it was a wanted poster, it didn't mean it was one of Adam's. Hell, this town was full of outlaws. It could be for anyone.

But if it was for him, if the man had been there to find him, it could mean Adam's respite was over. If that man knew who Adam was and told anyone he was here…it could bring Spurlock to his door.

To Nora's door.

*Damn it!*

*This* was why he should have never gotten involved with her. He should have fought her harder when she'd insisted they were married. He should have climbed on his grumpy pain of a horse and put Desolation behind him the moment he'd set eyes on her. Though the thought of doing that now made his heart ache. For a brief moment, he'd tasted a bit of happiness. He'd even dared to dream of the possibility that maybe they could have a future together. Maybe even a family.

But there was a reason he kept himself free from

entanglements. A reason he hadn't been to visit his own mother in years. A reason he tried never to get close to anyone. He was nothing but a curse to anyone he touched. He should have known better. He *had* known better.

But she'd been too damn hard to resist. And now his weakness had put her in danger.

He closed his eyes and took a deep breath, trying to get a grip on the anxiety and dread that slithered through him. That man could have been nobody. Did it look bad? Sure. But for all Adam knew, the man had been heading for one of the outhouses out back and it had just seemed like he was following Adam.

There had always been the possibility that his past would catch up to him at some point. That hadn't changed. But he also didn't have any surefire evidence that things had gotten any worse. There was no point in worrying everyone else until there was actually something to worry about.

He should probably pack up and leave. If he was gone, there wouldn't be anyone for Spurlock to find if he did come around. Then again, if he did come and Adam wasn't there, Nora could still be in danger. The thought of her confronting Spurlock, of the man even being in the same town as her, filled Adam with a fury—and a fear—so great, it made him shake.

So he'd stay. Though leaving was probably the better choice, he just couldn't make himself leave her yet. And he needed to be there to make sure she stayed safe. Because he didn't think he could survive this time if she was the one who ended up hurt.

• • •

Nora pulled another weed from the bed of thyme, her hand still tingling from the kiss Adam had given it before they'd gone their own ways. What was that man doing to her? She'd never pictured herself as the romantic type, and yet there she was, daydreaming in her garden with what she was sure was a besotted grin on her lips. Thankfully there was no one to see her but her chickens and the goats in the pasture.

Her happiness faded quickly when she saw her father's horse wander into the paddock and begin grazing. He must have just arrived. And she'd been too busy with her head in the clouds to notice.

She got to her feet and brushed off the dirt that clung to her clothes. That familiar feeling of dread sank like lead in her stomach. She hadn't realized how horrible that feeling was until she'd gone a while without feeling it. You could get used to anything, she supposed.

The last month, and the last several days especially, when her father had been gone more than usual and she'd either been alone or with Adam, she pictured a lifetime of that, and a longing hit her so intensely it took her breath away. She'd miss her father. But then, she already missed him now, even when he was there. Because the man he was now was not the man who'd raised her. But she couldn't avoid him forever.

She took a deep breath, straightened her spine, and then went into the house.

The moment she stepped inside, she knew it was going to be bad. Adam's things were strewn about the house, most at the bottom of the staircase where her father must have thrown them after finding them in her room. She tamped down the anger that flooded her at the thought of her father going through her room, her private things. In his mind, he was still the head of the household. He was her father. Even if she'd been the one taking care of him and everything else since the day her mother had died.

She found him rummaging about in the study, and her heart sank. "There isn't any more," she said.

His head jerked up, and his bloodshot eyes focused on her. "Isn't any more what?"

"Money," she said, weary to the bone with this scene. It had played out a dozen different ways over the years. "The money is gone. You took it all."

His eyes narrowed into slits. "I haven't taken anything."

She opened her mouth to argue. Normally, she'd give him an earful. But the sight of the man she'd once looked up to brought to such a state by his grief broke her heart. She hadn't thought it could break anymore. So instead, she just said, "All right, Papa," and turned to leave.

"You...you must have something put away. You sell your plants. You've got dresses in your sewing room. Someone must have paid you to make them."

"She'll pay me once I deliver the dresses. And the plant money is gone." Because he'd already taken it. She left the words unsaid, hanging in the air between them.

Her father's frown turned into a sneer. "What about that man you've got living here? He paying you anything for the food he eats? The bed he sleeps in? Or whatever else he's using you for?"

She sucked in a breath, a rage burning through her so hot, her eyes watered. "That's it. I've put up with a lot over the years. I've taken care of you, taken care of everything when you refused to do so. I've watched you drinking yourself toward an early grave. I've listened to your insults and your complaints and your drunken rages and I'm not going to do it anymore! I'm done. I refuse to stand here and take one more insult from you."

"I don't owe you any explanation, but out of respect for the fact that you are my father, even if you stopped acting like one a long time ago, that man you are so casually insulting has every right to be under this roof. He's my husband."

She hadn't seen her father so stunned since... well, ever. More emotions flew across his face than she could identify. Confusion. Sadness. But as was typical with him, he settled on anger.

"How dare you get married without my permission."

"Your permission? How were we supposed to ask for your permission? You are gone more than you're home lately, and even when you are here, you're too drunk to know what's going on most of the time."

She didn't bother trying to explain the real situation. He wouldn't understand. Hell, she didn't even understand it. Better to stick to the bare-minimum facts.

Most of the anger bled out of his face, but he still grumbled something about being there to give her away.

She shook her head. "I would have loved for you to have been there to walk me down the aisle and give me away. But even if you'd been here, that wouldn't have happened. If you'd even bothered showing up, you'd probably have been too drunk to walk me anywhere."

She let out a humorless laugh. "Within five minutes of getting to town, Adam was already helping me. Do you have any idea how good that felt? Do you know how long it's been since anyone has been there for me? What it feels like to finally have someone who makes my burden lighter instead of worse? I won't let you ruin that for me. Not this time."

Her father stared at her for a moment, then finally nodded. "You don't want me around, fine. I'll leave. Your husband can have you."

He flung down the papers he'd been riffling through and stormed out of the house.

Nora put a shaking hand to her forehead and took several deep breaths. She hadn't even asked him where the deed to the property was. Not that he'd have told her anyway. She'd ask him later, then. He'd come to his senses when he'd sobered up and would apologize as he always did. Maybe she could get some information out of him then. In the meantime…

She bent to pick up one of Adam's shirts that her father had flung down the stairs. A smile pulled at her lips when she realized it was the shirt from the first day they'd made love, the one he'd ripped all the buttons off.

She took the shirt over to where her sewing basket sat next to the fireplace and her favorite chair. She couldn't fix her father's problems just then. Or Adam's. Or know for a certainty that whatever it was that she and Adam were doing was the right decision.

But she could sew the buttons back on his shirt. So she'd focus on that. The rest…she just hoped she found some sort of solution before her life blew up in her face again.

# CHAPTER TWENTY-SEVEN

"Here's to your first day as a law enforcer," Sunshine said, raising his glass to Adam.

The men had found him holding up one of the posts out front, watching the street. Which they took as an invitation to haul him in for a drink and keep him company for the last hour or so. He should have gone directly home to Nora, but he wanted to make sure the stranger he'd seen was well and truly gone. Maybe the man had just been passing through or was another newcomer and Adam had scared him off. As long as he stayed gone, Adam wouldn't have a quarrel with him.

Doc and Preacher had raised their glasses as well. Adam and Woodson both grimaced but gamely held theirs up. Well, Adam did. Woodson sort of tipped his in their direction before taking another drink.

"Never thought I'd see the day," Adam muttered into his cider.

Woodson snorted. "I know the feeling."

Silence fell for a few moments before Sunshine cleared his throat. "So, you and Miss Nora seem to be getting along better."

Every man at the table turned and glared at him. "What?" he said, looking as innocent as any man Adam had ever seen. "It's true."

They all continued to stare at him. "You mean to tell me I'm the only one who saw him kiss her hand this afternoon? And the way she blushed?"

"No," Woodson said in that gravelly voice of his. "You're just the only one who refuses to mind his own business."

Sunshine just grinned. Nothing seemed to rattle the man. "Yes, well, if you all stopped having such interesting lives, I might pay a little more attention to mine."

Woodson grunted. "Then I'm going to take my interesting life and head home."

Sunshine stood as well. "I'll go check on things at the jailhouse. Brought a couple of brothers in after you left, and they are none too happy."

Adam frowned. "That's not unexpected, is it?"

"Oh, they don't mind being locked up. They just don't like being in adjacent cells," Sunshine said with a laugh. "But since we only have the two, there's not much I can do about that except calm them down when one of them gets riled. It's better than putting them in one together." He tipped his hat to Adam. "I'll see you in the morning, bright and early."

Adam nodded. "Thanks, Deputy."

"I'll say good night as well," Doc said, standing to take his leave. "Martha said something about fresh apple pie. I think I'll go see if I can scare up a slice."

"Sounds delicious," Adam said, though he had an idea that the good doctor might be after something a little sweeter than apple pie.

Adam glanced at Preacher, waiting for him to excuse himself as well. Preacher just smiled. "I don't have anywhere else to be."

Adam chuckled and drank the rest of his cider. He *did* actually have someplace to go. And someone who was hopefully waiting for him.

He stood to leave, but then he spied Nora's father losing a hand. And not his first, if the small pile of chips and the desperate gleam in his bloodshot eyes meant anything. When had he gotten back into town? Adam wondered if Mr. Schumacher had bothered to go see his daughter first or if he'd just come directly to the tavern.

The man had no business gambling when he couldn't afford to lose, especially when his daughter was killing herself to support him. If it weren't for Nora, Adam would walk away and let the man do as he would. Mr. Schumacher was a grown man and was entitled to make his own decisions, foolish though they were. But things were different now. Adam couldn't just sit and watch him lose all his money. For Nora's sake. Especially since the money was probably hers.

"I'd tell you to leave it alone if I thought you'd listen," Preacher said with a wry smile. "But I'm also getting tired of watching Nora deal with the brunt of the consequences of her father's mistakes. Just try not to get into too much trouble."

Adam smiled. "I can't make any promises." Then he left his glass on the table and went to join the game.

"Well, if it ain't my new son-in-law," Schumacher sneered at him.

Adam glanced at him in surprise. "Nora told you?"

"Did she tell me that she went and threw her life away on some two-bit nobody who's so piss-poor he doesn't even have his own house to move his wife into but has to live in her father's house?

Yeah, she told me."

Adam didn't bother arguing with the man. He'd believe what he wanted to believe. And since he himself had never made a decision solely to please Nora, Adam doubted he'd believe anyone else had.

"Do you have an objection to me joining the game?" Adam asked, not sure what he'd do if Schumacher said yes.

But the man just shrugged. "You got money to lose, I've got no problem taking it from you. Probably my daughter's anyway."

Adam bit his tongue, though the urge to call the man out on his hypocrisy was staggering.

The other men were a little wary. He was new, after all, and despite having been in town several weeks now, he'd never showed an interest in joining their games before. But money was money, and if he had it, they weren't averse to taking it. Or trying, anyway.

He watched them all carefully for several hands, keeping his bets small and purposely losing every one of them. The men started to relax, and the atmosphere grew more jovial. With all except Mr. Schumacher. The energy surrounding him grew increasingly frantic, and Adam wasn't sure how long he could hold disaster at bay. He'd been able to spin several hands in Schumacher's favor, hoping the man would take his winnings and leave before his "lucky" streak ran out. Instead, he grew bolder, bet more. And even Adam's skill wouldn't keep his chips flowing for long.

The man dealing shuffled the cards, preparing for another round, when the tavern doors banged open and Nora stormed in. She zeroed in on her father and marched over, stopping short when she saw Adam sitting at the table. Her eyes crinkled with surprise. And betrayal. Adam hoped that she'd realize he wouldn't do anything to harm her. But despite all they'd shared recently, they hadn't known each other long. And trust was a hard-earned thing for them both.

Yet he still had to choke back the explanation that hovered on his lips. He was actually helping... even if it didn't look like it. But he couldn't say anything without giving himself away. Her eyes narrowed, her face hardening as she turned from him and leaned over her father.

"Come on, Pa. Let's go home."

He shook her off. "Leave me be, girl."

Adam opened his mouth to say something, but what could he say that would help? He'd explain it to her later. If he couldn't keep her father from losing, Adam could at least make sure he won himself. Then he could return everything to her afterward. In fact, it might even turn out better that way. Her father would think the money was gone, and as long as she didn't tell him Adam had returned it, she could keep it safe from his disastrous gambling.

He tried to ignore her fuming and focus on the game. He needed to keep his wits about him.

The dealer dealt another hand of cards, and Adam's heart pounded when he spread them out in his hands, though he kept his face stone-still. He held the two of hearts, the seven of spades...and three kings.

He watched the others around the table, watching for their tells. Schumacher, unfortunately, was easy to read. Whether it was because he was too drunk to keep his poker face on or because he was just that bad at cards, Adam didn't know. Whatever the case, everyone at the table knew he held at least the beginnings of a good hand. A fact that was more solidified when he shoved every last coin he had into the pile in the middle of the table.

Adam glanced at the other men, trying to keep from looking at Nora, who was watching with increasing concern from a few feet away. He couldn't afford the distraction, even if every bone in his body was screaming at him to wrap her in his arms and wipe that fear from her face.

If the other men weren't holding anything, Adam could throw the game Schumacher's way and hopefully send him out the door with a nice pile of winnings.

They all called. Damn.

He waited until everyone had added their new cards to their hand. He'd dropped two cards and picked up the six of hearts and…holy hell, the fourth king. He kept his breathing calm and even, kept his body language as relaxed as he could, just as he'd been during the entire game. No one watching him would know what he held.

Whatever Schumacher had pulled sent the man's blood rushing to his cheeks, and even though he wasn't smiling, he still looked incredibly pleased. Adam hoped that it was the liquor making him so horrible at hiding his hand, because if he was always this easy to read, it was a wonder he hadn't lost everything he owned already.

Two of the other men folded. The third raised the stakes. Adam had enough chips to call. Schumacher did not.

That should have been the end of it. He should have folded.

Instead, he fumbled with something in his vest pocket and slammed a folded paper onto the pile.

"What is that?" the dealer asked.

"The deed to my property," Schumacher said, casting his drunken gaze around, daring anyone to reject it. Aside from a strangled gasp from Nora, no one said anything. On the contrary, the men still playing grinned, their eyes zeroing in on the deed.

"None of us is holding what that must be worth," Adam said, trying to stop the catastrophe unfolding before his eyes.

"It's worth what I say it's worth," Schumacher said. "The rest of you go all in and we'll call it even."

"Pa, you can't," Nora said, laying a hand on his shoulder.

He brushed her off. "Yes I can. It ain't yours yet. Now stay out of it."

Adam avoided meeting Nora's gaze, though doing so was nearly painful, and glanced at the other men. One he knew was bluffing. The man had been running his finger lightly over the backs of his cards since he'd picked up the new ones after discarding. A nervous tic. Every time he'd done it, he'd folded or showed a poor hand. Another he was relatively sure had nothing as well. A slight scowl flickered across his face for a breath of a second when he'd first picked up his cards. The third…Adam wasn't quite sure. He was doing a better job of hiding his emotions than he'd been doing the rest of the night. Which itself was a tell. He was most likely holding something good.

Only three hands could beat what Adam held. Four aces. A straight flush. Or a royal flush. No one could be holding a royal flush because Adam held all the kings. So that eliminated one threat. The chances that either Schumacher or the other man was holding one of those hands were slim. The chances of them each holding one, almost nonexistent. But there was still a chance.

Either way, his best bet was to stay in the game and hope either Schumacher won or he did.

The fidgeting man folded, as Adam had expected. The man on Adam's right also folded.

"The man's insane," he muttered, sitting back and shaking his head.

Adam agreed. Unfortunately, the remaining man either didn't agree…or did, but wanted to take advantage. Either way, he shoved all his chips into the pile. Adam couldn't back out now. He glanced quickly at Nora, his stomach dropping at the look of utter horror on her face, and pushed his chips into the pot.

Schumacher's eyes gleamed greedily.

The remaining man dropped his hand. A full house. Good hand. But not good enough.

Schumacher cackled and dropped his hand. "You lose, Bunson! I've got four pretty ladies, all lined up."

He laid out his four queens and started reaching for the pile in the center of the table.

"I'm afraid I've got you beat," Adam said quietly.

He laid down his hand, his eyes fixed on Nora. "Four of a kind. Kings."

Nora's mouth dropped open, and her gaze shot to his, her eyes glassy with unshed tears.

Schumacher lurched from his seat, his chair crashing to the floor. "You cheated!"

Adam sighed. "No, I didn't."

"You can't steal my property!"

Adam raised a brow. "I didn't steal it. You lost it." And as soon as he could, he'd make whatever arrangements were necessary to keep it safe for Nora, so her father could never do something so despicable again.

"No!" Schumacher screamed again. "You're a thief! First you steal my daughter and now you think you can steal my land?" He pulled a huge knife from his boot and started waving it in Adam's face.

Adam's mind faded to that quiet, blank place he'd hoped he'd never need to visit again.

And he reached for his gun.

# CHAPTER TWENTY-EIGHT

Nora gasped and staggered back against the table. Adam had gotten to his feet with his gun in his hand before she'd even had time to blink. She'd never seen anyone pull their gun so quickly before.

When she'd left her house to go searching for her husband and her father, she had feared something like this would happen. Adam was a gunslinger, after all, retired or no. And her father…well, her father was nothing if not adept at making people angry enough to want to kill him. Still, actually seeing it play out was a nightmare she wasn't prepared to deal with.

She couldn't even start to unravel the complications that Adam being in possession of her deed created. With their marriage in legal limbo unless Adam could sign the license, which he couldn't, her deed was now in limbo with him.

He couldn't transfer ownership of the property to anyone without going through legal channels, which would put his life in even more danger. He couldn't even just give it to her because one, that put her right back where she started—her father would just take ownership of it until she reached thirty. And two, too many people had seen Adam win. The story would probably be a town legend by the time the sun rose. And not all of those people were friends. She'd always be waiting for someone to take advantage of the legal ambiguity of the ownership records. So, everything she'd been through in the last month had been for naught.

And now, it looked as though she might lose her father as well. Again, at the hands of her...husband? Lover? She didn't even know anymore. No matter her father's faults, he was still the only parent she had left. She didn't want to lose him.

She looked to her father, who still hadn't seemed to realize that he was woefully out-weaponed. Her heart thudded in her chest.

"What are you doing?" Nora said, taking a step toward Adam.

Adam's eyes flashed to hers for half a second before returning to her father, who was starting to look a little green around the gills. "I'm trying to keep your father from making a bigger mistake than he already has tonight."

She frowned, not understanding his intentions. If he was going to just shoot her father, he probably would have done so already. Then again, he was still standing there holding a gun on him.

"Don't hurt him," she said, her voice coming out in a choked whisper.

"Don't hurt *him*?" he said with a slight squeak that had her raising her brows. "I'm more worried about him hurting me."

"You're the one with the gun," she pointed out, her brow furrowing with a frustrated frown.

"Well, sure, but he started it."

"Are you serious?"

"Hey, I was just trying to help, not start a fight."

Nora clenched her fists, trying to rein in the fury burning through her gut. "And how, exactly, does stealing our property help?"

Adam sighed deeply. "I didn't ste—"

"Put the gun away, Brady," a low, even voice said.

Adam's gaze flicked to Preacher, who had moved to stand halfway between Adam and her father, though he made sure to stay out of the line of fire. "So this is your idea of staying out of trouble?"

"This was not my idea. Besides, I did say I couldn't promise anything."

Preacher snorted. "So you did." He glanced at Adam's hand. "You're still holding your gun."

"Sorry, Preacher, but I have no desire to be holey," Adam said.

The preacher closed his eyes and shook his head, his mouth pinched together in what Nora was pretty sure was an attempt not to smile. They couldn't be serious.

"Holy? What is that supposed to mean?" she said, throwing her hands up.

Adam glanced at her briefly but kept his attention on her father, who was wobbly on his feet but still had a death grip on his weapon.

Adam gestured to the knife with his gun. "That means your dear father seems intent on poking me full of holes and I'd really rather he not. You tell him to put that pig sticker away and I'd be happy to stow my gun. My hide is pretty useless, but it's all I've got and I'm kind of particular about keeping it intact."

She opened her mouth to argue again when the sheriff's voice thundered from the door.

"What's going on here?"

Thank heavens. Someone had fetched the sheriff. Though…she wasn't entirely sure that was a good thing. The law was supposed to defuse these situations, and of course she didn't want any harm to come to her father. But with Adam being the newcomer and all, not to mention already being on the sheriff's bad side even if they *had* been sort of getting along lately, his chances of coming out of this unscathed were rapidly diminishing. And judging by the subtle tightening of his mouth, he knew it.

"Where's Sunshine?" the sheriff asked. "The Thompson boys still giving him trouble?"

"Probably. Plus, it's Frank's day off," Preacher said with a little shrug.

The sheriff sighed and rubbed his hand over his face. "Of course it is."

"Why is Frank's day off a problem?" Adam mumbled at Nora out of the side of his mouth, his eyes never leaving her father.

She raised her brows. "Frank is… He tends to be known for… He's…well, he likes to imbibe on his days off. Tends to get into trouble when he does, so he spends a lot of his free time in the company of the sheriff or Deputy Sunshine."

Adam's mouth quirked into a half grin. "Sounds like an interesting fellow."

"Sorry, Sheriff," Sunshine said, running in, his hair sticking up on end before he shoved his hat back on it. "Frank is a little quicker on his feet since he's been keeping the drinking to his off days."

The sheriff grunted at his deputy and then turned back to the issue at hand, his glowering gaze taking in the gun in Adam's hand.

"I've been gone less than an hour, Brady."

"I know, Sheriff. My apologies."

"Are you threatening one of my citizens?" the sheriff growled at him.

"Wouldn't dream of it, Sheriff," Adam said.

Nora had no idea how his voice remained calm, playful even, when he had both her armed father and the sheriff—once an infamous gunslinger, always an infamous gunslinger—staring him down. Her gut was roiling like a storm-churned lake, but Adam just shrugged.

"Mr. Schumacher here just lost a hand of poker and doesn't seem to be handling it well."

He nodded at her father, who leaned heavily on the table but kept his knife clasped tight in his trembling hand.

Nora's jaw dropped. Sure, technically that was the truth. But he was leaving a lot out.

"He didn't just lose a hand of poker, Sheriff," she said. "Adam just claimed the deed to our property, our home."

The sheriff jerked his furious eyes back to Adam. "You what? And put that gun away unless you intend to use it against me," he said, his livid expression turning Nora's insides to jelly even though it wasn't directed at her. She didn't know how Adam wasn't reduced to a twitching pile of sludge by that glare.

Adam sighed. "Fine, but if I end up looking like a pincushion, I'm going to be very cross."

The sheriff scowled at her father, marched toward him, and easily plucked the knife from his hand.

"Now, talk," he said, handing the knife behind him to Sunshine.

She and Adam both started talking, their words jumbling together and over one another. The sheriff held up an impatient hand.

"One at a time!" He took a deep breath and dropped into the nearest chair, rubbing at his forehead. "You," he said, pointing at her. "You say he took your property."

"Yes," she said. Then she frowned. "I think."

The sheriff blinked at her. "You think?"

She shrugged. "The way matters stand with our marriage makes things a little…complicated. But, just for the sake of argument, since he's not technically legally my husband and my father technically legally still has control over the property, yes, he took it. I think."

The sheriff closed his eyes and rubbed the bridge of his nose. Then he shook his head and looked at Adam. "That true?"

"Not entirely."

She cursed at him under her breath, and he blinked in surprise at her, opened his mouth to say something before snapping it shut, and then just blinked again before finally turning back to the sheriff.

"I did *not* steal anything. I won the property in a card game."

The sheriff's eyes widened and turned to her father. Unfortunately, once relieved of his weapon, all the fight had gone out of him and he lay slumped against the table, soft snores emanating from the recesses of his folded arms.

The sheriff shook his head and looked back to her. Nora's heart dropped at the look of pity in his eyes. "Your father put up the land in a card game? Is this true?"

She reluctantly nodded, her stomach twisting in a knot at the sheriff's deep sigh.

"I'm sorry, Miss Schumacher. But there isn't a law against doing something monumentally stupid. If Brady here won the game fair and square"—he paused and looked over at Preacher, who gave him an equally reluctant nod—"then I'm afraid there is nothing I can do about it."

Which meant the property was now Adam's. And if he wanted to, since they weren't legally wed, he could kick her out. Even sell it off if he kept it private. She didn't think he'd do either of those things. The man who had held her with such passion and tenderness wouldn't put her out on the street. Might put her in the chicken coop, though…

She tried to keep all that in mind. What she knew about Adam. How he was when they were together. But the fact that her future now depended on him… She closed her eyes against the panic that sent her head spinning.

Then she looked around, her frantic gaze taking in the pitying looks of those surrounding her, and she straightened her backbone. She wouldn't let them see her fall apart. She spared one glance for her father and, for a brief second, hoped he'd pull one of his disappearing acts—and not return.

She didn't mean it. She closed her eyes again, her hand pressing against her stomach in an effort to keep it from revolting. *I didn't mean it*. She loved her father. But what she wouldn't give to see him at least pull together a shred of the dignity he once possessed and walk out of there with her. So she didn't have to walk alone. Having just lost everything.

But he was too far gone to even notice she stood there.

Sweet angels in heaven, ever since her mother had died, he'd done nothing but make their lives more difficult than necessary. Drinking away the profits from her seamstress jobs. Being little to no help at home or with her business. Being forgetful, belligerent, embarrassing. But he had never done something so outright destructive before. Even with all their hardships in the past, she'd at least had some hope for the future.

Was this because of Adam? Because she'd married him, brought him into their home? Was being so blasé with their property her father's way of getting revenge? If so, he'd chosen well.

They didn't have much, but their small homestead was everything to her. Without it, she had nothing. No home, no place to work, no means to support herself, let alone her father.

She turned her furious eyes toward Adam. Deep down, she knew it wasn't his fault. Not really. Her father was the one who put up their home, and if it hadn't been Adam who'd won, someone else would have. But at that exact moment, she didn't care. All she could think of was that her home, her livelihood, her security…it was all gone. All her plans ruined. Because of *him*.

He stared back at her, but not with pity like the others. She couldn't read the expression on his face. She didn't even want to try and guess what he was thinking. But at least he didn't look at her like she was some helpless puppy who'd just been kicked.

She closed her eyes for another moment and then turned to leave.

"Nora...wait," he said, trying to stop her.

She didn't listen but pushed her way through the crowd and out into the street. He followed her, reaching out to grasp her arm.

She shook him off. "Don't touch me."

He held up his hands. "You've got to let me explain. I didn't plan any of this. I know you're upset, but—"

"You have no idea what I'm feeling right now. And don't pretend you care."

His jaw dropped with a pained grunt, like he'd just been socked in the gut. "How can you say that? After everything we've shared...do you really believe that?"

She slapped her hands over her face to muffle her scream of frustration, and then she dropped them, rounding on him. "I don't know what to believe anymore! Being with you has been...it's been..."

His face grew hard, the muscles of his jaw popping. "It's been what, Nora? A mistake? Is that what you were going to say?"

Her eyes searched his and her shoulders sank. She couldn't regret what they'd done. No matter what. "No. It wasn't a mistake."

His gaze locked with hers and held for a long moment before he nodded. "All right, then. Let's go home. We can talk there, away from prying eyes," he said, jerking his head at where most of the town were pressed against the windows and doors of the tavern not bothering to pretend that they weren't eavesdropping.

She didn't answer but followed him as he rounded up their horses. They rode home in silence.

Once they were inside the house, he tried to pull her into his arms, but she kept her body stiff and unyielding. She also didn't pull away.

He sighed. "I know what this looks like, but ending up with that deed wasn't my intention. I'll swear it on anything you wish. But if it hadn't been me, it would have been someone else," he said, echoing her own thoughts.

She scowled and folded her arms, refusing to meet his eye.

He tugged her closer. "I was just trying to help."

She choked out a laugh. "Really? Winning all of my father's money—"

"That he'd most likely stolen from you in the first place."

She ignored that, though he wasn't wrong. "And taking the deed to our home is you helping? I'd hate to see what it looks like when you aren't being so *helpful*."

He grimaced. "Yeah, I know it doesn't sound great, but yes, I was actually trying to make sure that he would walk away from the table with something in his pocket. I purposely lost nearly every hand I had. And it worked. All he had to do was take the money and walk away."

She folded her arms and glared at him. "Right. But instead, you walked away with everything and we're left with nothing."

"How are you left with nothing? You're my wife,

Nora. What's mine is yours."

She shook her head. "That's not how it works. What's yours is yours and what's mine is yours. And I'm left with nothing whether you intended it or not."

He threw his hands up. "If what's yours is mine, then this property would have been mine anyway, if our marriage was legal. If you were trying to prevent that so hard, then why insist on marrying me?"

She groaned out her frustration. "Because you weren't ever supposed to know about it!"

He raised his brows, understanding dawning on his face. "Ah."

"That's not… I mean it's not quite…"

"It's not what it looks like?" he asked, echoing his own argument.

She sighed and sank onto the couch. "I knew my father would end up doing something like this. I won't gain control of the property until I'm thirty. I was pretty sure he'd gamble it away, or outright sell it, long before that. In order to claim it before that, I had to marry. But…"

"But that would put the property under the control of your husband."

She nodded. "Unless I could find someone so opposed to the idea of marriage that it would be fairly easy to run him off once the deed was in my name."

"And the poor bastard would be none the wiser."

She just looked at him, guilt and shame twisting in her gut along with her anger. She shouldn't have to feel guilty about any of this. What choice was there if she wanted any hope of having something of her own, something some man couldn't take away from her when the mood struck him?

He didn't say anything for a moment, just took a deep breath and blew it back out, scrubbing his hand over his face. "We aren't going to figure all this out tonight. At least the issue with the deed. With our ambiguous legal status, all my issues, and everything else piling up against us…I just don't know what we'll do about it yet." He shook his head, his face drawn with regret. "We both know if I return the property, he'll just do this again."

She sighed. "I'll hide the deed. He won't even know I have it back. I can make sure that this doesn't happen again."

"Nora." He cocked an eyebrow. "You weren't able to stop it tonight."

His voice had been quiet, kind even. But it still sent a bolt of anger flashing through her. He wasn't wrong…and that just made her even angrier. She shook her head, too furious and upset to articulate anything else. Though it was less with him personally than the situation as a whole.

"I did, however, always intend on giving any winnings from the game back to you," he said, and a small spark of hope flared in her chest. "Here." He thrust a handkerchief full of coins at her. "It's everything he lost and then some. I would suggest finding a very good hiding place."

She stared at the bundle in her hand, surprised at the heft of it. There was a good amount of money in there. Enough to keep her from needing to panic too hard just yet. Over money, at least.

"Thank you," she said. She took a deep, shuddering breath and slowly let it all out. There was nothing more she could do about the situation tonight. And she was too exhausted to want to try, anyway.

"Is it your intention to turn me out of my home?" she asked.

The shock of the suggestion was clear on his face. "Of course not," he said, his eyes dimming with a lingering hurt. "Why would you ever think that?"

She gave him a slight smile, choking back the guilt that those pain-filled eyes of his sent skittering through her. "I thought you might want to give me a taste of my own medicine now that you hold the deed. I hear the chicken coop is newly renovated and mighty comfy."

His lips twitched. "Come here," he said, drawing her into his arms. "The only place you'll be sleeping is in our bed, right next to me."

She nodded and let him pull her close, keeping her gaze locked with his until his eyes started to blur. "Good," she said. And then she laid her head on his shoulder and let the tears flow.

When she'd cried herself out, he tucked her into bed, taking such gentle care of her that her heart ached. When he finally settled in beside her, she turned to him, pressing her body against him.

"Are you sure?" he asked. "After what happened, I didn't think—"

She stopped him with a kiss. "I don't want to think about that tonight. I don't want to think about any of it. Take my mind off it. Make it all go away, even if just for a few hours."

His fingers brushed across her cheek, and he stared into her eyes, searching. Whatever he'd seen must have convinced him, because he didn't speak again. He just leaned in and captured her lips.

He kissed her slowly, tenderly, until her head swam with the emotion of it. But that wasn't what she wanted just then. There had been too much of it already that night. If he kept being so lovingly kind, she'd never be able to hold it together.

She needed heat. Passion. Needed him to erase everything else in her head and leave nothing but mind-altering pleasure.

She threaded her hands through his hair, tugging just hard enough to break the kiss, and pushed him toward her breasts. When his lips closed over a tight peak, she threw her head back with a gasp.

Yes! This was what she needed. That fire he created within her to burn her up until there was nothing left. She arched under him, trying to bring him closer, make him suck harder. He growled low in his throat, and the reverberation sent tremors through her body.

He nipped and licked his way back up her throat, drawing her earlobe between his teeth just as he wrapped his arms around her and flipped them so she was on top, straddling him.

He sat up, keeping her locked to him. "Take what you need from me, darlin'."

She froze for a second, not sure…

His hands gripped her ass, and he hauled her closer, fitting them together. He took her hand and drew it down between them, wrapping her hand around him so he could help her guide him into her slick, wet heat.

She took over, sinking onto him until every hard, aching inch was seated deep inside. And then she wrapped her arms around his neck, pressing her body to his so there wasn't a breath of air left between them, and she began to move.

"That's it, darlin'," he said. "Take what you need. Make yourself feel good. Nothing else matters but this. Us."

She tried to breathe, tried to keep her movements controlled, but he growled at her again and fisted a hand in her hair, tugging to bring her face back to his. "You're thinking too hard. Dammit, Nora, just let yourself feel."

Then he ground his lips against hers and finally, finally she lost control.

She kissed and sucked and licked and rocked on him, moving with him until she didn't know where one began and the other ended, and she didn't care as long as the fire building in her continued to burn, incinerating everything between them but this. This was all that mattered. There was nothing else. No one else. No jobs or licenses or betrayals or plans or anything but that moment and the earth-shattering pleasure that built between them, wiping everything else clean.

And when that exquisite pressure finally exploded, it carried them both away until they were left trembling in each other's arms.

She drew in a shuddering breath and buried her face in his neck, keeping her body molded to his for as long as she could.

"Don't let me go," she murmured against his skin, not sure if she meant just for that moment or forever. Nor did she know what he meant when he whispered back, "Never."

# CHAPTER TWENTY-NINE

Adam tossed and turned most of the night, so when the sun rose bright and early the next morning, he greeted it with relief. Nora still slumbered by his side, the dark circles beneath her eyes gouging a hole in his heart. He slipped out of bed as quietly as he could, taking care to tuck the blankets firmly around her. She needed sleep. And he needed to think.

He let his mind wander as he went about the morning chores, collecting eggs and checking on the gardens. The post on the south fence line seemed a bit wobbly, so he went back to the barn to grab his bucket of nails and a hammer, taking his time about it as he got to work. Helping out around the house was the least he could do. If he could fix everything else for her, he would. How he could do that, though? He had no idea.

What he wanted to do was find Preacher, sign the damn marriage license, and do whatever he needed to do to get the deed to her land in Nora's name before her father came back to finish destroying her life.

It wasn't just the danger doing that would present to him that stopped him. Filing a marriage license and whatever paperwork needed to be arranged for the deed would alert his enemies to not only his location but also the fact that he had a weakness. A wife who could be exploited. Used to get to him.

He'd done enough damage to her life. He wouldn't bring his enemies to her door as well.

But if he didn't make everything legal, Nora had no security. Not even any respectability if she were to venture anywhere other than Desolation. Their marriage wasn't legal, but they were cohabitating. Fornicating. Frequently. Fabulously.

He couldn't keep the smile from his face at that thought, even though he wanted to kick himself for it. But damn, that woman was a walking dream come true. He'd never thought he'd be one for marriage. Hence his number one rule to avoid it at all costs. But then he'd never imagined that Nora was out there somewhere. A woman who wasn't afraid to call him on his shit and poor decisions and then turn around and help him fix them. Who could hold her own against anyone who went up against her. A woman he could count on to have his back and mean it. Maybe he shouldn't worry so much about his enemies finding him. Nora would probably make quick work of them and still find time to accomplish half a dozen other tasks by lunch.

She was also built for fierce loving, with mile-long legs that were made to wrap around him. He was starting to regret his decision to get out of bed so early when she was still warming the sheets.

He dropped his hammer in the bucket and turned to go back to the house. Then he ducked, jerking his body to the left just as a fist came flying at his face.

Mr. Schumacher stood there panting and raised his fists again. Adam didn't think he was still drunk, but he was definitely the worse for wear.

Adam glared at him. "I'm not going to fight you."

"Afraid to get beat by an old man?" he sneered, swinging again. Adam easily dodged him.

"I think we both know that isn't the case."

"Then what is it?" He swung again. But this time Adam caught his fist and held on tight.

"It would upset Nora. And one of us in this yard actually cares for her enough to make sure he doesn't do anything to make an already hard situation even worse for her."

All the fight went out of Mr. Schumacher, and he dropped his fist. "You took everything from me."

"No, I didn't, Mr. Schumacher. You gave it all away."

He just stared at Adam for a moment, his chest heaving. Then his shoulders slumped, and he turned, beaten, and walked away.

It wasn't Adam's fault. He knew it. But he still couldn't help the guilt that crept through him. Maybe he should have just kept his nose out of it. But he had to go and do it again. Try to help, and instead make an asinine decision that did nothing but make everyone's life worse. Like when he'd tried to help a certain nameless gunfighter gain a reputation for himself—thinking it was what every man wanted—and unknowingly destroyed his life instead.

When was he going to learn that his "help" never did anyone any good? All he could do now was hope that something turned out right, at least for the one who deserved it most.

• • •

Adam hammered the last nail into the board and gave the shelf a good tug. Solid as an oak tree. He was getting fairly good with the carpentry stuff. Perhaps

Mr. Vernice shouldn't have been so quick to fire him.

"That looks great, Adam, thanks," Sunshine said, admiring the shelf that he'd just hung.

Adam tried not to let the praise go to his head. It was just a shelf. But he was ridiculously proud of his fledgling skills, so he gave Sunshine a heartfelt thanks.

He put up his tools and then came out to join Sunshine on the walkway in front of the sheriff's office and jailhouse. It was situated right in the middle of town with Doc's clinic beside it and the tavern, boardinghouse, and general store directly across from it. Most of the action in town happened here. It was a good place to set up a law enforcement station. Of which he was a part. Him. An outlawed gunslinger.

Then again, their sheriff was another such as himself, so it wasn't like he was reinventing the saddle or anything. But it was surreal, to be sure.

"So how's married life treating you, Mr. Brady?" Sunshine asked.

Adam's eyebrow shot up and he opened and closed his mouth several times before shrugging. "I don't know how to answer that question."

Sunshine laughed. "Well, now that's the first time I've heard that."

Adam gave him a half grin. "No. It's just…" He sighed. "It's a long story."

"I've got nothing but time," Sunshine said with a shrug.

Adam leaned against the wall of the jailhouse and crossed his arms. "Well, for starters, I'm not a hundred percent sure we actually are married. No one seems to know. Preacher says we're married in the eyes of God. We said 'I do.' We live together. Do…other things together. So does a piece of paper really matter that much when everything else about our union says that we're married?"

"Have you asked Preacher about it?"

"He seems just as stumped."

Sunshine nodded a few times, and then he blew out a breath. "Would you like my opinion?"

"Yes. Please."

"You and Miss Nora seem happy enough together. You said 'I do' before Preacher, so you are good with God. It wasn't all that many years ago, a church wedding was all folks out here needed. So I don't see that the government adding some extra paperwork makes that much difference. If you are good with God and happy with each other, who cares what anyone else thinks? Do what makes you happy, Mr. Brady."

Adam blinked at him, the sheer brilliant simplicity of that echoing through him.

"Sunshine, you may have just solved a very large, complicated problem that I had twisted all out of proportion with a very simple, perfect solution."

Sunshine beamed at him. "I aim to please."

Adam pushed away from the wall. "Do you have anything else for me to do for a while?"

Sunshine shook his head, knowing before Adam even asked what he wanted. "I don't have any immediate tasks if you'd like to head on home for the afternoon."

"Mr. Sunshine, you're a saint."

"Be sure to tell the sheriff that. I just know he'll love to hear it," Sunshine said, laughing so hard his face turned red as he waved Adam off.

Adam hurried across the street to the general store first. Nora had mentioned stopping by there later to pick up a few supplies that Martha had ordered for her.

Martha just chuckled when he asked for Nora's order. "I'll be seeing her in just a few minutes for our weekly lunch, but if you want to take her order now, it's all ready for her." She indicated a basket at the end of the counter. "Tell her I tucked in that bonnet and dress from Mrs. Riley that needed altering. Ach, never mind, I'll tell her myself. Now shoo, I've got to get the rest of this order put away before I can head over to Mrs. DuVere's."

Adam nodded his thanks, gathered up the basket, and stepped back outside. He sucked in a lungful of clean, crisp air, feeling optimistic for the first time in a long time. He and Nora were going to sit down and have a long overdue conversation. Spill everything. No more secrets. No more hidden agendas. He wanted her. And if she wanted him as well, that's all he needed to know. They could work the rest out. Together.

Now all he needed was his damn horse…

He frowned, looking at the front of the sheriff's office where he'd left Barnaby that morning. And the horse had been there a few minutes before when he'd gone into the general store. But now…

He glanced down the street and shook his head with an amused snort.

"What is it?" Martha asked, following his gaze. "Ah," she said with a laugh. "I don't think you'll be going anywhere just yet. At least with Barnaby."

She was right. Because Barnaby was currently

busy trying to get Birdie's attention in front of Mrs. DuVere's. But as Birdie was in the middle of her midmorning nap, he was going to have to wait a bit.

"Oh well, it's a nice day for a wal—"

He jerked to a stop, his arm shooting out to grab Martha and pull her behind a porch post with him.

"What are you doing?" she squeaked.

"Shh," Adam said, peeking out from behind the post, his gaze focused on a gentleman who was slowly riding into town, his eyes scanning the street from side to side.

Adam cursed and swung back around to the store, which was locked. "Open the door. Quick, Martha, quick!"

"What is wrong with you?" she said, scrambling with her keys as she hastily unlocked the door.

The second it was open, he swept them both inside and slammed the door shut, relocking it and making sure the sign in the window showed Closed.

"You see that man," he said, keeping his voice low, though the man outside couldn't hear them.

She looked through the window where he pointed. "Yes, so?"

"So, that is Marshal Robert Spurlock."

"Really?" She pressed closer to the glass. "I've heard of him. People say he's worse than the criminals he hunts down." She sucked in a breath and glanced over at Adam. "Is he here for you?"

Adam nodded. "I assume so. Though I imagine since there's still a price on the sheriff's head, Spurlock would be happy with either of us. And probably a few other men in town."

Martha cursed under her breath, and Adam

looked at her with surprise. It was always the sweetest ones in the bunch who had the most impressive vocabularies.

"Come on," she said, grabbing his arm and hauling him toward the back of the store. "Out the back. And bring the basket," she said over her shoulder.

They wound their way through her kitchen, but she stopped before pulling the back door open, turning to grab the basket from his arms. She quickly rummaged through it and pulled out the skirt and petticoat to the dress Nora was going to alter.

"Take off your coat and vest and put that on," she instructed, opening the door a crack to peer through it. "Hurry."

He pulled his coat off. "This isn't going to fool him."

"It doesn't need to for long. We'll stick to the alleyway as much as possible, but a flash of skirt out of the corner of his eye will be easier to dismiss when he's looking for a man."

Good point. He yanked the skirt on over his pants and took off his hat, slapping the bonnet on his head.

Martha glanced back at him, opened her mouth to say something, and then just shook her head. "Let's go," she whispered.

They just needed to get to Mrs. DuVere's, which was thankfully only two doors down. But with Spurlock riding the streets, it was going to be a harrowing few minutes.

"Wait," he said, yanking on her arm to keep her behind the building.

"What?"

"You need to go to the sheriff's office. Make sure

he knows Spurlock is in town. He's in just as much danger. I'll get to Mrs. DuVere's and let Nora and Mercy know what's going on."

Martha nodded. "Be careful," she said, then turned to go back inside the store. Good thinking. It would look much less suspicious if she exited from the front of the store than skulking around the back alleyway. Like he was doing.

No help for it, though. He had to get to Nora, and his disguise definitely wouldn't stand up to any scrutiny.

He stayed to the back of the buildings for as long as possible and then darted up the alley between the two buildings, hurrying along the walkway as unobtrusively as he could, though he drew more than a few glances.

He'd almost made it to Mrs. DuVere's when his toe caught on the hem of his skirt, and he lurched forward. His attempt at yanking the material out of the way only succeeded in it tangling around his legs. A few choice curses left his lips as he stumbled again. He might as well just stand in the middle of the road and use the skirt to flag Spurlock down for all the good it was doing him. How a person was supposed to move about at all in the blasted thing was beyond him. He finally gathered up both sides of the voluminous frockery and near ran to Mrs. DuVere's. He had to get inside before his disguise did him in.

Nora was just entering the parlor house when he got to the front door, and he grabbed her and pushed her inside, his skirts swinging.

# CHAPTER THIRTY

Nora squealed, but Adam clamped his hand over her mouth until they were behind closed doors.

She lightly slapped at his arm, and he let her go.

"What do you think you are doing?" she asked, not giving him the courtesy of answering before she pummeled him for manhandling her. "Never mind that, what are you wearing?" Her eyes widened as she looked him over.

"What are *you* wearing?" he asked, his eyes raking over the blue dress that hugged her breasts but left the rest of her body hidden beneath its layers.

He seemed to like what he saw, though she hoped he wouldn't get too attached to her dressing this way. She did enjoy wearing her dresses when the skirts weren't going to interfere with her work. Afternoon teas with her friends were always a good occasion to gussy up a bit. But her trousers were definitely more suited to the harder labor she needed to do most days. Skirts just tangled around her long legs and made a nuisance of themselves.

"I miss your trousers," he said, and she chuckled. "Although…" He gathered a handful of her skirts and lifted them slightly. "This definitely has its possibilities."

She slapped his hand away and rolled her eyes. "That's not why I'm wearing this. Behave yourself."

"Why are you wearing it?"

Her lips quirked up. "I do wear dresses from time to time."

"Well, yes, but—"

"*You*, however, do not that I'm aware of. What is this?" she asked, gesturing up and down to him.

"Martha let me borrow Mrs. Riley's skirt."

Nora frowned. "The one I'm supposed to alter?"

"Yes. She—" Adam snorted. "Damn, woman, only you could distract me from something like this."

He yanked off the bonnet while he turned the lock on the door and went to peer through the curtain.

"Something like what?" she asked again, not bothering to hide her impatience. "I swear, if you don't start talking…"

"Remember when I said I was afraid that one of these days my past would catch up with me?" He turned to look at her, all amusement gone from his face, and her stomach dropped.

"Yes," she managed to choke out, though she already knew what he was going to say.

"It just rode into town, looking for me." He glanced behind him where Mrs. DuVere and Mercy stood watching them with wide eyes. "And he'll be looking for Woodson, too."

"What?" Mercy said, taking a step toward him.

Adam stood stoic under the weight of her furious stare, and Nora moved closer, ready to intervene. Oh, she understood the overwhelming desire to hurt the man. She felt it herself. Frequently. And most certainly at that moment. But, if necessary, she'd step in to defend him.

"Only if he finds out Woodson is here. I sent

Martha to the jailhouse to warn him," he said, trying to calm Mercy's obvious rising fear. "And Spurlock won't specifically be looking for him. He's here for me. Most people outside of this town assume Woodson is dead, so as long as he stays out of sight, he should be fine."

"And if this man does see him?" she asked, her voice low and tight.

Adam pursed his lips together like he didn't want to answer. He didn't need to answer, really. They all knew already. But he voiced it anyway. "There's still a price on his head. And Spurlock would love nothing more than to bring in the legendary Quick Shot."

Mercy took a step toward him, fury radiating off her. "And you brought this man here? He is here hunting *you*?"

Adam nodded, and Nora briefly closed her eyes against the onslaught of terror that threatened to overwhelm her.

Mercy's hands curved into claws, and Nora stepped between them, choking back her panic.

"Everyone, *stop*. We need to think. We can throttle him once everyone is safe," she said to Mercy, who blinked at her like she was coming out of a fog.

Nora relaxed a little when Mercy took a deep breath and stepped back.

"All right. So. We need to keep Adam and the sheriff out of sight and get this man out of town as fast as possible."

Mrs. DuVere folded her arms. "He won't find a place to sleep, I'll see to that, so if he wants to stay in the area, he'll have to camp outside town."

Nora nodded. "Good."

There was a brief ruckus at the back door that had them all turning, poised to fight, until the sheriff and Sunshine came marching in. Mercy flew to her husband with a little cry, and he wrapped his arms around her, murmuring something in her ear before moving farther into the room.

Nora stepped closer to Adam, ready to intervene if the sheriff threatened him. Adam put his arm around her waist and pulled her close, giving her a smile that tore at her heart. It didn't escape her notice that he put her a little behind him, keeping his body between her and any possible threat.

Sunshine glanced down at the skirt Adam still wore and pursed his lips, nodding appreciatively. "Pretty."

He flashed a brilliant grin. "Thanks. It has pockets! It's a bit too long though. I keep tripping over the damn—"

"Would you take that off before you rip it to shreds?" Nora asked, holding her hand out. "Mrs. Riley is expecting to get this back in better condition that it was. Not worse."

Adam gave her an apologetic smile while quickly untying the skirt and handing it to her. "Sorry," he muttered.

The back door closed again, and after a few moments, Doc and Preacher came in. They looked around the room, visibly relaxing to see everyone there.

"Glad you're all in one piece," Doc said, moving closer to Martha. "Someone said they spotted Adam running down the street in a skirt, and our interest was piqued."

Adam grimaced. "I wasn't running."

Sunshine laughed, and the mood lightened. Somewhat.

The sheriff turned to Adam. "Am I correct in assumin' the stranger who just rode through town is lookin' for you?" He didn't wait for Adam to agree. "Do I know him? Or, I should say, does he know me?"

Adam nodded, and Nora leaned against him, offering what support she could. Because she knew what came next was not going to go over well.

"Marshal Robert Spurlock."

The sheriff froze, his face tightening until he looked like he was carved from stone, save for the muscle that ticked in his jaw. He started pushing Mercy away from him, and Nora had the sudden realization that they were about to find out which of the gunslingers in the room was the fastest.

Mrs. DuVere stepped between them. "The first man who puts a bullet hole in my wall is going to be prying my dainty booted foot out of his ass. Am I clear?"

Both men scowled, but the tension between them dissipated somewhat, and she jerked her head in a sharp nod. "Good. Then let's move this upstairs," she suggested. "We obviously have some things that need discussing, and there's no need to do it down here where anyone might come through the door."

Nora sagged against Adam, relieved that his imminent death had been averted. For the moment. Of course, they still had a lot to talk about, and the sheriff wasn't known to be the most lenient man. And that was when he wasn't provoked. But for the moment, at least, he seemed willing to let Adam have his say.

Once they were situated upstairs, the sheriff pierced Adam with a glare. "Talk."

• • •

Adam's gut twisted, but the time for hemmin' and hawin' was over. He needed to come clean. About everything.

"I first came across Spurlock a year ago. There's a warrant out for me, but even still, I wouldn't normally be a case that interested him. He likes a challenge. Likes to bring in the notorious ones. The big names."

"Like Quick Shot?" Mercy said, her anger barely under control.

Adam hesitated a second before nodding.

"So why's he after you?" Woodson asked. "No offense, Brady, but you're small potatoes to a man like Spurlock."

"True." Adam wasn't offended in the slightest. He *was* small potatoes and wanted to keep it that way. "He didn't set out for me. He just sort of stumbled across me one night in a saloon just outside Denver. One of the men I'd beat in a card game decided to take his revenge by letting Spurlock know there was a warrant out for me. He must have figured he might as well, since I was there. Easy pickin's."

"Except?" Woodson said.

Adam gave him a small smile. "I'm not easy. And I'm good at getting out of sticky situations."

"So you got away from him before he could bring you in."

Adam nodded. "Spurlock is like a dog with a bone. He doesn't quit. And he has some sort of personal vendetta against me now for daring to escape from him the first time. I've managed to stay ahead of him so far. But no matter where I went, how careful I was, he'd find me. The last time, I got out only minutes before he arrived."

"And yet you came to my town, chose to stay," Woodson said, his voice laced with enough threat that Adam had to clench his fists to keep from reaching for his guns. But he didn't. Wouldn't have, even if Woodson had drawn on him. He'd deserve it. He put these people in danger. The people who'd taken him in. He should have left weeks ago, the moment he'd realized Woodson was there. Yet another mistake in his long history of making them.

He looked at Nora, though, his gaze taking in every inch of her. He was sorry that staying in Desolation had put his new friends in danger. But he'd never regret that it had brought him to her.

Her eyes locked with his for a moment, and she drew in a deep breath. And then turned to Woodson.

"With all due respect, Sheriff," Nora said, "you also came to this town, not so long ago, with a price that is still on your head. The only reason this lawman and others like him haven't come looking for you is because they assume you're dead. If Adam is at fault for his past putting the rest of us in danger, then so are you."

Adam sucked in a slow breath and reached over to take Nora's hand. When what he really wanted to do was wrap her in his arms and never let her go. That might have been the first time, ever, that someone had stood up for him. Even if he didn't deserve it.

Mercy, however, obviously didn't share his sentiment. She stared at her friend, horrified, before her eyes narrowed to dangerous slits. But Woodson put a hand on her shoulder and squeezed.

"It's all right, Mercy. She's not wrong."

Mercy looked like she wanted to argue, but Adam blinked at the sheriff in surprise. He completely agreed that Nora was correct in what she'd said. But he hadn't expected the sheriff to agree as well.

Nora squeezed his hand, and the sheriff continued. "I came to this town with a past that was hunting me. And almost immediately made another enemy who threatened the town. I haven't forgotten. We all came here to escape our pasts. So I won't fault you for that, Brady. However," he said—Adam had known there'd be a however coming. "I specifically remember telling you that you better not bring trouble to my town. You could have warned us before what hunted you was already here, breathing down our necks."

Adam nodded, but Nora was shaking her head. "There was no way he could have known this man would find him. And I'm sure he would have told us, at least me, I'd hope, eventually. He hasn't even been here a full month. Who of us here rode into town and immediately announced all our secrets to anyone who'd listen?"

He put a soothing hand on the back of her neck, lightly massaging it. His heart was so full that she cared enough about him to defend him, to Gray

Woodson of all people, that Spurlock could march in and shoot him right then and he'd die a happy man.

"None of us knows everything about everyone," Preacher said, and Adam's heart swelled even more. "That's one of the perks of this town."

Doc nodded. "It's unfortunate that this man has found him, but I don't think any one of us sitting here can truly cast stones."

Adam leaned forward. "Thank you. All of you. And for what it's worth, I am truly sorry it has come to this. I didn't ride into this town knowingly putting anyone else in danger. Hell, Woodson, you being here would have actually made me steer clear of this place if I'd known about it. I've spent years avoiding you," he said with a small grin at his old enemy.

Woodson snorted, but his wife still didn't look inclined to forgive him.

"Yes," Mercy said. "But once you realized Gray was here…"

Adam nodded, clenching his jaw. "I should have left, yes."

"I guarantee Adam isn't the only one at this table who might find himself staring down the barrel of his past one day," Nora said, pinning them all with a pointed look, "and it certainly isn't the first time that this town was in danger because of one us. But we protect one another. So instead of casting blame, I think our time would be better spent coming up with a solution."

"Agreed," Preacher said, nodding. "And the easiest solution would probably be to kill this Spurlock."

Adam's gaze jerked to the preacher, who was the

last one Adam would have suspected of the most bloodthirsty solution. But the man was already frowning and shaking his head before anyone could say anything else. "However, since we can't be sure whom he told about coming here, that could look too suspicious."

"Though we do already have a hole dug," Mrs. DuVere chimed in, with a wink at Adam. "Several, in fact. But I'm sure we can think of something. Perhaps if we made sure he was found far from town, it would avert suspicion?"

They discussed a few other options, discarding most as too problematic as they were dealing with a lawman, not just a regular bounty hunter. Listening to them, Adam sat stunned that these people—or most of them, anyway; Mercy was still glaring daggers at him—would be willing to go to such lengths to protect him, and Woodson, of course. And while he was touched beyond measure, he just couldn't let them do it. Not if there was a way to keep them all from danger.

Adam took a deep breath. "There's nothing to discuss. I already have a solution."

Everyone turned to him with polite attention. Everyone but Nora.

Whether she saw it in his face or heard it in his voice, he didn't know. He wouldn't have thought it possible for two people to understand each other so completely in the little time they'd known each other. But somehow, they did.

She was already shaking her head, her eyes stark in her pale face. "No," she whispered.

"I'm going to find him and give myself up."

# CHAPTER THIRTY-ONE

There was a general uproar while everyone spoke at once, saying why they were for or against Adam's plan, but Nora barely heard them. She didn't speak. Neither did Adam. They just sat and stared at each other while everyone around them debated options.

Finally, she sat back, putting some distance between them. And she shook her head again. "You are not giving yourself up."

The rest of the chatter quieted down, but she and Adam continued to stare at each other.

"It's the only way," he said.

She dragged in a breath through her nose and tried to remain calm. "No, it's not."

"Yes. It is."

She stood up, leaning forward a bit as she spoke. "*No*, it's not."

"I can do this all night, Nora. Yes, it is."

She gritted her teeth so hard, she was sure they'd crack, then let out a growl of frustration. She'd never met someone who made her want to literally tear her hair out, and beat them with it, until just then. "Would you stop being such a stubborn, bullheaded—"

"*Me?* If that's not the cow patty calling the co—"

"Don't you start that with me! You haven't even listened to the other options."

He jumped up from his seat and leaned in toward her until they were almost nose to nose. "Because there are none."

"Yes, there are!"

He threw his hands up. "Like what?"

"We leave."

He frowned and moved back a little. "What do you mean, we?"

"It's not that difficult of a word. You. Me. *We*. We pack the wagon and leave. Tonight."

His mouth opened and closed a few times, like he was trying to say something but kept discarding whatever was coming out. Finally, he gripped the back of the chair hard enough his knuckles turned white and shook his head.

"Absolutely not. The only reason we met in the first place is because you were fighting so hard to save your home. I'm not going to ask you to leave it now."

"You aren't asking me. I'm informing you."

"No, Nora. I can't let you do that."

"You don't get to decide what I do and don't do."

"I could use the same argument against you. I've made my decision. It has to be this way."

She slammed her hands on the table. "No, it doesn't! Stop trying to be a martyr!"

"Stop trying to be a saint!"

Mrs. DuVere leaned in, saying, "Why don't we all take a minute—"

But they both turned to her, glaring until she backed up. "Or not."

Nora swung back to Adam. "Why? Why is giving yourself up the only way?"

He sighed, sounding like it was being pulled from the bottom of his weary bones. "Because if I don't,

Spurlock will just keep hunting. I told you, he doesn't give up. And if I just leave, he won't move on until he's searched every corner of this town. That didn't matter in the other towns I was in. It *does* matter here." He looked at the sheriff, who was watching him with a steady gaze. "He won't stop until he's got someone in custody. And I won't let anyone else suffer my consequences. It's gotta be me."

Nora stepped back and then dropped into her chair, the fight draining out of her. Everyone else started talking again, offering up a few suggestions that wouldn't work. She just watched Adam. And he watched her.

The thing she hated the most was that he wasn't wrong. What he was suggesting *was* the best course of action. Well, actually, she thought killing Spurlock was the most efficient thing to do. But a bit morally gray and definitely illegal. Not that the whole legal thing had ever given anyone in this town pause.

"All right, all right!" the sheriff said, rubbing at his temples again. "I don't think anyone needs to run off half-cocked, fully loaded, or any other which way. As far as we know, Spurlock doesn't know for sure that Brady is in town. He hasn't seen him, and while it's possible someone gave him up, it's unlikely. And as far as we know, he has no idea I still exist. And I see no reason to remedy that. So as long as we both lay low, chances are pretty good he'll just move along and go search some other town."

Everyone nodded, murmuring their agreement. Well, almost everyone. Adam still sat, stone-faced but calm. Like he'd already made his decision.

The sheriff seemed to think the same thing, because he pinned Adam with his impressively terrifying stare. "If you simply cannot help yourself and insist on takin' some form of action, I'd highly recommend you just leave town. Turnin' yourself over to this man would be suicide. I'm sure you've heard the rumors as well as I have, but the vast majority of Spurlock's captures are on the dead side of 'dead or alive.' He seems to pride himself on it. So don't be a damn fool and sacrifice your life just to make yourself feel better."

Adam's lips pulled into a half grin, and he nodded. But Nora didn't think he was actually agreeing.

A small, miserable part of her wondered why he was so insistent on turning himself in. Because the sheriff was right. There was no reason to assume this man had any certain knowledge of Adam's where-abouts. And even less chance he knew of the sheriff's. He had no authority to go searching through houses—and there were more than a few hidey-holes spread across the town if it came to that. And this was Desolation. No one in this town would be traitorous enough to betray them.

So why? Was this some last-resort effort to escape their marriage? Did he want to get away from her so badly?

She tried to push the thought away. After all the moments they'd shared recently, she couldn't reconcile the man who held her so tenderly, came to her with such passion, with one who wanted to quit her presence so desperately that he'd turn himself over to his enemy.

Or just say he was going to...when he really

meant to simply disappear.

If he really thought the best course of action was to leave, then why wouldn't he want her with him? She'd offered to go, and she'd meant it. Yes, she loved her home. But she loved *him* more.

She froze, not blinking, not even breathing until her lungs burned so badly she had to suck in a breath. She *loved* him. When it had happened, she didn't know. Didn't need to know. The when wouldn't change the fact of it. That he'd burrowed his way into her heart, and nothing short of her death, and probably not even that, would dislodge him.

She loved the stubborn, aggravating, wickedly wonderful pain in the ass.

And it didn't matter a lick. He'd rejected her offer. His reasons seemed selfless, but it still felt like a rejection of *her*.

She shoved the thoughts away. Adam had done nothing to warrant them. Still, a lifetime of others treating her so made it more difficult than she would have liked.

Always the friend, never the lover. That was her.

And she'd been fine with that. Not content but… accepting. Until Adam had come along and changed everything. The thought that none of it had been real was too painful to contemplate.

But the nagging thought wouldn't leave her mind.

• • •

Doc and Preacher smuggled them to Nora's place in the back of the wagon. No one wanted to take the chance that Spurlock would spot them riding home.

They drove the wagon right into the barn, and Nora and Adam didn't get out until the doors had closed behind them.

Doc and Preacher helped unhitch the horses and then left.

Nora hadn't said a word since they'd left the others. Probably for the best. Because he could feel everything she wanted to say seething from her. He wished he could say something that would make it all better. Wished more than anything he could accept her offer, let her come with him. But he couldn't, *wouldn't* let her sacrifice everything she'd worked so hard for just because the consequences of his poor choices had finally caught up to him. This was his burden. He would not let her carry it.

He followed her into the house, his eyes darting all over the property, making sure everything looked as it should. Nothing appeared wrong. But everything *felt* wrong. He tried to shake the feeling. The last thing he wanted to do was go shooting at shadows.

The darkness of the house when he entered fit his mood, but it made him even edgier. Until his eyes met Nora's where she stood waiting for him in the middle of the kitchen. She didn't say anything, instead taking his hand and leading him up the stairs to her room, closing the door behind them.

She placed her hands on his chest, staring into his eyes. And he broke. He cupped her face, his thumb tracing the contours of her cheeks, her lips. She closed the short distance between them, brushing her mouth across his in a kiss so sweet, it cracked his heart wide open.

His fingers delved into her hair, and he kissed her, slow and deep, showing her without words everything that she meant to him. She drew him toward the bed, never breaking the kiss while they shed their clothes. He sank to the bed, and she straddled him, sinking down onto him while he wrapped his arms around her waist and buried his face in her neck. She held him close while she moved, her breath hitching. Though he didn't know if it was from pleasure or heartache.

Every movement was exquisite torture, wringing every last drop of ecstasy from his body while his heart screamed in agony.

How could he walk away from this woman? How could he stay?

All he could do was hold on to her while she loved him. Hold on tight while he showed her with every brush of his lips, every caress of his hand, every thrust of his body how much she meant to him. He memorized every shudder, every breath, every touch. Burned every second onto his soul so that later, when he was miserable and alone, he could think back and remember how he'd been happy once.

This...*this* moment was what he'd see when he closed his eyes for the last time. Her face as her climax overcame her. Her eyes, drowsy with sated bliss and love, though she'd never said the words. This. This was all he'd ever searched for in life. To realize it so late, to find it when he must lose it, was surely the cruelest punishment the universe could have dealt him.

Afterward, he held her close, his body wrapped

around hers, their breath mingling, until she fell into an exhausted sleep. He held her for as long as he could, for as long as he dared.

And then he pulled the blankets around her and slid from the bed. He dressed hastily, gathered his things. Pausing, he stood over the bed, watching her sleep. He needed to leave, now, before she woke. But he couldn't make himself move.

Adam didn't know if he'd be able to find Spurlock, but he'd been riding south the last time they'd seen him. If Adam traveled that direction, doing what he could to make himself as visible as possible, hopefully Spurlock would find him. And this would all be over. And Nora would be safe.

Walking away from her would be the hardest thing he ever did. Compared to that, prison, or even execution, would be easy. And he would die a happy man, knowing his love lived.

And love her he did. Good God, he loved her so much it hurt. It startled him a little to realize it. Not just that he loved her but that he trusted her. Enough to want to risk being with her. Hell, if he had his choice, he'd sign that damn paper right then. Happily. Dive headlong into matrimony and wallow in it. With pleasure.

There were still no guarantees. But she was worth the risk.

He'd made a lot of truly horrible decisions in his life. Maybe he was getting ready to make another. But of one thing he was entirely sure—she was the one *good* decision he'd ever made. The best decision. And if he had the choice, he'd choose her all over again. Choose her sooner. Choose her forever.

Choose to keep her alive, safe.

He took a deep breath and then a step backward. And another. He gritted his teeth, a sudden fury flooding his system so thoroughly, he shook. The cruelty of losing her just as he'd found her ate at him.

Enough. He'd made his decision, and he'd stand by it.

He spun on his heel and walked out the door just as she began to stir.

• • •

Nora took a deep breath, a small smile touching her lips at that faint woodsy scent that was uniquely Adam's. She stretched, her hand reaching for him.

But his side of the bed was empty, his pillow cold.

Her eyes flew open, and she jerked upright, frantically looking about the room.

He was gone.

She cursed under her breath, throwing off the blankets so she could yank her clothes on, shoving her legs into her pants so hard, she thought they'd rip.

Of all the stubborn, foolish, reckless decisions— what the *hell* was she going to do with that man?

She knew exactly where he'd gone, what he was going to do. And she'd be damned if she was going to let him. He couldn't have made it that far.

She thrust the door open and strode through the house, outside, and toward the barn. Barnaby was gone, and she cursed again. Her horse, Teddy, thrashed his head and stamped his feet, and she tried to calm herself, not wanting to pass her panic to the poor horse.

She reached gently up to him. Heard the footstep a moment too late.

Blinding pain shot through the back of her head, and blackness claimed her vision as she fell.

# CHAPTER THIRTY-TWO

Adam had put several miles between him and the town when he spotted something in the road.

He frowned. He wasn't lucky enough for it to be Spurlock. He *was* lucky enough, however, for it to be a trap set for him. As far as he could tell, it was a person, though there was no sign of a horse, unless it had wandered into the small copse of trees lining the road. Which was a possibility, since there was also nice, sweet grass in there.

Adam took a deep breath and blew it out, his eyes scanning his surroundings, looking for anything out of the ordinary. Minus the body in the road, of course.

Finally, he nudged Barnaby closer, then kicked him into a trot when he realized what, or who, he was looking at. He dismounted and dropped down next to Nora's father.

"Mr. Schumacher?" he asked, leaning farther to make sure the man still breathed.

He did, thank God. Nora had her issues with her father, but Adam wouldn't want to have to tell her that he'd died. He ignored the spike of pain that pierced his thoughts at the reminder that he wouldn't be telling Nora anything anymore and tried to focus on her father.

Then again, maybe he would. Because he could hardly leave her father lying in a ditch.

He didn't seem to be injured, though the fumes

coming off him left little mystery as to what had started his little adventure. Adam patted at his cheeks, rousing him.

"Mr. Schumacher?"

The man groaned and blinked up at him. "Brady?"

Adam's eyes widened, more than a little surprised that Schumacher knew his name.

"Are you all right?" Adam asked.

"Aside from the fact that I apparently drank myself into a ditch? I'm fine." Schumacher grunted and rubbed at the back of his head. "What do you care?"

Adam grasped one of Schumacher's arms and helped him sit up. "Your daughter cares about you, and I care about her."

Schumacher frowned and glanced down at himself, his face twisting in disgust. "I'm not worth caring about. Just…leave me here. At least out here I can't drink." He pulled a flask from his pocket, shook it until it rattled, and tossed it aside. "I'll be better off if I stay out here. So will my daughter."

Adam just stared at him. If Schumacher was finally starting to gain a little clarity about his life, well…it was about time. However, time was something they really didn't have just then.

He leaned down and ducked under Schumacher's arm to help him to his feet. "Worth it or not, your daughter loves you. And she's going to need you, so get up."

Schumacher raised red-rimmed eyes to Adam's. "What do you mean, she's going to need me? She doesn't need anyone."

Adam snorted. "Nora is the most capable woman I've ever met in my life. But everyone needs someone, Mr. Schumacher."

"I'm no good to anyone like this."

"Are you sober?"

Mr. Schumacher took a deep breath and let it out slowly. "At the moment."

"Good. If you care about your daughter at all, try and stay that way for at least a few hours."

Schumacher glared at him. "My issues got nothin' to do with my daughter."

Adam looked at him for a hard moment before answering. "We both know that's not true."

Schumacher frowned but didn't say anything. Adam wasn't sure if he was thinking or just staring off into space. They had no time for either. He scrubbed a hand over his face. Why did nothing ever go to plan?

"Come on, let's get you home."

Schumacher glanced at him in surprise and hesitated before finally nodding. Adam sent up a quick prayer of thanks to whoever was listening. He'd had to haul Mr. Schumacher into a wagon once, and once was enough. He really didn't want to have to try and wrestle the man onto a horse when he was actually conscious.

Speaking of horses… Adam looked around, frowning. "Where is your horse?"

They spent a moment looking for his horse before it became clear that she had either run off or been stolen. Since Mr. Schumacher had no idea how he'd gotten so far out of town, he was little help.

"Barnaby can carry both of us," Adam said,

mounting and holding out a hand to help Schumacher up behind him.

The horse grunted when the man swung up. "You sure about that?"

Adam chuckled. "Not exactly. But he should be fine for a mile or two. He just likes to complain."

Schumacher barked out a quiet laugh, and they headed back toward town. It seemed there was no escape for Adam after all. Not that he wanted one.

"We've established why *I* was out here, but what are you doing out here? Last I heard, you and my daughter were hitched. You abandoning her already?"

Adam belatedly realized that putting a man who hated him at his back might not have been the wisest decision. But why break his streak now?

"No. Quite the opposite," he said. "I'm trying to protect her."

"Right. You're going to have to explain your thinkin' on that one," Schumacher said, understandably not believing him.

Adam spent the ride back into town filling Schumacher in on the whole Spurlock situation while keeping an eye out for the aforementioned devil.

Schumacher quietly snorted when he was finished. "Well, I can't say that I'm happy you did something that most likely hurt my girl." Adam could feel Schumacher sag against him, like what little fight he'd mustered had fled. "I've hurt her enough." He dragged a sharp breath in through his nose. "Still. Even if she hates me, I'm still her father. She's been through enough."

"She doesn't hate you," Adam said quietly.

"Wouldn't blame her if she did," Schumacher muttered. "Still. You're giving yourself up to keep her safe. I can admire that. Maybe you aren't so bad after all."

Adam's lips twitched. "Thanks."

They'd reached the house, and Adam pulled up suddenly, quickly dismounting and leading Barnaby behind a couple of trees that were nearby. They wouldn't hide the horse by any means, but they wouldn't be so obvious if someone from the house were to look out.

"What are you doing?" Schumacher said, sliding down from Barnaby.

"The gate to the garden is open," Adam said, keeping his voice low. "Nora would *never* leave it open. Something's wrong."

He pulled the horse farther behind the tree. "Stay here with Barnaby. I'm going to see what's going on."

Schumacher grabbed his arm before he could leave. "She's my daughter. I should go."

Adam shoved his impatience down. The man wasn't wrong. Still… "I know you want to help her, Mr. Schumacher, but you're in no real condition to do so. Let me see what's going on. I'll be right back, and we can come up with a plan."

Schumacher reluctantly nodded, and Adam crept back over to the fence, keeping hidden behind trees and bushes as much as possible.

The house looked quiet, but there was noise coming from the barn. He moved as quickly as he could to the nearest wall, inching along it until he came to a knot in the wood he could look through. And what he found had him seeing red with a fury so strong, his body shook with the force of it.

Nora sat slumped in a chair, her legs and arms tied, her head limp on her neck, obviously unconscious.

He was nearly to the barn door, his gun in his hand, before he realized he'd moved. Cursing under his breath, he stopped short and crept back a few feet. As much as he wanted to slaughter the man where he stood, Spurlock wasn't some green boy. The only reason to take Nora was to draw out Adam.

He tried to choke back the terror clogging his throat at the thing he'd always feared finally coming to pass. He'd been trying to avoid this exact situation his whole adult life. From the moment he first saw her, he'd known he should just walk away. Being with her, staying with her, *loving* her…had done nothing but put her life in danger. And he had no one to blame but himself.

He gritted his teeth so hard, his jaw popped, but he made himself walk away, back to where Schumacher waited. Charging in there without a plan in place would just get them both killed.

He didn't know what his face looked like, but Mr. Schumacher's drained of all color, then flashed bright red the moment he saw him.

"What's happened? What did you see? Nora…"

"Spurlock has her," Adam ground out.

"What?" Schumacher lurched forward, and Adam grabbed his arm. "I need to go get my daughter. I know I'm a sorry excuse for a father, but

I'm not going to just sit here while some criminal has her."

Something had definitely changed in Schumacher since Adam had won that deed from him. Maybe it was losing everything in that poker game that shocked some sense into him or finding himself left for dead in a ditch. Or maybe the threat of truly losing the last person on earth he loved and who loved him. Or hell, a combination of everything, Adam didn't care. He was glad, for Nora's sake, that *something* had changed. Whatever it was, Adam just hoped it was permanent.

But for the moment, he needed Schumacher clear and focused. Not charging in half-cocked.

"We're going to get her, but we've got to be smart about it. I've got a plan, so you need to sober up quick. I need your help."

Schumacher dragged in a ragged breath, his eyes wild, but he finally nodded.

"Good," Adam said, grabbing Barnaby's reins. "Now, I need you to go to the south wall of the barn. There's a knot in the wood there where you can watch, keep an eye on her. I'm going to go in and get Spurlock to follow me."

"What's going to keep the man from just shooting both of you? Or killing her and riding off with you?"

"I'm the only one he wants. Killing her serves no purpose, especially if he thinks she doesn't mean anything to me."

Schumacher's face turned thunderous at that. "And does she?"

Adam met his gaze, fury and fear and frustration

tearing him to pieces from the inside out. "She means everything," he said, biting out the words. He closed his eyes briefly, using every ounce of willpower he had to bring himself back under control. He wouldn't do Nora any good if he lost it. "But Spurlock can't know that."

Schumacher watched him for a moment and then slowly nodded. "All right. I'll keep watch."

Adam let out the breath that burned in his lungs. "Good. Good. All right." He took Barnaby's reins again and then pulled a paper out of his pocket, handing it to Schumacher. "Give this to Nora."

Schumacher nodded, putting it in his pocket without looking at it. "What are you going to do?"

"Draw him out. He should follow a few moments after I leave. If he doesn't, you go in and make sure he follows me. I don't care what you have to tell him. Just get him out of there."

"And if I can't? If he doesn't listen?"

Adam pulled one of his guns and slapped it into Schumacher's hand. "Then shoot him. Tell everyone I did it. I'm already a wanted man. I can take the blame for one more death."

Schumacher's eyes widened, but he pinched his lips together and just nodded.

Adam nodded back. And then went to save his love. Even though he'd have to destroy her to do it.

He could only pray one day she'd forgive him.

# CHAPTER THIRTY-THREE

The pounding in her head dragged her out of the darkness. The moment she tried to crack an eye open, she wished she could slip back under. Her head seemed too heavy for her neck to lift, but she worked at it a few minutes and finally got it upright. She needed water. The desert her mouth had become tasted like copper, and her tongue seemed too large for her mouth.

Of more concern was the fact that she couldn't lift her arms. It took a few seconds to register the ropes that bound her hands to the chair. Still not an ideal situation but decidedly better than paralysis or missing limbs.

After a few minutes of blinking and stretching, she finally got everything not tied down in relative working order. Though she was still in desperate need of a drink.

"There you are. I was beginning to think you'd never wake up."

Nora's head jerked up at the unfamiliar voice, and she groaned at the sharp, stabbing pain that splintered through the back of her head.

"Careful. Might want to keep your movements minimal for a few days."

Nora glared at him. He didn't need to introduce himself. She knew exactly who he was and why he wanted her.

"Spurlock," she said, putting as much contempt

into her voice as she could. "What did you do, crack the back of my skull?"

"Naw, it's not cracked. Just a bit bruised," he said, leaning against one of the posts in the barn. Her barn.

Now that her head was starting to clear somewhat, she could see that she was being held in her own barn. Something about that just felt so... insulting.

"If you're going to go through the trouble of kidnapping me, you might at least hide me somewhere no one can find me. Put a little effort into it."

Spurlock laughed. "You've got some fire in you. I can see why he likes you."

"Who?" she asked, not holding out much hope the ploy would work. But there was no reason to give the man all the information he was after too easily.

"Come now, don't play coy."

She just blinked at him like the most innocent baby angel who'd ever flown in the heavens.

He huffed. "Your paramour, of course."

"Husband," she snapped before she could stop herself.

"Husband, is it?" Spurlock rubbed his chin. "No, I don't think so."

She raised a brow, though even that small movement sent a twinge of pain through her head. "Why not?"

"There's no official record of any wedding, for one."

She knew that would come back to bite them one day.

"And if he was really your husband, and you were his devoted wife…then where is he?"

Nora frowned and looked around. There was daylight streaming through the gaps in the slatted walls, though the light was muted. That side of the barn was always in the shade during the morning. Which meant…

"Trying to calculate how long you've been my guest? I'll help you. I brought you in here a little after eight in the morning. And it's now well after midday."

All day. And no one had found her?

Spurlock's grin made her skin crawl. "Ah, now you're understanding. You have been missing all day, yet no one seems to have noticed. Not your friends or your father—though, to be fair, he doesn't seem to notice much of anything these days, does he? And not your errant lover. My apologies," he said, clapping a hand on his chest and giving her a little bow. "Your husband."

Nora rolled her lips between her teeth and bit down, using the pain to distract her from the almost overwhelming desire to spit in Spurlock's face. Somehow, she didn't think antagonizing him to that degree would keep her alive longer. Though the temptation to unleash her rage and see just how far she could take it was strong enough to make her hands shake.

Instead, she sucked in a shallow breath and prayed for composure. "You seem to know a lot for a stranger to this town."

Spurlock lifted a shoulder in a lopsided shrug. "Just because this is the first time you're seeing me doesn't mean it's the first I'm seeing of you. I don't just ride into a town without scouting it first. And I've got more eyes than my own keeping a watch out."

She should have known. He seemed to be waiting for some sort of response from her, but she wouldn't give him the satisfaction. Instead, she sat and waited until he tilted his head, regarding her a little more closely, before shrugging and continuing on.

"The fact remains, not one single, solitary person has come looking for you. It's not like I've made it difficult. I want them to find you, after all. Well, I want one person to find you. I hope you don't take offense. But he belonged to me first. He escaped from me once. It won't happen a second time."

She snorted. "Seems like a lot of trouble to go through just to draw one man out. Maybe he'd come if you just asked him really nicely."

Spurlock gave her a cold smile that didn't reach his dead eyes. Then he shrugged. "Or perhaps I should have used something he actually likes as bait. A nice apple pie, maybe. He'd at least get a few moments of enjoyment out of that before it was gone. You, on the other hand…"

He looked her up and down, the disdain dripping from his face enough proof of what he thought of her. "I don't know how he brought himself to touch you. And I mean that literally. Most men prefer their women to be…delicate. Feminine. Not built like they could fell an oak tree just by passing it."

She tried to tune out his words. Keep her face neutral, trying to look as bored as possible.

He was only saying what he thought would hurt

her the most. She'd dealt with men like him her whole life. They were all the same. Especially if they were around a woman who intimidated them. Though for a man who didn't know her at all, he was doing a very good job.

"Coming from a man who'd need a ladder to look me in the eye, I suppose I can see why you wouldn't understand my appeal."

Spurlock's face changed in an instant, going from mildly bored to raging fury. The back of his hand connected with her face before she had time to brace herself for the impact, and her head snapped back. Black spots swam through her vision, and she gasped at the pain screaming through her skull. Her mouth filled with blood, and the tangy, metallic taste made her stomach churn. She spat it out on the floor, wiping her chin on her shoulder the best she could. Another hit like that might do her in.

"No one understands your appeal," he hissed into her face. "That's why the only man who's ever touched you was a desperate criminal who was just passing through."

"Alleged criminal, Spurlock," Adam's voice said from the doorway. "You haven't proven anything against me yet."

Nora's heart jumped. Adam stood at the door of the barn, his gun trained on Spurlock.

"Toss your gun over here, Spurlock. Nice and slow."

Spurlock cursed and glared at Adam, but he did as directed. Happiness and hope rushed through Nora. He'd come for her!

Wait. No. This was bad. Very bad. He shouldn't be

here; he needed to leave.

She tried to catch his gaze so she could convey to him somehow that she was fine. Despite Spurlock's taunts, someone would find her. But Adam…wasn't looking at her at all. He slowly entered the barn, all his attention focused on Spurlock, who sneered at him.

"I don't need to prove anything against you. That's for the courts to decide. If you make it back to Denver alive, that is. So many accidents can happen along the trail. So many escape attempts gone wrong."

Adam snorted. "Which is why I think I'll just gather my belongings and be on my way. And you," he said, gesturing with the gun for Spurlock to…to stand closer to her? What was he doing? "You can stay here and keep her company for me."

Spurlock was obviously just as confused, though he made an effort to not show it.

"Didn't you come to claim your *wife*, as she calls herself?"

"God, no." Adam laughed, the cold reverberation sounding foreign coming from him. "She's been calling herself that since about five minutes after I met her. She's delusional."

Nora sucked in a breath, the pain shooting through her chest sharp enough to draw tears. He didn't mean that. He couldn't mean that. He…he was just trying to throw off suspicion. Trying to make it seem like he didn't care about her.

He was doing an incredibly good job.

But he had to do it, right? So Spurlock would think… Though what did it matter what Spurlock thought now? Adam had won. He was the one holding the gun on Spurlock. He was the one controlling the situation now. If he wanted, he could make Spurlock untie her, and she could hogtie him instead or run to get help or whatever else he wanted them to do. They had to do it because he held all the cards.

So why wasn't he letting her go? Why was he still acting so cold?

Unless he meant it.

Her throat ached from the emotions that she tried to choke down as her eyes swam with unshed tears. But she wouldn't let them fall. Not in front of them.

Adam was brushing aside the dirt and hay with his foot, looking for something. And her stomach sank farther.

"I went along with her delusions for a while," he said, finally finding what he was looking for.

He knelt down and finished brushing off a section of flooring, though he took care to keep his eyes and his gun trained on Spurlock.

"She was a nice diversion for a few weeks. Definitely cheaper than visiting the brothel, since she thought we were actually married. And she was amusing enough for a time. A bit clingy, though." He finally looked at her and frowned.

"You didn't need to hit her so hard," he said to Spurlock, and for half a second, she thought maybe there was some part of him that did care about her, no matter what he was saying. "She's got a hard enough time getting men to notice her as it is without adding a big scar to her face. Oh! There we are," he said with a smile, finally managing to pry a floorboard loose with one hand.

He reached inside the hole, and she closed her eyes to block out the look of triumph on his face when he withdrew a large bag of cash and coins. She didn't want to know what betrayal looked like.

"That's what you came back for?" Spurlock said with obvious surprise.

Adam raised his eyebrows. "Wouldn't you? This is her life savings. Every penny she's been able to hide from her drunk of a father over the years. She's been squirreling it away, saving it for...what? An emergency? A rainy day?" He snorted, and his obvious disdain for all her hard work, her hopes and dreams, shattered what was left of her heart.

"Thanks, wife," he said, jiggling the bag as he started backing up. "This will do nicely to get me set up someplace neither of you can find me." He made it to the doorway and paused. "Do me a favor, Spurlock. Keep her tied up for a few more hours. Give me a little head start."

"Why don't you just kill her if you really feel so little for her?" Spurlock asked, and the sick dread that had settled in her belly sent a fresh wave of fear through her.

Adam shrugged, his gaze raking over her as if he were actually considering it before sighing with regret. "For much the same reason I can't kill you, much as I'd like to. It would keep her from following me, true. But she does have a few friends here and a father who can't seem to keep himself alive without her. They'd come after me eventually if I killed her. And who needs that hassle, really? I already have one warrant out for me. As you well know," he said with a wink at Spurlock.

"Now, if you two will excuse me, I've got somewhere else to be." He touched the rim of his hat with the tip of his gun in a mock salute and disappeared out the door. Seconds later came the sound of horse hooves thundering down the road.

"Heh," Spurlock said. "That son of a bitch actually left you to die. No. He stole your money and then left you to die. He didn't even untie you or take my gun with him so you'd have a fighting chance. You know, I actually feel kind of sorry for you. I mean, sure, I was going to kill you, but I wouldn't have ripped your heart out before I did it."

He sighed and scratched at his beard and then shrugged. "Well, if you'll excuse me, I've got an outlaw to catch."

He picked his gun up off the ground and shoved it back in his holster.

"You're just going to leave me here?" she asked. It probably would have been wiser to keep her mouth shut rather than reminding him he hadn't killed her yet. But at that particular moment, she didn't care anymore. Kill her, don't kill her. He couldn't hurt what had already been completely destroyed.

Spurlock grabbed his hat from where he'd hung it over a post and shoved it on his head. "Under normal circumstances, no, I wouldn't. But Brady did make a few good points about your people coming for me, if you even have any, because they still don't seem to have noticed you're gone."

"Plus, that man has proven more than capable of

disappearing at the drop of a hat, and I don't want to let him get too far ahead of me. My associate who found him for me in the first place met with an unfortunate accident a few days ago, so I'm on my own for the moment. Which means I'm afraid this is where we say goodbye. Sorry your lover turned out to be such a coldhearted bastard. If it makes you feel any better, he'll never get to Denver alive."

He was out the door and on his horse before Nora could release the shuddering breath she'd been holding. It blew out of her in a long, slow exhale, and when she tried to suck in more air, it caught in her throat in a silent sob, the pain of Adam's betrayal ripping through her so fiercely, her body shook with the agony of it.

Him leaving was always going to hurt. But if he had just walked away, it would have merely broken her heart. Instead, every word he'd uttered had sliced at her until she'd been left sitting there, her very soul shredded beyond repair.

She'd opened up to him. Told him her deepest, darkest fears, the pain she hid from the rest of the world. She'd stripped her pride for him, given him access to the soft, secret pieces of her that she kept safe from the rest of the world. She'd let him in. And he'd burned her down. It would have hurt less if he'd simply stabbed her through the heart. But he hadn't killed her.

He'd completely destroyed her. And the pain was too much to survive.

She dragged in a ragged breath so sharp, it was like breathing glass, and when she let it loose again, it tore from her with a wail that made the very heavens bleed. Once she started, she couldn't stop the tears from flowing. They left her in great racking sobs that set her body shaking.

She hadn't cried when her mother had died. She hadn't cried the first time she couldn't rouse her father from a drunken stupor. Or the first time he'd stolen her money. Or the first time a man had laughed at the thought of courting her. Or any of the other hundreds of times strangers or even her own friends had looked at her and joked about her size, her strength, or any of the other dozen reasons no one would ever want her before going about their day like they hadn't just carved out another piece of her heart.

But she cried now. She cried for it all. All the lost love, the lost innocence, the lost dreams.

And Adam. The biggest dream of all. The one she'd been foolish enough to actually believe in. She'd known better. She'd *known*. And she'd fallen anyway.

And now she'd pay the price.

"Nora?" A voice finally filtered in past her shuddering breaths and the noise roaring in her ears, and she squinted through wet, swollen eyes.

"Baby? Can you hear me?" Gentle fingers brushed across her cheeks, wiping away the tears that still leaked from her eyes.

"Pa?" she whispered, her voice hoarse like she'd been screaming. Maybe she had been.

"It's me, baby." He'd untied her without her even realizing it, then he shoved his shoulder under her arm and helped her stand.

"We need to get moving," he said. "Can you

walk? I...I don't know how much help I'll be..."

The familiar scent of whiskey clung to him, but he seemed much more lucid than he usually did. He helped her across the yard and into the house, where he deposited her on a kitchen chair. A moment later, he pressed a cup of water into her hand and wiped at her face with a damp cloth.

His face scrunched into a grimace when he dabbed at the cheek Spurlock had hit.

"It doesn't hurt that bad," she said, and he nodded and moved on to the rest of her face, though he didn't look like he believed her.

She meant it, though. It smarted, sure. But it was nothing compared to the pain that still throbbed in her heart like it was a living, breathing entity trying to consume her alive.

"I'm sorry I took so long getting to you. Adam—"

She flinched at his name, and her father frowned and dropped to his knees in front of her.

Her eyes widened. Her father had never been one for coddling when she was younger and seemed pretty much of the mind that trials and pain only served to make one stronger and should be embraced. Until he'd succumbed to his own demons, that was.

But this...this was different. She'd never seen him so earnest.

"I know you're not going to want to hear this right now, not after what all just happened. But you need to know the truth. That man loves you—"

She jerked away from him and tried to stand up, but her father pushed her back into the chair.

"No. You need to hear this. He left earlier this

morning, intending on finding that lawman who's been after him. Instead, he found me sprawled out on the trail just outside town."

He looked down, shame burning through his eyes. He shook his head and rubbed at the back of his neck. "He could'a kept riding, left me there in the dirt. I'd have done it if I were him, especially after the way I've treated him, both of you. But he didn't. He hauled me out of that ditch, put me on his horse, and rode us both back here. But when we got back, we could see that the door to the garden had been left open."

"I'd never leave it open," she murmured.

"That's exactly what he said. He knew the moment he saw that gate that something was wrong. He left me with the horse while he crept over to the barn and took a peek at what was going on inside. I don't know what he saw, but he hurried back right quick. I've never seen a man so…crazed. He was more than mad. He was furious. And afraid. For you," he said, gently wiping away another tear she hadn't even felt falling.

"He came back over to me, told me I had to sober up quick because he needed my help if we were going to get you out of there safe. He has a plan. He didn't bother explaining it to me…" Her father frowned and he rubbed at his head. "Or if he did, I can't quite remember it. But he set me to watching you through that hole in the south wall. He said he was going to make sure the lawman left you alone and followed him, and that if he didn't, I was to make sure the lawman went after him. Say whatever I had to. And if I couldn't get him to go, he told me to shoot him, and he'd take the blame."

Her father shook his head like he couldn't believe it. She felt the same way. If it had all been an act…it had been a damn good one. *Too* good.

"I heard him, what he said. I know he said terrible things."

"Yeah, he did," she said. "And then he stole all our money." She blew out a deep breath. "He might not have wanted my blood on his hands, but if he actually loved me, would he have done any of that?"

"To save you, to make that lawman believe that he didn't feel anything for you so he'd let you go? To make sure that he followed him, for the money if not for himself, yes. He would."

She shook her head and he scowled. "He loves you," her father said again. "So much that even a sorry excuse for a man like me could see it plain as day."

She turned her head, squeezing her eyes shut as if that would make it so she couldn't hear what he was saying anymore. It certainly didn't keep more tears from spilling out.

"He loves you," he insisted. "He sacrificed himself for you."

She shook her head. She'd believed it once. She wasn't going to make that mistake again.

Her father sighed. "All right. I know you don't believe me. And I don't blame you. But just…think on what I said."

She hesitated, but she nodded anyway.

"Good. Oh, and he said to give you this." He held out a paper with another sigh. "I should have given it to you a long time ago."

She took the deed to the property in a trembling hand and didn't know whether to laugh or cry some more.

It seemed she finally had everything she'd wanted.

Everything but him.

She drew in a deep breath and strode out the door, her father at her heels.

"Nora! What are you doing?"

"We're going to go save my husband from his reckless attempt at martyrdom. And we're going to need reinforcements."

Her father's brows raised. "You're going to ask for help?"

She took Adam's gun from him and shoved it in the band of her pants. "From every damn person I can find."

• • •

If Nora had realized it was going to take as long as it did to gather everyone up, she'd have gone on her own.

Asking for help wasn't something she was very good at. But she wanted their help with this. Needed it. It was too important to risk going it alone. *He* was too important. And Spurlock was too dangerous to try and take out by herself. She had to give it to them, the moment she'd ridden into town, asking them all to drop everything to go chase down a murderous marshal with her, not one of them had hesitated to say yes.

But now, everyone was gathered in the sheriff's

office, throwing out one strategy after another. And if one more person offered up one more suggestion that didn't begin with *let's go now*, she was going to scream.

When Doc raised a hand and started with yet another *what if we*, Nora jumped up from her perch on the desk.

"Nope! No more!"

Everyone in the room turned and stared at her.

"I'm sorry. I know everyone is trying to help. But the longer we stand around discussing things, the farther away they get. If Adam is even still with him," she forced herself to say. She looked over at the sheriff. "You said it, Sheriff, and Spurlock himself confirmed it. He prefers to bring his bounties in dead. Adam's hours are numbered the moment Spurlock finds him. The longer we wait, the more of an opportunity we are giving him to make that happen."

Preacher stepped forward. "I know you're worried for him, but the odds are pretty good he's still alive. For now."

She frowned and folded her arms across her chest, as if that would somehow help contain the roiling pit of emotion that was threatening to boil over at any second. "How do you know?"

"Because it's a lot easier to travel with a live man than a dead one," he said, not bothering to soften the blow. She'd always appreciated that about Preacher. Sure, it stung when you were on the end of whatever bluntness he was slingin', but she still appreciated it.

"Good. I hope you're right," she said. "But the

longer we wait, the worse his chances get."

"I'm a little surprised you're so fired up to go and get him," the sheriff said. "Considerin' how he left things."

She cringed, cursing her father for telling everyone *everything* that had happened in that barn.

Mercy quietly admonished her husband as Martha spoke up. "I know he couldn't have meant any of those things he said. He needed to get Spurlock out of there. And needed you to stay put. I know it was horrible but…I've seen the way he looks at you."

Mrs. DuVere nodded. "So have I. Whatever else might be going on, that man loves you."

Sunshine, Doc, and even Preacher nodded in agreement. The sheriff sighed and gave one jerk of his head, joining in with the others.

Nora took a deep, shaking breath. "My head knows that. It might take my heart longer to catch up. But regardless of how I feel about him right now, I know I'll never be able to live with myself if he gets killed because my feelings were too hurt to come save him. Or worse, if we are too late because we were too busy sitting around making grand plans."

She grabbed her hat off the desk and clapped it on her head, her limited patience at an end. "I'm riding out now. I'd love to have some company. But I understand if anyone wants to stay behind."

She didn't wait to hear any more arguments, statements, declarations, or admonitions. It was past time to leave.

Teddy pranced beneath her, picking up on her

agitation as she pulled herself into the saddle. Her father was right behind her. And so was Doc, and Martha, and Preacher, and Sunshine. Mercy and the sheriff came out last, followed by Mrs. DuVere, who had apparently volunteered to stay behind with little Daisy.

Nora swallowed hard past the sudden lump in her throat at the sight of all her friends surrounding her. "Thank you," she said, her voice hoarse.

Doc nodded at her with a smile. "He's one of us now."

"And we take care of our own," Preacher added.

Her heart swelled again, and she took a deep breath and turned Teddy toward the road out of town.

"Let's ride!"

She kicked her horse into a run and thundered out of town, her friends at her side.

# CHAPTER THIRTY-FOUR

It had taken a bit longer than Adam had expected for Spurlock to catch up to him. Especially considering he'd done everything except draw the man a map showing exactly where he was going. He'd even walked his horse as slowly as Barnaby would go—and that was saying something, because Barnaby was slow even on a good day.

Now Barnaby was tied to Spurlock's saddle, and they plodded along behind him, Adam in iron handcuffs. He hadn't put up much of a fight, though he'd done enough to make it look like he wasn't just giving up. Barely. Luckily, Spurlock believed in his own legend enough that it didn't occur to him that Adam was making it easy for him.

Frankly, he was surprised that Spurlock hadn't just ridden up and shot him in the back. Adam hadn't been doing anything to prevent that exact scenario from occurring. After what had happened in the barn, death would have been welcome. He deserved it.

He couldn't get the image of Nora's face out of his head. It would haunt him for the rest of his days. That mixture of shock and betrayal etched on her face, the hint of despair in her eyes that she couldn't tamp down fast enough. And worst of all, the pain. It radiated from her as he'd used everything she'd shared with him against her. Hurting her like that had almost been more than he could bear. It was like ripping his own heart clean out of his chest.

But Spurlock wouldn't have believed anything less. The man was heartless, cruel. It was all he understood.

Adam hoped Nora's father could make her understand, could help her move past it. Past him. Find some happiness, even though it would destroy something in him that it wasn't with him. But she'd be better off. Hopefully, he hadn't hurt her too much. He'd needed her to hate him, though. That woman was as stubborn as her legs were long, and she loved more fiercely than any wild tiger. She never would have let him go if she thought he was in danger. Even to save her own future, her own life.

Better that she hated him. She could move on with her life. He could trust her father to help him, to tell Nora what he wanted him to. Tell her that Adam had used her and left her, and she was better off without him. The pain of his betrayal would fade eventually, and she'd find someone else. She'd need to, because his own life was over. Even if he made it to Denver alive, and he very much doubted he would, he'd spend years in prison, decades if Spurlock decided that would be more fun than just killing him and had anything to say about it.

There was no hope for them. It was better if she accepted that.

Spurlock stopped to camp for the night just as the sun was setting. He got a fire going and gnawed on some hard biscuits and jerky, which he didn't seem inclined to share. Adam did his best to ignore him. The night was actually pleasant, if he didn't think too hard about the fact that he'd broken the heart of the woman he loved and was sitting there ignoring small talk from the man who'd forced him to do it. He tilted his head back and watched the stars.

After several minutes of silence, Spurlock shook his head and let out a bark of a laugh. Adam glanced over at him, and Spurlock just shook his head.

"If I'd known you were going to be this miserable, I'd have brought your little plaything along, just for some entertainment," Spurlock said. "Though there really isn't anything little about her, is there?"

Adam's stomach dropped. "Excuse me?"

Spurlock waved him off. "Don't worry. I don't mean that kind of entertainment. I prefer my women a little less…mountainous. But I did enjoy watching you break her heart. Even though she tried to hide it. Honestly, though, I didn't think you had it in you. I've been following you for what…the better part of a year now? You're a surprisingly well-liked man for all that you're a gunslinging gambler."

"Better be careful with all those compliments, Spurlock. I might start to think you like me a little."

Spurlock snorted. "You're a pain in my ass, Brady. I'll be glad to be rid of you. I've got bigger game to catch. You've been nothing but a waste of my time and energy."

"Gee, Spurlock, I'm flattered. That a man of your caliber has deigned to hunt down a small-time man like me. I think I'm honored."

"You should be," he sneered.

"Hey, the last thing I want to be is a burden. I'd be happy to remove myself from your presence. Just toss me the keys to these shackles here and I'll be on my way. You won't ever hear a peep out of me again."

"Cute, Brady. Real cute."

Adam shrugged. "Just trying to be helpful."

Spurlock shook his head. "Don't you ever get tired of hearing yourself talk?"

Adam frowned and thought it over. "Not really, no. I mostly find myself delightful."

"I should just shoot you now and put myself out of my misery."

Adam gave him a slow smile. "Careful there, Marshal. That doesn't sound like a very law-abiding thing to do."

Spurlock got up and stalked toward him, pulling his gun from the holster. Then he squatted down beside him and jammed the gun up under Adam's chin. "Whoever said I was law-abiding?"

Adam shrugged, using the movement to align himself just a little bit better. "Not me."

He jerked his head back, out of the way, and slammed his hands upward, knocking them into Spurlock's elbow and sending the gun he'd held flying. Spurlock cursed, but Adam was already swinging his leg around. It caught Spurlock perfectly in the back of the knees, swiping his legs out from under him.

Adam jumped up and gritted his teeth, letting his leg fly again. He hated to kick a man while he was down, but in this case, he'd make an exception. His boot caught Spurlock right in the head. The blow didn't knock him out, but it stunned him just long enough that Adam was able to grab the gun that Spurlock had dropped. He had it aimed on the lawman before the man could draw another breath.

Adam just stood, gun trained on his new prisoner, and waited for their change in position to catch up with the man. It took longer than he expected. Either Spurlock wasn't as brilliant as he liked to think of himself, or Adam had kicked him a little harder than he'd thought.

Eventually, though, he noticed that Adam was standing over him with a gun, and he was lying on the ground, helpless. He scrambled into a sitting position but kept his hands held up as he eyed Adam warily.

"This is why you should handcuff a man's hands behind his back, not in front."

Spurlock glared up at him, though he reeked of fear. It never failed to surprise Adam just how much of a coward most bullies were.

"What are you going to do, Brady? Shoot me and leave me in some ditch somewhere?"

"Naw," he said with a shrug. "That's something you would do. I've got a bit more class."

Spurlock snorted. "Then what are you planning on doing?"

"You know, I'm not sure. I figured I'd let them help me with that," he said, jerking his head toward the small grove of trees they'd stopped beside.

"What? Who's *them*?"

The rustling that Adam had been hearing for the last several minutes grew louder, and several people separated from the shadows, trees, and boulders they'd been hiding behind.

Nora wasn't among them. That hurt a lot more than he would have thought. After the things he'd said, he wasn't surprised and truly didn't blame her for not coming to his rescue. But it didn't stop the pain from spearing his already shattered heart.

"Ah," Sunshine said, "I thought we'd been quieter than that."

Woodson snorted. "Most of us were. Some of us need to work on our stealth skills."

Sunshine waved him away and turned to rummage in Spurlock's saddlebags.

"Stay out of there!" Spurlock yelled.

Preacher walked over and glanced down at him with surprise. "Bit of a nuisance, isn't he?"

Adam snorted. "You have no idea."

Doc clapped him on the shoulder. "This all feels a little anticlimactic, Brady. We were all set to come stage this big, dramatic rescue, and then you went and essentially rescued yourself."

"Sorry?" Adam said. "I could use help with these, if anyone is still inclined to be helpful," he said, holding up his shackled hands.

"I don't know," a voice said behind him, and he spun around, coming face-to-face with Nora. "I kind of like you shackled."

# CHAPTER THIRTY-FIVE

Nora hadn't been sure how she'd feel seeing Adam again. The words he'd hurled at her still burned through her mind. He'd played his part a little too well.

And now, here she stood, face-to-face with the man who'd brought her the greatest happiness and pleasure she'd ever known in her life — and the greatest pain. It was enough to make a girl's head spin clean off her shoulders.

"Nora," he breathed. Adam brought his hands up to cup her cheeks, chains rattling, and pulled her close enough he could press his forehead against hers.

"I'm sorry," he whispered. "So, so sorry. I didn't mean it. None of it. I had to make you think I did, couldn't let him know what you mean to me. I'm so sorry," he murmured over and over again, pressing kisses to her temple and forehead.

She brought her hands up to hold his and closed her eyes, just breathing in the scent of him. Her body reacted to him as it always did. She wanted to curl around him and never let go. Just his presence calmed her, and the tension that had kept her taut as a bow seeped out of her.

Even as her mind replayed every horrible, hateful word he'd hurled at her.

She stepped back, needing to put a little distance between them. His eyes searched hers, but she dropped her gaze, focusing on unlocking the shackles that bound his hands.

She dropped them at his feet, and he took a cautious step toward her, stopping just shy of touching her again. Part of her mourned that. Wanted him to just grab her and haul her against him. The rest of her appreciated that he was leaving it up to her whether she came to him or not. Even though she still didn't know what she wanted.

No, that wasn't true. She knew exactly what she wanted. What she'd always wanted, from the moment he'd first stepped up to help her load her father into that wagon.

*Him.*

But her bruised and battered heart couldn't take any more if she was wrong.

"Why did you come?" he asked quietly, his words for her ears alone.

She flinched. "Do you not want me here?" she asked, though she was afraid of the answer.

He exhaled sharply, like someone had just knocked the wind out of him. "Want you?" He heaved in a breath, his fists clenching and unclenching, and finally he cursed, reached out to wrap a hand around the back of her neck, and hauled her to him with a groan, caging her in his arms. He dropped his face into her neck, inhaling with a shuddering breath, his entire body trembling against her.

"I will always want you. Always." He drew back enough to meet her gaze. "Maybe not standing right by my side while I'm dealing with corrupt, murderous lawmen, because I want to keep you safe," he said, aiming for a smile. "But otherwise, always." He brushed a tendril of hair off her face. "You are the only good decision I've ever made."

Was it possible for her heart to break and heal at the same time? Oh, what this man did to her.

"I just meant…after what I did…I didn't expect…"

She shrugged and gave him a weak smile. "I couldn't let some jackass come in and steal my husband."

A ghost of a smile crossed his lips. "Am I still your husband?"

Her smile faded, and she blew out a tremulous breath. She wanted to say yes. Her whole being screamed at her to say yes. But the pain that he'd caused still rippled through her with every breath she took. She wasn't sure she could trust what was real and what wasn't anymore.

"I don't know," she whispered.

He nodded, his face tightening like he was fighting not to say something else. "I understand," he finally said. "I'll be here. When you're ready."

The sheriff cleared his throat. "Sorry to intrude," he said. "But we need to get this wrapped up before anyone else comes along."

Adam nodded, and Nora followed him over to where Spurlock was on his knees in the dirt, his hands tied behind his back. She stood in front of him, letting a cruel smile spread over her lips as he craned his neck to look up at her.

"I think I underestimated you. Interesting company you keep," he said, nodding at the sheriff and Adam, who stood at her side. "Maybe I should put you on my payroll. You seem to have a knack for collecting outlaws."

She didn't bother to answer him, instead looking at the sheriff. "What are you going to do with him?"

Preacher and Sunshine hauled Spurlock to his feet. He sneered at them all, though Nora had no doubt the man was afraid. And he should be.

"He's seen you," Adam said to the sheriff.

"Yes, he has," the sheriff said, giving Spurlock a cold smile.

The lawman thrust his chin in the air. "I'm sure you've killed people for less. So go ahead. Do what you're going to do."

The sheriff turned to Adam. "See, that's the problem with bad people. They assume everyone else is just as evil as they are."

Adam snorted and looked at Spurlock, who glanced back and forth between them, forehead creased with confusion.

"You aren't going to kill me?"

The sheriff studied him for a minute, letting him sweat, then released a long sigh. "I'd really love to, Spurlock. Truly. Despite my general distaste for violence, some men just need killin'." He moved a little closer to him. "But I don't need to kill you to keep you from disturbin' any of my people again."

Spurlock, apparently feeling a little more sure of himself now that the sheriff hadn't immediately put a bullet in him, gave him a look oozing with scorn. "Is that so?"

The smile the sheriff leveled at Spurlock had even Nora shivering in her boots. She didn't know how Spurlock was still standing under it.

"Absolutely. See, I know what really happened in Abilene."

Spurlock's bravado disappeared between one breath and the next, his face immediately leaching of all color. "I don't know what you're talking about," he managed to say, though there was a tremor in his voice he couldn't hide.

What the hell had happened in Abilene?

She glanced at Adam, but he just shrugged.

"I've got witnesses and signed affidavits," the sheriff continued. "All I have to do is send word. And I have people who will do it for me if I ever fail to check in with them."

"You've kept all that all these years?" Spurlock asked.

"You sound surprised," the sheriff said. "I like to be prepared for any possibility that might arise. And a few of my friends in town are even better than I am at diggin' up dirt. So you might want to tread carefully from now on."

Spurlock swallowed audibly, and the sheriff smiled again.

"So here's what you're gonna do. You're gonna get on that horse of yours, and you're gonna ride out of here. You're gonna forget you ever found Mr. Brady here. You're gonna forget you ever even heard of the existence of Desolation. Because if you or anyone else ever shows up, lookin' for me or any of my people again, I'll make sure every ounce of evidence I have on you goes public. And I've got more than just Abilene. You've made a lot of enemies, Spurlock. And they'd all love to see you fall. You leave me and my people alone, or I'll give them the rope they need to hang you."

Spurlock stared at the sheriff, his gaze flicking back and forth between him and Adam, and Nora held her breath, waiting to see what he'd decide. She had no doubt if he made the wrong choice, he wouldn't be riding anywhere. Preacher and Doc were already standing ready with their hands at their holsters. So were Adam and Sunshine. And Spurlock finally seemed to get it through his thick skull that he'd been beat.

He jerked his head in a nod, and Nora released a breath of relief.

The sheriff nodded at Preacher and Doc, and they released Spurlock from their grip. Doc moved away, and the sheriff turned to speak to Sunshine. Adam wrapped his arm loosely around Nora's waist as Preacher untied Spurlock's hands.

Nora wasn't sure what happened next. One minute Preacher was removing the rope binding Spurlock. The next he was flying backward, and Spurlock was spinning around, a gun glinting in his hand.

She opened her mouth to shout, but it came out in a grunt as Adam shoved her behind him.

Two pistol shots fired, one after the other, and Nora pushed away from Adam, trying to make sense of the scene before her.

Everyone stood frozen. Everyone except Spurlock, who lay unmoving on the ground, a bullet hole in his chest, his gun lying beside him.

All those not lying dead on the ground turned to Adam, who stood, feet braced, gun smoking in his hand.

Spurlock had pulled his gun, aiming at the sheriff. And Adam…he'd pulled his weapon so quickly she hadn't even seen it. But he'd managed to get his shots off just before Spurlock pulled his trigger.

"Did you…did you just save the sheriff?" she asked.

Sheriff Woodson looked at Adam and the gun he held, looked down at Spurlock, then back at Adam. He sucked in a deep breath and let it out slowly.

"All right," he said with a shrug. "I guess I forgive you."

# CHAPTER THIRTY-SIX

Adam stood in Nora's front room, his heart thudding in his chest. He'd never thought to see this place again. This house that he'd begun to think of as his home. Never thought he'd have the chance to be standing before her again. He'd ridden off with Spurlock, not sure he'd ever even see the sunrise again. Yet here he was. Miracles did happen occasionally, it seemed. He could only hope he'd get another one.

Nora had been mostly silent as they'd ridden home. He hadn't wanted to pry into her thoughts, wanted to give her time to process what she was feeling. He'd done his job a little too well when he was trying to convince Spurlock he didn't care for her.

But he didn't think he could take the silence anymore.

"Nora, I…"

She held up a finger to stop him and took a deep breath. "I understand why you did what you did. I even agree with the plan to a certain degree. It worked, so it's hard to argue with it too much. However," she said, keeping him from interrupting. "What I'm having a hard time with is that you went behind my back. Came up with this plan of yours that revolved around destroying me and sacrificing yourself."

"I was trying to protect you," he started, and she

held up a hand again.

"I'm aware. Very noble. But I don't need you to protect me."

He sucked in a breath, desperately wanting to argue that point. Oh, he completely agreed that she was more than capable of holding her own. But that didn't mean he'd ever stop wanting, *needing* to protect her.

"What I want is someone who I can trust to tell me the truth. Who I can trust to not hurt me," she said, the small crack in her voice reaching inside his chest and shredding a piece of his heart. "Who I can trust to trust *me*. I want a partner. Not a keeper."

God, this woman staggered him. His heart swelled with pride as he watched her. How had he been lucky enough to find her? What had he ever done in his miserable life to deserve her? This incredible woman, this queen standing before him, strong and commanding? He didn't know. But he'd gladly spend the rest of his life proving that he was worthy. He wanted nothing more than to fall to his knees and worship her.

"Can you do that?" she asked. "Can you be that for me?"

He came toward her, stopping a breath away. "I will be anything you need me to be. Gladly. Proudly. Your partner. Your lover," he said, leaning forward to brush his lips across hers. "Your husband," he said, pressing his forehead to hers. "If you'll have me." He pulled back enough to meet her gaze.

Her breath caught in her throat, and she lifted a hand to his cheek. "Is that what you really want?"

His lips pulled into a slow smile. "More than

anything I've ever wanted in my life."

"I thought your number one rule was to avoid matrimony at all costs."

"It was." He shrugged. "But I was wrong."

That startled a laugh out of her, and he nearly closed his eyes and groaned at the pleasure that sound sent crashing through him. He would happily spend the next fifty years of his life making sure she was happy enough to laugh like that every damn day.

He gently cradled her face. "Marry me."

Her eyes searched his, and the smile that touched her lips made his soul sing.

"All right."

Adam gripped her thighs and lifted, wrapping her legs around his waist. Nora held on tight to his shoulders, laughing.

"What are you doing?"

He turned, heading for their bedroom. "You agreed to marry me. It's only fair that we have a wedding night."

"Except you're supposed to have a wedding before you have a wedding night."

He kicked open the door to their room but didn't put her down. "We sort of had a wedding. Just because we didn't realize it doesn't mean it doesn't count."

Her jaw dropped. "You've been arguing the exact opposite for a month now."

"Well, yes, but arguing *for* it is more to my advantage now."

He dropped her to the bed and tugged off her boots. And then her pants.

She laughed but made no move to stop him. He made quick work of her clothing and even quicker work of his own. But he didn't touch her right away. Instead, he stood over her and sucked in a shuddering breath.

"My God, woman. Do you have any idea how incredibly beautiful you are?"

He shook his head and swallowed hard, his eyes shining so brightly as he looked at her that she had to fight back tears of her own.

When he finally came to her, moved over her, in her, she wrapped her body around him, and he held her close. They showed each other without words what they meant to each other. Illustrated with every kiss, every caress, every stroke, that they belonged to each other, heart and soul, from that moment on.

And when that overwhelming, undying pleasure swept them both away, they stayed locked in each other's arms.

Nora pressed her forehead to Adam's neck. "Husband," she murmured, her body trembling against his.

"Wife," he said, lifting her face. He pressed a gentle kiss to her temple and sighed against her skin. "My darling wife. I love you so much."

She smiled up at him, her soul singing. "I love you, too."

• • •

Nora and Adam stood in front of the Town Council, awaiting their verdict. It was the last day of the month. Time was up.

The sheriff leaned back in his chair, crossing his arms over his chest and pinning Adam with his sternest look. Though the effect was a bit ruined by the smiles from everyone else at the table.

"Time's up, Brady. Do you have a permanent job yet? Because if I'm not mistaken, nearly everyone in town has fired you. Some of them more than once."

"Gray. Really?" Mercy said. "We just broke a dozen laws to rescue him and bring him back here. You wouldn't really make him leave." She frowned, scrutinizing her husband. "I don't think."

The sheriff shrugged. "Rules are rules. Everyone else has to follow them." He turned back to Adam. "So?"

Sunshine cleared his throat, and the sheriff glanced over at him. "Don't you dare say it."

Sunshine just grinned. "Sorry, Sheriff. But he's done really well. He's completed every task I've given him and shown a great aptitude for the work. I think he'll make a fine assistant deputy."

The sheriff closed his eyes and rubbed a hand over his face. "Sweet lord in heaven, help me. Whatever did I do to be cursed with your presence?"

Everyone laughed, and Mercy bumped his shoulder with hers. "I thought you forgave him for... all that past stuff," she said, waggling her fingers.

The sheriff sighed. "I did. That doesn't mean I want to spend every day working with him."

Nora smiled, and Adam laughed. "Sorry, Sheriff. I did try to get fired, but Sunshine there just wouldn't take the bait."

The sheriff glared at his deputy. "Really?

Everyone else managed to make his employment so despicably hard he'd have quit if he hadn't gone and gotten himself fired. But you somehow can't manage to get rid of him?"

Sunshine just shrugged with that infectious grin of his. "I'd say sorry but…"

"Wait," Adam said. "You all were *purposely* making the jobs harder?"

Everyone glanced around, trying to look as innocent as possible, but the guilty grins gave them away.

Adam closed his eyes and let out a long-suffering sigh, and Nora laughed along with the rest of them.

"That's all right," Adam finally said. "It turns out, it doesn't matter if I have a job or not."

He threaded his fingers through Nora's and reached inside his coat, pulling out a piece of paper that he slid along the table to the sheriff.

"What's this?" the sheriff asked.

Adam smiled down at Nora again and squeezed her hand. "Our signed marriage license. We were remarried, legally this time, last night."

The rest of the Council broke out in cheers and congratulations. Even the sheriff smiled. A little.

"And if you'll indulge me," Adam said to the Council before turning to Nora, "I have a wedding gift for my wife."

He looked over at Preacher, who handed him a folded sheet of paper. Adam handed it to her and waited until she opened it up.

Her forehead creased, and she glanced up at him, her heart thudding. "A death certificate? For you?"

He smiled and pulled her to him, wrapping his

arms loosely about her waist. "Yes. One certificate so you can claim your deed," he said, nodding at their license. "And one so you keep it in your own name, not your husband's," he said, nodding at the other.

"And so you can live in peace," Preacher added. "No one will come looking for him again if he's legally dead."

"You're lucky you're gainfully employed, Brady," the sheriff said. "If she's legally a widow, I could technically toss you out of town."

Mercy rolled her eyes, and Sunshine just shook his head and laughed.

Nora, however, hesitated only a second longer, and then she threw herself into Adam's arms and started laughing.

"What?" he asked.

She shook her head. "You managed to somehow get officially married and legally absolved from matrimony all in one swoop."

He laughed. "Not my intention, I promise." He pulled her close and kissed her. "As long as matrimony involves *you*, I am all in." He paused, pursing his lips in thought before he spoke again. "I would like to keep avoiding *him*, though," he said, jerking his head at the sheriff.

Sheriff just snorted. "Finally, something I can agree with."

# EPILOGUE

Adam hammered in another nail and then stood back to admire his handiwork.

"That's coming along nicely," Mr. Schumacher said. "You might want to add a few extra nails, just to make sure it's sturdy."

"It'll hold," Adam said, tugging on the shelf he'd just hung in Nora's new potting shed.

Ever since the night Spurlock had shown up, and consequently disappeared, Mr. Schumacher had been making a concerted effort to stay sober. From what Adam could tell, losing what was basically all his and his daughter's worldly goods in that poker game had shocked him. Nearly losing his life in that ditch had scared him. And nearly losing Nora, in part because he'd been in no shape to do more than wait for others to help her, had driven home a change of heart and mind that had been truly miraculous to watch. Adam was just sorry Schumacher, and Nora, had had to go through so much for her father to get to the point where he was ready to rebuild his life.

It had been nearly six months now since the man had had a drink, and he'd been helping out more and more on the farm. It would take time, but he and Nora had also been repairing their relationship. Some days were better than others. But they were making progress.

Now that the property was officially in Nora's

name, they'd been working on expanding her businesses, and her father had actually been a lot of help, teaching Adam what he needed to know so he could take over more of the agricultural side of her business and she could concentrate on expanding her sewing. With more time on her hands, she'd been able to make ready-made clothing as well as doing her commissions. Adam and her father were building her a shop adjacent to their house where she could meet her customers and display her goods.

Mr. Schumacher was still gruff with Adam, but Adam was sure he liked him. Even if it was begrudgingly.

They worked peaceably side by side for a few more minutes before Mr. Schumacher cleared his throat. Adam glanced at him, eyebrows raised in question.

"I…" He cleared his throat again. "I never thanked you," he said.

Adam frowned. "For what?"

It took the man a minute. He wasn't one for words, so Adam patiently waited.

"I was lost for a long time. When my wife died, I didn't handle it well. She'd been everything to me and when she was gone…well…"

Adam nodded. He could imagine all too well how it would feel to lose the love of your life, what you might do if you found yourself suddenly facing decades without the person who made your world turn round.

Mr. Schumacher cleared his throat again. "Nora was still so young. But she stepped up, took on all the responsibility, took care of everything. She made it look so easy. Nothing ever seems to fluster her. She just deals with whatever needs doing. It made it easy, I guess, for me to just let her put everything on her shoulders."

He rubbed his forehead, his pain and regret palpable. "I didn't realize what kind of toll it was taking on her until you came along, until I started seeing her smiling again, enjoying life, that I started realizing how long it had been since I'd seen her that way. It woke me up," he said, finally looking at Adam with a small smile.

"Then watching you start to fix the place up, seeing how happy it made her to have you helping her…made me realize how much I'd put on her. How little I'd done to help and how much I'd been doing to make it worse."

Adam wanted to stop him, tell him it was all right, but the man clearly needed to get it all off his chest. So Adam just waited and listened.

"Then that night, that night you left to draw out the lawman." His jaw clenched so hard it made a popping noise, and Adam briefly closed his eyes. He'd never forgive himself for the things he'd said to her that night, for what he'd done to her. Even if she'd forgiven him.

Her father blew out a long breath. "I'd never seen her cry before that night. Not ever. Even after her mother died. She was always so strong. To see her cry like that…it broke something in me. I should have been able to protect her. Maybe if I hadn't been so…if I'd been better…I could have helped. I could have done something so that you wouldn't have had to...do what you did." He took a deep breath again and blew it out. "I don't ever want to see her like that again. Anyone ever makes her feel like that again and I'll deal with them," he said, pinning Adam with a stare that he had no trouble mistaking.

"She'll never feel another ounce of pain if I can prevent it," Adam said. "I swear it."

Mr. Schumacher nodded. "Good." He clapped a hand on his shoulder and squeezed it. Maybe a little harder than necessary.

"Anyhow. I just wanted to say thank you. For helping to open my eyes. For being there for my daughter when I couldn't be. For making her happy since then."

Adam nodded. "It's my great pleasure."

Mr. Schumacher just nodded and left to go back to his chores.

Nora came to stand beside Adam, sliding her arm around his waist so she could lay her head on his shoulder.

"Husband," she said, giving him a smile that warmed his very soul.

"Wife." He leaned down and gave her a lingering kiss.

She looked out over the gardens with their new fences, the new paddock behind the barn, and the potting shed he'd built. "You know, you're getting surprisingly good at building things. Mr. Vernice would be proud."

He chuckled. "I don't know if I agree with the surprising part, but thank you. Practice makes perfect, I suppose."

"That's true. You've actually managed to make several pies now without burning down the kitchen."

He gave her a mock glare. "Keep teasing and I'll stop making them."

She held up her hands. "I won't say another word."

Her father crossed the yard toward the barn and waved at them along his way.

A loud crack echoed through the air, and Adam and Nora jumped, looking toward the garden just in time to see a bright blue ribbon fluttering in the opposite direction of a cracked fence post.

"Damn it, Lucille!" Mr. Schumacher took off after the errant goat, shouting curses at it until he and the goat had disappeared down the lane.

Nora and Adam held on to each other and laughed until their sides hurt. Then Adam pulled her close and pressed a kiss to her temple.

"How much did you hear?" Adam asked. "Before Lucille showed up, that is."

"Most of it." She snuggled closer to him. "He's going to be all right, isn't he?" she said, smiling up at him.

"Yeah. I think he will be."

He leaned down to give her a soft kiss, and she sighed, hugging him tighter.

"Now, what was that you were saying about something being your great pleasure?" she asked, looking up at him with a suggestive smile.

"Oh, that. Well, I was talking about how making you happy was my great pleasure...or maybe it was that giving you great pleasure is what made me happy..." He frowned, tilting his head as he pretended to think about it. "You know, I think it'll be easier if I just show you."

He bent and tossed her onto his shoulder, grinning as she squealed out a laugh. Matrimony had never felt so sweet.

# ACKNOWLEDGMENTS

To my fabulous editor and publisher Liz Pelletier, thank you for starting this crazy journey to Desolation with me. I love these books so much and I love you for always being there with soul-cheering encouragement or a swift kick in the pants, depending on what I need LOL. Lydia Sharp, my wonderful editor, I couldn't do any of this without you. Thank you for always being there and working so hard to make these books shine! And to the amazing team at Entangled, Stacy, Jessica, Riki, Debbie, Curtis, Meredith, Heather, Katie, and all the incredible people behind the scenes—thank you so much for your hard work and support from start to finish and in between. To Elizabeth, Bree, and Toni—thank you for making this book gorgeous inside and out! And Toni, thank you so much for always being there for me. I think it's fifteen years now? That you are still a part of my life and a part of my publishing journey is something I thank my lucky stars for on the daily. I love you, lady!

Thank you to my wonderful agent, Janna Bonikowski, for all your support, guidance, and hard work on my behalf. And for always reading my novel-length emails and responding with a laugh and a smile. I love that you get me as well as you do.

To my historical gals—Lexi Post, Sapna Bhog, and Heather McCollum—I love our chats so much! It's been wonderful having your support and friendship. Thank you, all! To Eva Devon, I have so loved getting to know you! Thank you for all your encouragement, your cheering, and your Regency knowledge! And to Lisa Rayne, I truly could not do this without you. Our chats keep me motivated and sane LOL. This writing world can be tough and lonely sometimes and I am so grateful to have found such an amazing friend to share the journey with. Thank you for always being there to cheer me on, help me brainstorm, and make sure I'm actually working! Truly couldn't do this without you and wouldn't want to!

To Tom, who keeps things running when I am overwhelmed, who dropped me off at a hotel and kept everyone away (aside from feeding me occasionally LOL) so I could finish this book, and who keeps our kids healthy and happy when I'm buried in deadlines. Thank you so much. I love you, babe. To Connor and Ryanna, I love you more than you will ever know. Thank you for being my rocks, my biggest cheerleaders, for making me laugh and enduring my clingy hugs – I love you two! To Kyelie, Andy, Matt, Mindy, Axton, Casen, Novalee, and Alix, I love you all so much! Thank you for always supporting me and cheering me on. To my parents, siblings, and family who have loved and supported me from day one—you'll never know how much it means. Thank you all!

And most of all, to my dear readers—you guys are why I get to do what I do. Thank you for all the love and support!

# A Matter of Temptation

Miss Wilhelmina "Mina" Crawford is desperate. Having been ruined in the eyes of society years ago for one foolish, starry-eyed mistake, she spends her days secreted away at her family's crumbling estate, helping her brother manage the land but not able to truly live life the way she's always dreamed. When her brother admits to just how dire their finances have gotten, she takes it upon herself to procure employment...but the only one who will even consider the scandalous idea of a female secretary is the brilliant, ruthless, and infuriating Earl of Creswick.

Simon Loughton, the Earl of Creswick, needs help if he wants to finally pass the reform bill he's been championing for years and secure the vote for England's most vulnerable constituents. Too bad help comes in the form of a woman with breathtaking nerve, fiery red hair, and a sense of humor to match.

Now temptation—disguised as a lovely, clever-mouthed devil—lives and works under Simon's very roof. And Mina finally feels as though she's truly living life to her wildest dreams. But even the most incendiary of kisses can't incinerate Mina's past...or the shocking secret that could ruin them both.

*Shakespeare meets* Bridgerton *in this witty and lively marriage-of-inconvenience romance.*

# MUCH ADO ABOUT DUKES

USA TODAY BESTSELLING AUTHOR
## EVA DEVON

As far as William Easton—the Duke of Blackheath—is concerned, love can go to the devil. Why would a man need passion when he has wealth, a stately home, and work to occupy his mind? But no one warned the duke that a fiery and frustratingly strong-willed activist like Lady Beatrice Haven can also be a stunning, dark-haired siren who tempts a man's mind, body, and soul.

Lady Beatrice is determined to never marry. Ever. She would much rather fight for the rights of women and provoke the darkly handsome Duke of Blackheath, even if he does claim to be forward-thinking. After all, dukes—even gorgeous ones—are the enemy. So why does she feel such enjoyment from their heated exchanges?

But everything changes when Beatrice finds herself suddenly without fortune, a husband, or even a home. Now her future depends on the very man who sets her blood boiling. Because in order to protect his esteemed rival, the Duke of Blackheath has asked for Beatrice's hand, inviting his once-enemy into his home...*and* his bed.

*Without mercy, there is no love in this third
installment of the Sons of Sinclair historical
romance series by award-winning author
Heather McCollum.*

# HIGHLAND
## JUSTICE

As the new chief of Clan Mackay, Gideon Sinclair knows
the importance of maintaining order at any cost. To keep
the conquered clan in line, Gideon must mete out ruthless
justice or risk losing their precious new peace. But from
the moment he meets Cait Mackay—aye, from the
moment the sweetness of her lips captures his—all of
Gideon's careful objectivity is well and thoroughly
compromised.

Cait knows that kissing the brawny Highlander is a
dangerous game. It was bad enough she picked his pocket
to feed the children in her care, but sometimes a desperate
woman must disguise her crimes any way she can. Only
her act of deception has made things worse… Because one
kiss with the Highland's most brutal chief leaves her
breathless and out of her depth.

Now Gideon must choose between his duty and his
heart when his lovely thief is accused of treason against
the king himself.

*Fans of* Bridgerton *will love these two Regency romances for the price of one, featuring two best friends, each determined to advertise for love.*

# The Brides of London

## VANESSA RILEY

**The Bittersweet Bride**: Widow Theodosia Cecil needs a husband and needs one fast to protect her land, so she places an anonymous ad in the paper. She's delighted she spends her remaining weeks exchanging flirtatious letters with the perfect man... Until she meets him and realizes he's the son of the man trying to steal her land.

**The Bashful Bride**: When sparks fly between timid heiress Ester Croome and a handsome actor, they're quick to elope. But when she discovers there is so much more to him than meets the eye, in order to save the marriage the shiest woman alive must publicly woo the most desirable man in England...her husband.

AMARA
an imprint of Entangled Publishing LLC